Challenge
of
Choice

By Betty Briggs

Sunrise Selections

ISBN 0-9656307-3-0

Sunrise Selections
P. O. Box 51602
Provo, Utah 84605-1602

This book is dedicated to my family, both immediate and extended, whose continued interest in my projects nourishes any faith I have in myself.

Heartfelt thanks to my husband, Scott, for his long hours and exceptional photographic and computer skills which molded *Challenge of Choice* from snapshots and manuscript to cover and novel with visual sparkle.

Special thanks to models: Tressa Johnson, Shaun Briggs, Ryan Bunker, McKenzie Wolz, Lani Homan, April Briggs, Josh Clift, Heather Johnson, Shelly DeWitt and Suzanne Senser, and to equine models: Flashy Red Money (Red), Bimini Midnight Star (Midnight), Nobel Witch (Nobel), Streakin Red Minx (Minx), Bimini Sunrise (Sunrise), Gunsmoke's Lucky (Jasmine), Krustie Loma (Ash), Sheka Zulu (Prince) and Magnum. I acknowledge horsewoman, Shelly Johnson, who provided many of my models, both two-legged and four.

Thanks also to great friends and fellow writers: Rebecca Crandell, Linda Orvis, Lisa Peck, John Thornton, Milt Briggs and Ben Bracken. Their creative brainstorming constantly sparks my imagination.

The photo on page 150 is courtesy of Misty Kay Hutchings—Makeup and Hair Artist/Photographer

Betty continues to work as a legal secretary, ferreting time away each day for her two passions—horses and writing. She finds great joy in her husband, two grown children, five grandchildren, and three horses. She loves watching her two oldest granddaughters mature in the "horse world" and has purchased an old, ranch gelding named Partner to share their growing up experiences. Betty is the author *A Tuff-to-Beat Christmas, Quality Concealed* and *Image of Deception*. Next year, look for a new and improved edition of *A Tuff-to-Beat Christmas.* Then, as a change of pace, she will venture into the realm of mystery/adventure with a whole new cast of characters, including, wouldn't you know, horses.

Partner & Betty

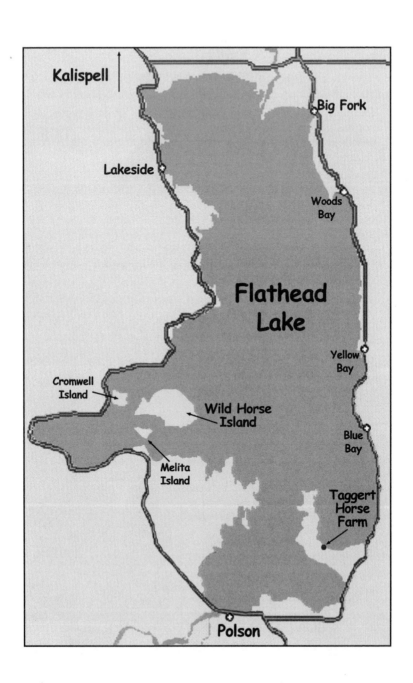

CHAPTER
ONE

When Heather Chambers saw Tyler Taggert after ten months, one week and two days, she fought the impulse to slip David's ring off her finger and hide the diamond in her pocket. After all, David Cane was the man in her life now. She hadn't dreamed she'd run into Ty again, let alone find him here, in this spectacular horse barn, on the shores of Montana's Flathead Lake. After what he'd done, how could she still feel such a rush of warmth?

Ty stood in the middle of an indoor training arena. A chestnut stallion, secured by a long lunge line, cantered in a wide circle around him. A muscle in Ty's jaw flinched when he noticed her, but he kept the horse moving several more revolutions before he shouted, "Whoa!"

Coiling the lunge line as he walked, Ty led the chestnut from the arena. Something about the way Ty carried himself, the straight stance of his taut body, the stomach so flat it was almost concave, made Heather light-headed.

"Heather," he said, reaching for her hand. He pulled her closer, curling her fingers around his. The diamond flashed. "What's this?"

Even in faded blue jeans, worn cowboy boots, and a white T-shirt with horse slobber smeared across the front, Ty was handsome, more so than she remembered, and he'd regained the weight—all in the form of muscle—that he'd lost when he'd been injured the summer before.

The summer before. Darn him! Double darn him! What had happened? Why hadn't he? . . . "A ring. Do you like it?" The edge to her voice reflected the hurt she'd meant to hide. When she'd left him last year, she believed he cared for her.

"Not really." He let go of her hand. "Mine would have been bigger." His face betrayed no emotion.

Her brows raised. They'd never know, would they? Ty had seen to that. "It's a promise ring," she said.

"Promise?" He stared at her with topaz brown eyes flecked with gold.

Heather had never seen eyes that color before. Once they'd reminded her of a puppy's. Now their steady, unyielding glare was every bit wolf—lean timber wolf—like the rest of Ty.

"Did you promise him the same thing you promised me?" Shoulders squared, he seemed poised, ready to attack.

"Wait a minute. You're acting like this is my fault." Her back stiffened.

"Isn't it?"

"I don't see how."

The red-colored stallion at Ty's shoulder tossed his head and moved forward.

"Whoa!" Ty said again, gathering the slack in the lead.

"Maybe we should discuss your promises." Heather attempted a steely stare of her own. "I seem to recall you promised to come see Image and me compete at the fair last fall. What about your promise to write? And I would've thought you'd have let me know when you moved another three hundred miles away. This is your place, isn't it?" She realized she was shouting and lowered her voice. "Let's do talk about promises."

"I came to the fair."

She blinked. "You what?"

"Katie and I came to watch you at the fair."

"You and your sister came?" Thoughts bombarded her brain like hailstones on pavement. "Where? Why didn't you let me know you were there? I didn't see you." Oh, no! Chewing her lip, she remembered David's actions right after she'd won. She shook her head. The Utah State Fair . . . AGAIN. It had marked the beginning of her relationship with David almost two years earlier, before she'd met Ty, and it was at the fair ten months ago that David had reappeared in her life, after her summer with Ty.

"It's no wonder. That big buff guy smothering you with victory kisses probably blocked your view. I wasn't about to interrupt." He stared at her, eyes smoldering, teeth almost bared. "I had hoped it would take you longer to forget me. What was it? Two weeks?"

Heather's mouth fell open. "I didn't forget you. He wasn't smothering me. . . . It was one kiss—well, maybe two. He surprised me." She swallowed once, then again. "That was the first time I'd seen him in months. When he left we were kinda going together."

Keeping a close hold on the lead rope, Ty led the stallion forward. "Like you and me?"

She followed him out of the arena, down a dirt aisle into the stall area of the huge wooden barn. The wet sand smell of freshly raked and sprinkled ground rose up to greet her nostrils.

A horse whinnied.

"No. Not like you and me." Heather's shorter legs took two steps to Ty's and the stallion's one. "Quit putting words in my mouth."

"Someone should. You don't seem to know what to say to whom."

Another horse whinnied, followed by a chorus of three or four more. Heather noticed that most of the stalls in the barn were occupied, but she didn't stop to look. "I've known David a long time."

Ty snickered. "Did you have a lapse of memory last summer when you were with me?" He tied the chestnut stallion's lead to a hook in the cement wall of the washing enclosure, picked up the end of a hose, and squirted off the animal's sweat-stained body.

"That's not fair," Heather shouted between squirts. "I thought David and I were broken up."

She noticed the way Ty's broad shoulders tapered down to lean hips and how the muscles in his arms stretched the fabric of his short-sleeved shirt. David had a good build too. He worked out at a local health club every day, and he was smart. Someday he'd really be somebody.

"You didn't know for sure if you were broken up? Do you know now?" Ty shut off the water.

Sighing, Heather held up her left hand, wiggling her fingers.

"Oh, yeah. The tiny ring."

She opened her mouth then shut it without saying something she'd regret later.

"I know. I know. It's a promise ring." Ty grabbed a metal shedding blade and ran the smooth side along the stallion's back, scraping off standing water. The horse sidestepped, but Ty kept working. "So are you going steady? Getting married? What?"

"Kevin says I'm too young to get married." Heather shifted from one foot to the other, bending to adjust her stone-washed jeans at the tops of her knee-high riding boots.

"There's a Kevin too?" Ty asked.

Heather slapped at him. "My stepfather. You remember him—the guy I set my mother up with, now the father of my baby brother, and in his spare time, my acting horse trainer and jumping coach."

"I remember." A smile twitched across his face. "He came with you, I take it."

"He sure did." Heather scratched her head. Kevin had tricked her into coming to Montana. That's what he'd done. They'd been showing Royal Image in Utah and planning trips to California. Now, with only a week's warning, she found herself here. Even though she was excited that her black Thoroughbred had just won his first Montana championship, she knew now it had been a setup. Kevin had wanted her to see Ty again before telling David she'd marry him.

"Eighteen is pretty young," Ty said, drawing Heather out of her thoughts, "especially if you're planning to marry someone you don't know if you've broken up with or not."

"We're not broken up anymore. He loves me." She ran her hand through her hair. "I think."

"You think?" He almost growled. "Well, does he or doesn't he? Where was he last summer? How come you thought you had broken up?"

She pulled at the neck of her white knit shirt. "At college."

"So?" The shedder fell from Ty's hand. He picked it up quickly. "Didn't he keep in touch?"

"No. He kinda dropped out of sight . . . like you."

"Me?"

"Yes. I'd about decided I'd never see you again. You'd quit writing. I had no idea where you'd moved. Kevin, . . ." she shook her head, "evidently Kevin figured out where you and your family had gone. He has sources you wouldn't believe." Sources . . . connections . . . finaglings. Boy, did he ever! That devil. He probably thought it fair to meddle in her love life since she had in his.

"I don't keep in touch with girls who two-time me." Ty led the stallion out of the stall. "Excuse us." He stepped between her and the chestnut. "Careful. Don't get too close."

"Oh, don't worry." Heather's chin raised.

"To the horse." Ty grinned.

Heather straightened to her full five feet three inches. "I knew that and I didn't two-time you. I didn't start dating David again until several months after the fair. . . ." Her voice trailed off while her mind retrieved a memory. "That's when you stopped writing, wasn't it? Your last letter came two days before the fair."

He tipped his head. "Do you blame me? You two looked pretty friendly."

"The fair. The fair. Forget the fair!"

"Easy for you to say. That's where I saw my girl kissing another guy."

"But David didn't know I was your girl. He thought I was his girl." She closed her eyes and grimaced. This was not going well—not well at all.

Ty stopped short. The stallion kept walking. Ty pulled him back. "Well, I guess that's part of the problem, isn't it? You don't seem to know whose girl you are."

Heather shuddered. He made her sound like her once-best-friend, Sheila, who continually surrounded herself with a bevy of boys, never actually deciding between them, but usually preferring the ones who belonged to someone else. Once David had been Sheila's prey. "I'm my own girl," she said through clenched teeth.

"Really. Does David know that? How come he didn't write? What . . . did he know you were two-timing him with me? Does he know about me?"

"Yes, no and yes," she answered as she watched Ty and the stallion walk down the aisle in front of her. Great looking guy. Great looking horse. Had Ty brought the stallion from the ranch? The beautiful animal looked familiar, but she couldn't place him. She wrinkled her nose. How could she forget a horse that looked like that?

"David didn't know about me at first, but he does now?" Ty called back over his shoulder.

"Yep. He does now. He didn't decide not to write to me because of you, though. He didn't know about you then. He didn't write to me because he got scared."

"Scared?" Ty stopped the horse and waited for her to catch up. He peered down at her from his six-foot height. "Of you?"

She hugged her middle. "Not of me—exactly. He said he got scared of . . . of falling in love with me." Her voice tapered off.

"That is risky."

Heather raised her brows. "He said he liked me too much and we're so young and he's got so much school ahead." She shrugged. "He sorta sounded like my mother. He said he thought we'd better cool it for a while."

"Okay . . ." Ty paused, his lips thinning. "So you'd decided to 'cool' it for a while. . . . What changed?"

She forced herself to look at Ty. "David said he missed me too much."

Ty's eyes flashed. "So you immediately forgot about us." He turned the chestnut into a stall then stepped back, securing the gate. The layer of wood shavings covering the floor crunched under the horse's hooves.

"I didn't forget about us. No way. I told him about you and how much you meant to me, but then you didn't come to the fair—uh—I didn't think you came to the fair—and you didn't write—and then I didn't know where you'd gone and David kept coming around . . ."

Ty grasped the top of her arm. Heather pictured a wolf pouncing on a chipmunk's tail. "Do you love him, Heather?"

"Yes. Probably. I don't know. I thought I did until . . ." She traced the side of the stall door with her nail.

"Until?"

She had to tell him. She couldn't have him thinking last summer meant nothing to her because . . . because it meant everything. "Until just now when I saw you again."

"So you do remember us?" he said in the soft, tender voice he reserved mostly for talking to his horses, and before she had left him last summer, to her. His grip on her arm relaxed.

"Of course I do. How could I forget? I watched for you at the fair. I didn't see you, honest. When David showed up, he was so sweet and I guess I was feeling a little rejected." Yes. First David had left her, then it appeared that Ty had followed the trend. Once she'd kidded fifteen-year-old Katie about the girl's fear of being an old maid. Now it seemed as if she herself at eighteen was so afraid of having no one, that she'd let David back in her life without question. She frowned, not particularly liking this revelation about herself.

"I was happy to see him." Heather started out whispering, then continued with more confidence. "And when you didn't write, you didn't call, I thought you didn't care about us anymore—that I was just a summer pastime to you."

"I'm not like that."

"I know . . . now. I thought it was happening again. David didn't write—you didn't write. I don't know. I'm so sorry."

Hands on her shoulders, Ty turned her to face him. "Where do we go from here?"

"I wish I knew." She analyzed the dirt on the ground. "Do you think it's possible to have strong feelings for two people?"

He lifted her chin with his finger. "You're living proof." His eyes narrowed.

They faced each other. Heather's heart raced. She longed to lay her head against his chest and feel his strong, safe arms around her.

"I've got fourteen horses to feed and water," he said finally. "Wanna help?"

Relieved at the change of subject and glad Ty would let her stick around, Heather replied, "Love to. Oh, shoot! I forgot about my horse. He's still outside in the trailer unless Kevin's unloaded him. Would you like to have fifteen horses for dinner?"

He grinned, allowing her a glimpse of the old Ty. "I've got a stall just his size." He continued down the aisle to stand beside a double-wide stall, one probably designed for a mare and foal. "You're . . . you're just staying the night?"

"I'm not sure."

"About a lot of things . . . lately," Ty said.

Pulling a tissue from the pocket of her jeans, Heather waved it like a white flag. "I give up. Can we call a truce?"

Ty chuckled. "For now."

Across the aisle from where Image would stay the night, a beautiful sorrel mare stretched her neck across the stall gate.

"Is that Lady Roxanna? Oh, my gosh. She's incredible." Walking over to stroke the mare's velvet nose, Heather remembered how she'd helped Ty acquire the gorgeous, registered Quarter Horse the summer before. "Image will be pleased." She smiled.

Ty smiled too.

"This is a beautiful barn," she said. "You'll have to tell me why you're here and fill me in on how everyone is."

"You'll see for yourself at dinner tonight, except for Colton. He's at school and working on his instrument rating. He got his pilot's license, you know."

Heather felt Ty's stare. Since she tried so hard to show nothing, she knew her face went scarlet red. Apparently neither of them had forgotten that she'd fallen for Ty's older brother last summer before she'd noticed Ty. Colton had called her "green eyes" even though his eyes were darker green than hers. No wonder seeing her with David had made him so angry. He probably felt she fluttered from guy to guy without so much as a backward glance. "Great," she said, intentionally ignoring his reference to Colton. "I can't wait to see everyone again."

Ty grabbed a hose hooked to an inside water faucet and handed it to Heather. "Here. You can fill up Image's water barrel and fetch him some hay from the stack just outside that door." His arm brushed hers and she felt her pulse race.

The chestnut stallion snorted as she passed his stall. Heather stopped. She studied him from nose to tail. "Beautiful animal," she told Ty. "Boy, does he ever look like that racehorse who disappeared about a year ago. You know . . ." She snapped her fingers, trying to remember.

"Freedom's Choice?" Ty said.

"Right. It isn't him, is it?" Heather teased.

All expression faded from Ty's face. "I don't see how he could be. You don't really think he looks like Freedom's Choice, do you?"

CHAPTER TWO

As if he'd had a run-in with a streak of lightning, Royal Image bolted down the ramp of the four-horse slant, aluminum trailer. Heather scurried after him, hanging onto his long lead rope.

"Some things never change." Ty slipped the rope from Heather's hand and pulled the black Thoroughbred into a tight circle around them. "Whoa, boy. Steady. That's a good black-hearted devil." His voice never shifted from its kind, gentle tone.

Heather laughed. "Careful. You'll hurt his feelings."

Ty brought the horse up next to him and patted the gelding's long neck. "Heaven forbid."

"I can't blame him for being frisky." Heather glanced up at tall pine trees stretching into a cloudless blue sky. "He's been traveling in cramped quarters."

"Not too cramped. This your rig, Heather?"

The extra-wide trailer sported a dressing room up front—not that Image had any use for it—but the padded walls and rubber matted floor of his accommodations were nearly as nice. Two red stripes, one wide, the other narrow, ran the complete length of the twenty-foot trailer and matched the shiny Dodge diesel that pulled it.

"It's Kevin's. Looks like he's in the horse business again." She grinned. "He's happy, really happy. Mostly because of Mom and my new brother, Robby, but I like to take credit too, and, of course, there's the horses."

"Good for him," Ty said. "He deserves it."

Heather remembered Ty's reaction last summer when she'd told him about her stepfather's background. Once a member of the U.S. Equestrian Team, Kevin had nearly resigned from the human race after his daughter's fatal fall from a horse and the messy divorce that followed.

Bringing her back from thoughts of a year ago, Ty continued, "You remember my trailer, I trust." His hand brushed Heather's as they led Image toward the barn.

She smiled, only partly from thoughts of the dilapidated green and rust two-horse trailer.

A wind chime clanged in the distance. Birds chirped and sang until they grew impossible to ignore. Image answered a whinny from inside the large, cedar-sided barn.

"You're smiling. You must remember my trailer." Ty pulled Image away from tufts of grass alongside their pathway.

"It's not that bad," Heather giggled, "but I did notice you tried to hide it in those trees over there." She pointed. "Gosh. It's beautiful here. Everything's so green. There are ferns growing under those pines."

"Yeah. It's something all right. Wait until you see a sunrise on the lake." He gestured to their left. "Actually, I just parked the trailer over there to get it out of the way. I'm gonna buy a fancier one as soon as I get this barn paying."

Heather got the impression they were discussing horse transportation to avoid talking about what really troubled them.

Ty opened the sliding front door to the stable so they could pass through. Image's hooves clomped against the packed dirt floor. At the sight of the other horses, the gelding whinnied again.

This time as Heather moved down the aisle in the barn, she paid more attention to the horses stabled there.

Next to the stall where Image would stay, she saw one of her favorite horses from the ranch, a stocky Palomino who belonged to Ty's sister, Katie.

"Partner!" Heather stepped to the stall door for a closer look. "You brought Partner. I'm so glad."

"No way could we leave him." Ty and Image joined Heather at the Palomino's stall.

The geldings sniffed noses.

"Katie doesn't ride much these days, but I can put anyone on Partner for lessons and the old boy takes care of them. Besides, he's part of the family. Some days I'd take him over Katie."

Heather laughed, remembering the Katie of last summer—red pigtails, braces, fifteen years old and still no figure. She was full of imagination and mischief, usually the center of some drama, more often creating it. A year ago, Katie had thought the neighboring ranch house was haunted and nearly gotten herself, Heather and others killed when her "ghost" turned out to be an escaped murderer. Ty had come to their rescue. Come to think of it, he'd always been there when Heather needed him.

Of course, lately David had too. Now in Utah attending Brigham Young University along with Heather, he'd helped her register, shown her to classes, and introduced her to all the right people.

Image poked his nose through the rails of the stall and nipped at Partner.

"You won't recognize Katie," Ty said. "She's pretty cute now and since she's been acting, she wears makeup and stuff. She's filled out too." Immediately Ty's face turned red. He glanced away.

"Katie's acting? Where?" Heather sensed color rising in her cheeks too. Always the gentleman, Ty probably felt uncomfortable mentioning Katie's figure. Katie, on the other hand, would have discussed anything. At times it was difficult to keep the redhead quiet. Last summer she'd continually bird-dogged Heather and Ty and made it no secret how happy she was when they'd finally gotten together. How would Katie react when she found out about David?

"She's working at Bigfork. It's a summer theater about thirty miles north of here, right at the top part of the lake," Ty answered. "They're doing *Bye Bye Birdie*. Katie plays Kim. If you were staying longer, we'd go watch her." He studied Heather as if searching for some reaction. Then he led Image into the stall and removed the gelding's halter.

The big horse lay down and rolled, then stood to shake himself off. Wood shavings slipped from his sleek body. True to his Thoroughbred breeding, the gelding was tall and lanky, with strong shoulders and hindquarters for running, but this Thoroughbred used his muscle for show jumping.

"You'll have to admit Image is quite pretty now."

Ty nodded. "Not bad for a big sissy."

Heather rolled her eyes. "We won quite a few trophies on this 'big sissy' last season. Kevin even rides him in some classes. We owe you a lot."

"Me?"

"Yeah. Before we came to Montana last summer, Image was a total . . . a total wingnut."

"Early mornings, mud, mountains, sweat . . . It's amazing what a summer on a ranch can do for a fellow." Ty buckled the top of the halter he'd taken off Image, coiled the lead rope and handed them to Heather.

"No. I think it was more than that. It really was you. You never let me give up. You made me believe in myself again." Her eyes met his and couldn't pull away. She wished things could be as they once were when she and Ty were best friends. Of course, David would never approve of her having Ty as a best friend.

"There's my little cowboy," someone said.

Heather turned to see Wells Taggert, Ty's father, and her stepfather, Kevin Quinn, walking into the barn. Although the two former college buddies were approximately the same age and both noticeably handsome, the contrast between them immediately struck Heather. Wells, in his weathered Stetson and boots, looked like he'd just stepped out of a John Wayne movie; while wearing close-fitting tan riding pants and knee-high English dress boots, Kevin appeared as if he had spent the afternoon watching polo with Prince Charles.

Kevin extended his hand to Ty. Wells, displaying none of Ty's earlier restraint, wrapped his arms around Heather. Although she hugged him back, his reaction caught her by surprise. Kevin had probably not mentioned David to Ty's dad.

"I see you brought along that ill-mannered renegade of yours?" Wells favored her with a lopsided grin.

"Yes. Kevin wanted to come." Heather leaned out of the embrace.

Her dark-haired stepfather cocked a brow. "These youngsters nowadays have absolutely no respect for their elders. . . ." He jerked his head toward Ty, ". . . with the possible exception of this young man."

Ty chuckled, stole a quick glance at Heather, then stared at the dirt floor.

As if any of Kevin's apparel would ever need straightening, Heather adjusted the lapel of his tweed English-cut jacket. "You're just not elder enough, I guess."

Rubbing the back of his neck, Kevin replied, "I'd say she wiggled out of that one, wouldn't you, gentlemen?"

He'd addressed both father and son, but only Wells answered. "I'd be willing to wager she could charm herself out of a rattlesnake den."

"I wish," Heather said. She knew now that when it came to Ty's state fair experience, she'd been about as charming as skunk spray.

Ty opened the gate to Image's stall and disappeared inside.

The gelding walked to the far side of the enclosure.

"Oh! You meant my ill-mannered horse, didn't you? Yes, we had to bring him along." Heather grinned at Wells and followed Ty into the stall. "Image is a much better boy these days. Did Kevin tell you he won the jumping championship in Helena?"

Cornering Image, Ty leaned down to check one of the gelding's leg wraps.

"Championship, huh? He must be good." Wells stared at Image's sixteen-hand-high shoulder. "If only he weren't so short. How do you get on him?"

"Fence posts are handy, buckets, Kevin. . . ." Heather rubbed the gelding behind his long, narrow ears.

"That's why she keeps me around." Kevin joined Ty at Image's feet.

Wells laughed, a big belly laugh from deep down. That was the way these Taggerts were—big-hearted and friendly. They accepted everyone for who they were and respected others' opinions even if they didn't share them.

Heather loved Ty's family almost as much as she once thought she loved Ty, but she loved David's family too, particularly Matthew Cane, David's father, who was her main boss at the legal office where she worked part-time. Mr. Cane had always been so kind—making extra time for her in his busy schedule, continually helping her hone her secretarial skills, not to mention allowing her extra time off whenever she needed it to show her horses.

"Do you want to leave these leg wraps on, or shall I take them off?" Ty asked Kevin. He was strictly business now. Image was in his barn and he seemed to feel utmost responsibility.

"Let's take them off," Kevin said.

Only after they had Image settled in and he'd begun to care for the other horses did Ty open up. He retrieved a wheelbarrow from a storage area in the barn and filled it with a bag of grain and a can of food supplement. "Wanna come along?" he asked. "I'll introduce you to all the ponies." The trio followed after him. "Let's start with Image. Does he need grain?"

"No!" Kevin and Heather said in unison. The big horse didn't need extra energy right now.

"I'll take that as a definite no. Sorry, Image," Ty said.

They headed away from the building's entrance to the next stall.

"You all know Partner," Ty said. "Oh, except for Kevin. Kevin, this is Partner, Katie's horse from the ranch."

"Partner," Kevin said, nodding.

The Palomino received a small portion of grain.

They walked by a passageway which, according to Ty, led behind the first row of stalls to a tackroom and grooming area.

The next three stalls contained horses in training for other people in the area.

Six stalls ran up the center of the barn, the first two of which were empty. Then came the ones containing Ty's new purchases—three registered Quarter Horse mares—a sorrel, a bay and a buckskin. Roxie stood in the end center stall, across from Image. The four mares received grain and food supplements.

"Look at the shoulder on that buckskin and the hip on the sorrel," Kevin commented.

"Beauties, aren't they?" Ty smiled, clearly pleased by Kevin's approval.

Soon the two of them were so engrossed in conversation that Wells and Heather followed along, back down the aisle they'd just come through, as mere spectators. A twinge of uneasiness taunted Heather. What was it? Silly girl. She felt left out.

Six stalls on the opposite side of the barn had fenced runs out the back so the horses could go outside if that door was left open. A chorus of whinnies greeted Ty and his three companions as they walked along that row of stalls.

A mature sorrel mare, heavy with foal, peered out at them from the first stall on the far side. She received a generous portion of grain and supplement. Next came the four geldings Ty had brought with him from the ranch: Sage, Joker, Drover and Arab.

"I just couldn't leave these guys behind." Ty gave each of the horses a loving pat and a can full of grain. Heather noticed Ty's hands with their long slender fingers—gentle hands—now with a deep scratch across his left index finger. She remembered those hands holding hers. She shook her head. Snap out of it, girl. Remember whose ring you're wearing.

When they came to the last stall where Ty had put the stallion, Heather had to stop for another look. The huge horse was so unbelievably beautiful and brawny. Image was taller, but the stallion probably outweighed her horse by a hundred pounds or more, and he was a deep chestnut—red from the tips of his short, fine ears to the end of his flowing tail—with only a tiny spot of white on his forehead. Actually, Heather thought with a smile, the stallion's perfect conformation reminded her of David, who was also big, solid and handsome. Ty was more like Image—a slender, trimmer version of perfection.

The chestnut horse stood with his head turned away from them. Heather stepped closer and extended her hand through the bars in the gate to coax the horse over.

"No!" Ty grabbed Heather. She fell back against him.

Charging the gate with teeth bared, the beautiful red stallion had become a raging demon.

Wells stepped between the horse and Heather. Kevin looked from one to the other with a perplexed frown on his face.

"I'm sorry, Ty, I didn't mean to upset him." Heather felt his heart beating against the back of her shoulder.

"It's not your fault," Ty said into her hair. "He's just plain ornery. I should've warned you." Then, as if realizing for the first time how close he held her, Ty dropped his arms to his sides.

"Whoa," Kevin said. "Where'd you get this fellow?"

"I don't think he needs extra grain, do you?" Ty checked the gate to see if it was secure. "The man we bought this place from, McCade Saxton, left him behind."

"I don't wonder." Kevin peeked around Ty to the pacing stallion.

"He's pretty, though, don't you think?" Ty asked.

Kevin grinned. "I don't know. It's hard to see past the mouth."

"Yeah. I'm beginning to wonder what to do about him. He's not bad under saddle, but, as you can see, he has terrible stable manners." Ty glanced over his shoulder. His gaze fell on Heather but switched to Kevin when her eyes met his. "I call him Rocky because he's always picking a fight. His registered name is Red Rock's Last Chance. I've been thinking about getting him gelded, but look at him, and he's got a pedigree that won't quit. He's out of that famous Quarter Horse stallion, Red Storm. I think McCade paid a fortune for him."

"And then he ran off without him." This from Wells.

"Strange, huh?" Ty said. "But I wasn't going to argue. He left the stallion and that old sorrel mare. She's in foal to Rocky, and if what I hear is true, I'm in for it."

Kevin started over to look at the mare again. "How do you mean?"

"I guess all Rocky's foals are just like him—all chestnut, all solidly built, all mean."

"Ooh," Heather said.

"That gelding I'm training for Mitch Jeffreys two stalls down from Partner is Rocky's colt too," Ty said. "He's chestnut, solidly built and mean, I mean, mean. I've been working with him twice as long as the gelding next to him and sometimes it's like I've never touched him." He shook his head.

"Bad mind, huh?" Heather asked.

"Actually no, I think he's smart, real smart. If only he wasn't so ornery. I'm about to suggest that Mitch sell him for rodeoing. That horse would make one heck of a saddle bronc."

"It sounds like you have your hands full," Kevin said.

They were all by the outside door of the barn. Wells started out. "Better get back to work now. I've got a pump that's been acting up and the lawn's burning."

"I'll go with you," Kevin said. "Thanks for the tour, Ty, and for putting Image up for the night." He made a wide circle around the red stallion. "Do you need any help here?"

"No, I'm fine. Heather's already volunteered."

Kevin smiled, a strange twitch of a smile, Heather thought.

"That was before I met Rocky." Heather followed Kevin out the door.

Grabbing her arm, Ty pulled her inside the barn. "Oh, no you don't. You're not backing out on me now just because you've met a man-eating . . . uh, a woman-eating horse."

Heather laughed. "I remember when you thought Image was a challenge. Times have changed."

"They sure have," Ty returned.

CHAPTER THREE

Later that evening, Wells and Bea Taggert, Ty, Kevin and Heather gathered for dinner around a large bricked fire pit about twenty feet from the shores of Flathead Lake.

Cherry wood popped in the fire, waves swished against the cement retaining wall that separated the huge front lawn from the lake, the moon reflected silver on the black rolling water and Heather felt like she'd passed through the Pearly Gates.

Wells distributed his own specially designed wienie roasting sticks—half-inch metal tubing with wooden handles attached to one end and sharpened forked rods to the other. Bea, Ty's mother, heaped a picnic table with various temptations, including potato salad, fresh fruit—cut up bite size, homemade buns and bottled mustard pickle.

The only thing that kept it from being a totally awesome event was that when they all pulled up lawn chairs around the fire, Ty chose to sit on the other side of Kevin instead of next to Heather. A chill of rejection forced the smile from her lips. Why had she thought Ty would seek her company? Wasn't she all but engaged to David? She chewed her bottom lip.

In the barn earlier Ty had been sweet, even kidded with her as they finished the chores. Now he ignored her. She stared across the lake into the darkness as a vision of David's face flashed through her mind. She smiled, but the likeness instantly vanished.

Bea opened a bag of hot dogs and offered one to Heather.

"Thank you," she said, her mind still on Ty and David. Then remembering her manners, she jumped to her feet. "Oh, here, let me help."

"No, dear, you're tired. You just sit and relax." Bea touched Heather's shoulder and smiled. "I have everything under control." A little over five feet tall, Bea was one of the few adults who looked at Heather face to face. The woman's eyes twinkled. Actually, Heather remembered, they generally did.

Heather adored Bea. She had a heart as big as a washtub and a smile wider than a sickle blade. She was kind like Ty, and full of energy, information and advice. Heather remembered at the ranch the summer before Bea had known everyone in the valley, all their children and pets by name, and all their problems, and had figured out ways to be of service to all. Heather knew it would be the same here, once Bea had a chance to work her magic.

Following Bea's hot dog passing path, Heather's glance fell on Ty. Firelight flickered across his tanned face and made his hair appear golden. Golden? At the ranch, under the huge cowboy hat he always wore, Ty's hair had been dark. Now, longer and bleached by the sun, it seemed more the tawny brown color of his brother, Colton's.

Ty must have sensed her gazing at him for he gave her a quick smile—nothing special, but nice. She almost wished he'd treat her mean if he felt she deserved it, but Ty wasn't like that. How would she ever learn his true feelings—and what of her own?

Good grief, here she was moping about Ty's brush-off when it was David she loved. Wasn't it?

Ty laughed at something Kevin said. Heather's attention peaked when she tuned in to what they discussed—why the Taggerts had left their ranch and settled here in this paradise farther to the north.

Spearing a wienie with his roasting stick, Ty explained, "I'd been dealing with this guy by the name of McCade Saxton on a couple of Quarter Horse mares." He gestured with his free hand. "Actually, you've seen the mares—that buckskin and bay in the middle stalls."

Kevin followed Ty's lead, placed a hot dog on a stick and stuck it next to a burning log. "Nice mares." He paused. "You know, I've heard of McCade Saxton."

"When I was looking for mares last year, I found that most Quarter Horse people had," Ty said. "It was like Quarter Horse and McCade Saxton were one and the same name."

Heather watched their hot dogs bubble and blister in the fire. Juice dripped onto the coals, enhancing the already wonderful scent of pines and bonfire.

Ty had to walk in front of Heather to get to the mustard, relish and other goodies. "Dig in," he told her. "We don't usually have to ask a person twice." Piling his plate with food from the picnic table, he went on with his story. "That's why I came up here in the first place—to buy those mares. McCade and I became friends and I started visiting on a regular basis. I bought the mares while we still lived on the ranch." He slipped by Heather only to return to his seat next to Kevin.

"If I'd known we were going to end up here anyway, I wouldn't have hauled them all the way to the ranch." He shrugged. "Of course I had no idea what McCade planned."

Wells cleaned another of the wienie roasting sticks, poking it into the pebbles at the lake shore and sloshing it up and down. "Boy, is that ever right. I was as surprised as a kid on Christmas morning when Ty came home and told me about McCade's offer. He said he'd been thinking about getting out of the horse business for years and why didn't we make him an offer." Wells rejoined the group.

Bea handed him a hot dog and he placed it on the freshly cleaned stick, then stuck it in the coals. After watching what Wells had done, Heather readied her stick for a hot dog.

"Since at the time we hadn't sold our ranch, I suggested a deal I thought he'd flat refuse," Wells went on, talking more directly now to Heather than to Kevin. "I'll be darned if he didn't accept it."

Although the fire warmed Heather's face, the breeze off the lake made her glad she'd worn a sweatshirt. She smiled at Wells as she stepped to the picnic table.

He grinned back and followed. "Afterwards," he went on, "since we'd been able to come up with that adjoining ranch along with its water, we sold the two ranches together for a fairly decent profit. I still can't figure why McCade would part with this place for less than it was worth. Must have been that since he's gettin' on in age some—being around sixty I'd figure—he was just plain tired." He passed Heather the mustard. "Of course he'd taken a liking to Ty. Imagine that." Wells winked at her for some reason. "And since he didn't have any kids of his own, I guess he wanted Ty to have it. Makes a fellow wonder, though. Why such a hurry? He even left behind two horses rather than taking time to sell them like he'd done the rest."

Heather and Wells filled their plates. She sat down on the other side of Kevin, Wells on the opposite side of Ty.

Ty stopped chewing and said, "The sorrel mare was his favorite. Maybe at first he was planning on taking her along, and the stallion . . ." He rolled his eyes. "We all know about him. But the place is ours now, all sure and legal, and that's what matters."

After making certain everyone was comfortable and getting fed, Bea settled into the empty chair next to Heather, placing her own plate on her lap. "Tell me about yourself, dear. I understand there may be a wedding in your near future."

Heather choked on potato salad and began to cough. She drained her entire cup of hot chocolate and glanced at Kevin, who stared at her. Actually, everyone was staring.

Kevin and his big mouth, Heather thought, then wondered at her own reaction. If she'd decided to marry David, shouldn't she be getting it out in the open? Of course, since everyone knew what she and Ty had meant to each other last summer, it would be a little uncomfortable for both of them for a while, but so be it. David was the important one, wasn't he?

Off in the distance dogs barked. It surprised Heather how far across the lake sounds carried. For a moment, she wished she were far away with the barking dogs. "I've been asked," Heather began.

"Twice," Ty mumbled.

She studied him, trying to read his thoughts. "I've been asked, but Kevin thinks I'm too young." Placing her unfinished meal on the ground beside her, she slid back in her chair. "Eighteen is young."

"Well, I'll be . . ." Kevin burst out. "Progress."

"Bea was seventeen when we married," Wells offered.

"That's enough out of you," Kevin said.

"You want to be sure, dear," Bea told Heather. "You'll be married for a very long time."

Heather lay her hand on Bea's arm. "You're right about that." She retrieved her plate from beside her chair, walked to a garbage sack near the table and tossed in what remained of her dinner. Folding her arms tightly against her body, she edged closer to the fire. No one else seemed to be, but she was shivering.

"Well, if it isn't Little Miss Two-Timer."

Whirling around, Heather watched Katie pace down the sidewalk from the house.

When Ty said his sister had changed, he hadn't been just stretching his vocal cords. Pigtails, freckles and braces—all gone. The youthful cocoon had fallen away to reveal a confident sixteen-year-old beauty with generous curves and brownish red hair tumbling to the middle of her toned five-foot-seven-inch body. The once vulnerable blue eyes flashed in the firelight and the darkly painted scarlet lips curled in contempt. Katie still wore her theatrical makeup which, for as pretty as she looked, made her seem even more the stranger. Heather had rarely seen this side of Katie's temper.

"Hi, Katie," Heather said, picturing an excitable chestnut filly with flowing mane and bared teeth.

"I can't believe you'd really come here, after what you did to Ty." Her nostrils flared.

"That's enough, Kate." Ty stepped between Heather and his sister. "Don't go running off at the mouth until you know what's happening."

"How can you protect her? Are you forgetting how bummed you were?"

Heather felt the weight of an anvil at the back of her neck.

"I said, that's enough." Ty's eyes narrowed.

Heather's face burned like the bonfire she stood beside. "Give me a break, will you? I can explain." If only she could.

Wells, Bea and Kevin sat speechless, mouths ajar, like they witnessed the approach of an oncoming train and couldn't get off the tracks.

"I'm listening, but this better be good." Katie lifted her chin. "Were you or were you not kissing that other guy?"

"Do we have to go into this right now? Right here?" Heather lowered her voice. She would've much preferred to explain to Katie in private.

"You won't bother us." Kevin looked up innocently.

"Go right ahead," added Wells.

Heather could have strung both of them up by their thumbs and felt good about it. Some help they were.

"I'm waiting." Katie folded her arms.

"Kate!" Ty warned.

The redhead clenched her jaw.

"Okay, okay, I'll tell you. Looks like I have no choice." Heather swallowed a couple of times, then began.

She told about David coming back from college, about the friendly victory kiss at the fair, her trips to the empty mailbox and her fear that Ty had changed his mind. David had been extra sweet, Heather reported, even when they'd discussed her feelings for Ty, and he'd been there to comfort her after it appeared Ty's interest had strayed.

"Hmm. Now let me get this straight. First there's David, then there's Colton, then there's Ty, then there's David—again. Are there more? How do you find time for your horses?" Katie flung her arms out, palms up. "My love life should be half as exciting. So now who's number one?"

"Don't you see?" Heather choked. "I don't know. David's a wonderful guy. He really is, but Ty . . ." To her total humiliation, when she glanced at him, she burst into tears.

Both Bea and Ty stepped closer, but Heather held up her hand and backed away. "I'm sorry. I can't do this right now." She turned and started for the house. The Taggert home stretched along the crest of the hill for what seemed a half a block or more. Heather was running when she reached it. She kept right on going. When she felt like this, she always sought the comfort of her horse. She wished Possum, her favorite, were here. Image would have to do.

Ty flipped on the light and walked inside the barn. "Are you okay in here, Heather?"

She sat cross-legged in the corner of Image's stall. The big Thoroughbred stood with his neck extended over her, like a mare protecting a foal.

Before Image's ranch training last summer, she would have never trusted him enough to share his stall. Since then, however, they'd spent countless hours together at horse shows and in the practice ring. She and David had even taken Image and Possum, Heather's other horse, on a ride in the mountains last spring. An attorney-in-training, David wasn't comfortable around horses, but he loved Possum and the gray gelding had always taken a fancy to him—rooting in his pockets for the treats David brought. Image, ignoring David completely, took treats only from Heather.

"I'm fine," Heather answered in the most normal voice she could muster, "but thanks for checking." Heat rose in her cheeks. Ty had known right where to find her. Running off to hide in a horse's stall wasn't the most grown-up thing to do. But she couldn't help it. Darn it. How was she supposed to feel? How could she love David and still have her heart nearly leap out of her chest whenever she saw Ty?

"Shall I leave the light on, or not?" Ty continued down the aisle, visiting with each horse as he passed.

"Off's fine," Heather said, instead of what she really wanted to—something like, *Stay here and talk for a minute. Help me sort out my feelings, maybe just hold me for a while.*

"Okay. See you tomorrow." He flipped off the light as he left.

Heather bumped the back of her head against the side of the stall, bumped it again, then again as if that would clear her mind. What was wrong with her? Wasn't Ty just a dear, kind friend—she sighed—who was far too handsome for anyone's good? Stop it! Her thoughts should have been of David, not Ty. She wore David's ring and his necklace. Necklace! Actually she had two—David's, a silver chain and running horse charm, a gift to her as he headed off to college two years ago, and then there was Ty's . . . Remembering that day about ten months ago, she smiled.

She'd been lingering in the doorway, trying to memorize the details of the room that had been hers during her summer stay at the ranch. Ty had come up behind her.

"I have something for you," he said. "Turn around and close your eyes."

Heather did as Ty suggested, sensing his arms pass in front of her face before he secured something around her neck.

"There." He took her hand. "Come look in the mirror."

A silver key—like a smaller version of ones used to open doors in old English mansions—hung suspended on a matching chain around her neck. It was beautiful.

"Is this the key to your heart?" Heather had tried to make her voice sound light.

"You could say that." His liquid brown eyes told her he'd not been kidding.

"You have mine too," she'd said.

Now her hand clenched into a fist and she pounded her leg. There she went again. "David! David! David! Not Ty," she almost shouted.

Image's head bobbed.

"Sorry, boy." Relaxing her hand, she rubbed her leg. "Go back to sleep."

There was a word for girls like her. She couldn't think of it now, but it was no compliment.

Here she was wearing David's necklace . . . yes, wearing David's necklace, but she'd brought Ty's along, nestled in her suitcase. What had she been thinking? When she'd packed the other night, she'd not known she'd be seeing Ty again. Maybe coming to Montana had triggered the impulse. She wouldn't wear it, though. It would remain safely in her suitcase. What could be wrong with that? David's ring on her finger and necklace around her neck would keep him close to her. She'd make certain of it.

Now, what was that word she couldn't think of earlier? Ty had said something about two-timing. Heather grimaced.

All at once more words popped into her mind—two-faced, deceitful, double-crosser. How about fickle? She didn't like the sound of that.

Whatever happened to the days before David and Ty, when all she had to worry about romantically was . . . was, well, nothing. She hadn't even had a boyfriend before David and Ty. How pathetic was that? She yawned. It had been a very long day.

The next thing Heather knew her head jerked. She must have fallen asleep. She rubbed her arms to take away the chill and wondered how long she had been here in the stall.

Her eyes began to adjust to the darkness. She could make out Image's dark form still on guard above her.

She stood, brushed sawdust off her pants, patted Image and headed out of the barn. The full moon cast its glow on the grassy pathway leading to the cedar-sided home.

Turning the knob on the door, Heather entered the house through the side door by the garage. She tiptoed into the hall where an old rifle leaned against the corner of an exposed coat nook, a coiled lariat shared a hook with a Levi jacket, and boots sat beside tennis shoes on the floor. Framed photos of scenes from the ranch decorated the walls of the hall, as well as a Charlie Russell calendar upon which someone had inked birthdays, anniversaries and other important events on the appropriate dates. In spite of herself, Heather lifted the June page of the calendar to peak beneath. She grinned, happy that her July 16th birthday had been circled and labeled. She'd be nineteen then and, according to Kevin, probably still too young to get married, but considering how seeing Ty had affected her . . . Stop it. She wasn't going to let herself think that way again. Tonight she felt ninety instead of nineteen.

She moved down the hall past a laundry room, a half bath and a small study, which was decorated with wallpaper depicting various breeds of horses, into a cheerful kitchen. The aroma of bread baking greeted her. She grinned as she recognized an antique table from the ranch—the table that had once belonged to Wells's parents, the table Bea had never particularly liked. It was big and bulky—especially for a kitchen of this size—but Heather knew Bea put up with the heirloom to please Wells.

A dining room came next in Heather's wanderings. She doubted this room would ever be used. As hard as Bea tried, the Taggerts rarely ate formally, preferring instead to gather around the kitchen table or to picnic outside.

Heather noted Bea's beautiful ceramics displayed throughout the house, reminding her of the cherished figurine of a girl and horse that Bea had created as a gift for her last summer.

Lights on the dock illuminated the rolling water as Heather stood in the Taggert front room gazing out of the large picture window, across the abundant lawn, to the lake below. All was silent except for the ticking of the grandfather clock behind her. Its intricate hands read ten after one. Heather had been in the barn for over an hour.

Since Bea had shown her around the house before dinner, Heather knew that three bedrooms and two baths lay beyond the front room where she now stood. The master bedroom, Katie's room and a guest room, where Heather would be staying during her visit, completed the house's main level floor plan.

An oak banister and stairway led to a finished basement, where Kevin probably now lay snoozing in a room next to Ty's.

Still unable to sleep herself, Heather sank into an overstuffed armchair. Her gaze settled on framed photos of Ty, Colton and Katie on top of the TV. Bea and Wells certainly had beautiful kids. What a surprise Katie had been. The butterfly had truly shed her cocoon. Butterfly. Heck. A wasp with stinger pointed.

Heather dragged herself from the chair, walked a few steps to the bedroom, pulled down the bedspread, kicked off her shoes and without even removing her clothes, collapsed on top of the covers. Her eyes closed.

Pine-laden air from the open window flowed in over Heather's face the next morning and the sound of wind chimes rewarded her ears. Warmed by the memory of Bea's excitement the day before over her earlier purchase, Heather chuckled, knowing that whenever she'd hear a similar sound in the future, it would remind her of this wonderful place. Glancing at her watch, Heather sat up straight. Seven forty-five! Much later than she usually got up. Image would be pacing the stall, whinnying for breakfast.

The bedroom window faced the lake. Heather stood for a moment, taking in the unspoiled beauty of the shimmering water, tall green pines and jagged mountains. She wondered why Katie hadn't chosen this room instead of the one across the hall with no view of the lake. Probably that room's outside door and full wall of bookcases had influenced Katie's choice. Heather remembered that Ty's sister loved to read and had already collected boxes of books.

Searching through the clothes folded in her suitcase, Heather selected a pair of cutoffs, a knit top and sandals. Maybe today would be her chance to get a tan on her legs. Kevin usually insisted that she ride in long pants and boots and wear that miserable riding helmet to protect her head. He worried too much.

Heather pulled a brush through her light brown hair. She smoothed the bedspread, straightened her clothes and put her suitcase in the closet.

As she opened the bedroom door, Katie came out of the bathroom. She looked almost herself today—a subdued version of the night before. The heavy makeup and exaggerated hairstyle had disappeared, but not the new-found beauty. Katie was even prettier this morning with her red hair hanging loosely around her shoulders and her face freshly washed and natural. She wore shorts and a T-shirt and walked barefoot across the plush, rust-colored carpet. Heather knew she would have to confront her friend eventually, so she smiled and said, "Hi, Kate, are we speaking today?"

Stopping, Katie twisted her mouth in thought, then slowly grinned. "More than likely, I expect. I've been thinking about you all night, but don't go assuming you're off the hook. I'm still ticked—real ticked."

Heather grimaced. "I'm sorry, Katie, but try to understand. I thought things were over between Ty and me." She glanced up and down the hall.

"So you just bounced back to Darwin." Katie folded her arms and leaned back against the hall wall. "What did you do with Ringo, the kitten we gave you? Feed it to Darwin's dog?"

"David. His name is David and he doesn't own a dog. Besides dogs don't take Ringo on. He's king of our barn and he's huge. He loves David."

"I never said he was a smart cat." A smile flashed across Katie's face, then she sobered. "I just keep thinking about Ty. You really hurt him, Heather. He wasn't the same for months. He would hardly even talk to me." She straightened.

"I didn't know." Heather's throat tightened. She returned to her bedroom and crooked a finger for Katie to follow. "I felt pretty awful myself. I even tried to call once, but that was after you moved. It wasn't until Kevin talked to someone who knew someone who knew your dad that he figured out where to find you. I guess I could have done some detective work too, but I figured if Ty wanted to get in touch with me, he knew where I was. After a while David was there and he kind of helped take the hurt away." Heather closed the bedroom door. "David's really sweet too. You'd like him."

"I sincerely doubt it." Katie plopped onto the bed. "So, how do you feel now?"

Heather shook her head. "I . . . I don't know. Honest, I don't." Staring at nothing in particular, she eased down beside Katie. "David's a great guy and I care about him lots, but I gotta tell you, when I saw Ty yesterday, it was like . . . like I'd never left. Now my mind's having a boxing match. I feel guilty when I think about Ty and I'll be darned if I don't feel guilty thinking about David." She shot Katie a sidelong glance. "I don't even know if Ty still cares about me."

Katie frowned. "Don't look at me. He never talks about you anymore."

Jumping to her feet, Heather began to pace. "See, that's another problem. What if it turns out I can't forget Ty, so I don't marry David, and then Ty doesn't want anything to do with me."

"Beats me." Katie shrugged. "I guess you'll just have to be an old maid like me."

Heather stopped and whirled around. "You're impossible." She threw her hands in the air. "I mean it, Katie. I don't know what to do."

"I should have such problems."

"You will." Heather dropped back onto the bed.

"Not me. I'm never getting married."

"Have you looked in the mirror lately? You can run, but you won't be able to hide."

"Who's hiding?"

Heather laughed. "At least you're not mad at me any more." She paused. "Are you?"

Drawing her long legs up under her chin, Katie hugged them to her chest. "I guess not. I can see you're suffering. Actually, time was when I wanted to see you miserable—down and out, tear-your-hair-out miserable." Mischief showed in Katie's large blue eyes.

"Stick around." Heather giggled, then leaned over and gave the taller girl a squeeze. "I've missed you."

"Me too." Katie dropped her legs over the side of the bed and returned the hug. "Now, let's go see what trouble we can stir up. I don't need to work until this afternoon." She jumped up.

"Work?" Heather rose to straighten the bedspread where they'd been sitting. "I hear you're a big star."

"Oh, yeah." Katie rolled her eyes. She opened the door and nodded toward the opening. "After you, my dear. Our public awaits."

"Let me make a quick trip to the bathroom and then there's this guy I've got to see first," Heather returned.

"Ty?"

"Image."

"I knew that," Katie said.

Heather sniffed the wonderful scent of sizzling bacon and of bread, fresh from the electric bread maker, before she and Katie wandered into the sunlit kitchen.

"More eggs?" Bea asked, spatula in hand.

Wells and Kevin sat at the large oak table, eating a breakfast of bacon and eggs, fresh squeezed orange juice, bread and strawberry preserves.

"Morning," Heather said and chuckled. "Those are great." On the wall behind Bea, little decorative plaques displayed their messages. They described anyone but the meticulous and hospitable Bea: "You can touch the dust, but please don't write in it," "If you want breakfast in bed, sleep in the kitchen," and "This is a self-cleaning kitchen, clean it yourself."

Katie greeted the adults with a smile.

Below them, outside a large picture window which comprised one end of the long, narrow kitchen, the sparkling blue lake rested mirrorlike in its bed of cliffs and pines.

"Sit here, you two." Bea pulled out a couple of chairs.

"As delicious as everything looks, I believe I'm going to pass this morning." Heather glanced around the room. "But I'll take a rain check."

"Rain checks are readily accepted at this table." Wells paused, then grinned. "Ty's already come and gone."

Heather's brows raised. "Oh. Okay." She studied her manicure, trying to appear nonchalant.

"I better not eat either." Katie laid her palms across a flat stomach. "I still have to be able to squeeze into my costumes each night."

"Since when have you had to squeeze into anything?" Bea slid another fried egg onto Kevin's plate.

"Yeah," Wells said.

Kevin winked at Katie.

Pulling her gaze from the outside door, Heather stared blankly at her friend. "What did you say? Customs?"

"Costumes." Katie grabbed Heather's hand and patted the back of it like she was trying to bring her back from a faint. "This girl's totally out of it today."

Kevin leaned back in his chair, grinning. His dark hair was combed but still damp, probably from an earlier shower. Heather's mom, Laura, had often commented that being married to—she called him her GQ model—had elevated her own appearance stress level to Olympic proportions. Kevin had always laughed and said, "I only dress up so I'm able to tag along with my beautiful wife." Now he waved his hand in front of Heather and said, "I think he's with the horses."

She blinked. "He who?"

Kevin raised his glass of orange juice. "I'd look in the barn, if I were you."

"Well, I do need to check on Image." Heather smiled.

"Yeah. Yeah. Tell him hi for me." Taking a sip of juice, Kevin returned his attention to breakfast. "Bea. You're spoiling me. Could I have one more egg?"

The barn, spotless as ever, smelled of sawdust and alfalfa. Coming in through the arena door, the girls strolled down the aisle, glancing from side to side at each of the horses. When they came to the red stallion's stall, without even communicating what the other would do, they both eyed it warily and gave it a wide berth. Then they looked at each other and laughed.

"Brave, aren't we?" Katie said.

"Yeah, right," Heather returned.

They walked out through the main entry, crossed in front of the barn and started down the opposite aisle.

"Hi, Partner." Katie greeted her horse, who barely glanced up from his hay.

"Image, old boy. How are you doing this morning?"

Her horse didn't even raise his head.

Heather put her hands on her hips. "I can see we're sorely needed here."

"Yep. You have to get up pretty early in the morning to beat Ty. Let's hit the lake. I think some serious suntanning and gossip are in order." Katie turned for the door.

With the intent of returning later to work Image, Heather followed Katie out of the barn. At the top of the hill overlooking the lake, Heather saw Ty and even though she knew her heart had no right to do so, it raced.

"What's he doing?" She held a hand to her forehead to shade her eyes from the sun.

Katie sighed. "Who knows. He's always doing some fool training thing with his horses."

Fully dressed, Ty headed down the boat ramp leading Roxanna, his favorite mare, into the water.

"Dad says Ty's getting quite a reputation as a trainer." Katie twisted a lock of her long red hair around her finger. "Let's go harass him." Her eyes glistened.

By the time the girls reached Ty, Roxanna was shoulder deep in the clear blue water. Heather imagined the tug of war she'd experience trying to coax Image into the lake. Nothing short of a backhoe would be able to persuade him.

The girls were leaning against the metal rail fencing that separated the sidewalk and lawn from the lake when Ty noticed them.

"Hi," he said to Heather, grinning. "Wearing anything you don't want to get wet?"

Relieved he'd not said anything about her display of emotions the night before, she answered. "Not really."

Ty, riding Roxie bareback, turned the chestnut filly back toward the cement boat ramp. The water in the lake now came just below her belly. "Ever gone swimming on a horse before?"

Heather glanced at Katie, then back at Ty. "Not in recent memory."

"It's about time you gave it a try then. You can too, Kate, if you must."

Ty and Katie, Heather remembered, were never above giving each other a hard time.

"That's okay, but you go, Heather." She nudged her friend.

Creeping around the end of the railing, Heather began her descent down the ramp. "I don't know, Ty, are you sure about this?" She glanced up at him. The breeze blew his thick brown hair across his tanned forehead, giving him an appealing earthy look. "What are you doing anyway? I know. Is this your idea of a sea horse?"

"Cute, Heather." He flashed a dazzling grin. "No, this is therapy and conditioning. Racehorses are worked in swimming pools after leg injuries and show horses are conditioned in pools designed especially for that purpose." He swept his arm to the side, gesturing. "Welcome to the world's largest swimming pool—and Roxie loves to swim. I'd like to show her in some halter classes this year. We're focusing on getting into show shape."

Heather stepped into the water with her sandals. The sudden cold chilled her feet and legs, but she quickly got used to the water temperature. "Looks like the exercise is working. I wonder if swimming would do the same for me."

Ty's gaze traveled up and down Heather's form. "You're already in show shape, but come here, we'll give it a try." He reached down and scooped her up with one arm, placing her in front of him astride the big Quarter Horse mare. His arms hugged Heather's sides as he guided Roxie back into the lake.

Staying close to the shoreline, Roxie did not swim at first, but picked her way along through the water as it washed over Heather's and Ty's lower legs.

"Catch you later, Heather," Katie called from the shore.

Katie was at it again, Heather realized. How cleverly she'd maneuvered Ty and her together.

"I can't believe Roxie likes to swim." Heather fingered the mare's mane.

"A lot of horses do." Ty chuckled. "Even old Rocky."

"Rocky? You kidding me?" She peered back over her shoulder.

"Nope. I left him in the corral one night—the last time I'll ever do that, mind you. When I came out the next morning, he was gone." Ty drew out the last three words.

Heather sucked in a quick breath of air. "Oh, no!"

"I had visions of destroyed fences, torn-up lawns and flower beds, mangled passers-by, but guess where I found him?"

"Where?" Heather said, relieved that Rocky hadn't been out of his stall unsupervised when she and Image were out wandering.

"Right there," Ty pointed to the end of the boat dock, "standing in the water, surveying his kingdom."

"No way. Did you have to go in after him?" She pulled a face. "Scary thought."

"No. I guess he'd finished looking around. I just shook the grain bucket I was carrying and out he came, dripping wet. After he helped himself to the grain, he let himself be haltered and settled in his stall. I've ridden the old boy in the lake a couple of times since then, but I don't completely trust him yet."

"Gosh. I wonder why."

All at once, horse and riders came to a deeper spot in the lake and Roxie began to swim. Heather had expected a rougher ride, but as the mare sank deeper, she glided across the water with just her head, neck and a small portion of her sorrel back above the surface. Her riders were wet to the waist as the water flowed against them. Her heart threatening to pound a hole in her chest, Heather felt Ty's strong body behind her and his legs against hers as they gripped their knees to the sides of the swimming mare.

Powerful sorrel shoulders worked beneath Heather. A final stroke and Roxie's hooves reached solid ground along the lake's shallow edge.

Water washed over their feet and ankles as the couple rode in front of a large parcel of virgin land. Tall pines bordered the shoreline and extended into a forest where no homes marred the landscape.

"An old bachelor owns all this property. He's had hundreds of offers, I hear, but won't sell." Guiding the mare, Ty's arms rested against Heather's sides.

"It's so beautiful. I don't blame the guy." Her eyes widened as Ty leaned forward into her back and a smile crossed her lips as she felt the strength of him against her.

"I guess I don't either." Ty turned Roxie toward the shore. Water streamed from all three as the horse found her footing and walked out onto dry land. Arms still encircling Heather, Ty grabbed the horse's mane as she shook moisture from her sleek body like a giant greyhound.

A trail led into the forest and Roxie trotted along it, her hooves snapping fallen twigs on the ground. Ty slid back, making room between himself and Heather. In the shadow of the dense trees and without him close behind her, she shivered.

"Fine thing." Heather hugged her arms to her body. "After soaking me to the bone, you won't even keep me warm."

"I didn't think you wanted me to keep you warm anymore." His voice carried an edge to it.

Well, what did she expect? Here she was, a visitor in his world, flirting with him while she was supposed to be promised to someone else. She needed to tell him how she felt. One problem. She didn't have a clue. The only thing she knew for certain was having him close, with his arms wrapped around her, meant much more to her than it should. "I asked, didn't I?"

He propped his chin on her shoulder. "Do you always get what you want?"

As Heather tried to figure out what to say, Roxie walked into a clearing in the forest where spears of light broke through the trees. "Oh, there's the sun. I'm all right now."

"Look over there." Ty pointed.

Against the backdrop of lush green, a doe and twin fawns lifted dainty heads from their grazing. Big ears stuck out from the sides of their faces and curious brown eyes stared.

"Oh, aren't they gorgeous?" Heather whispered.

"You wouldn't think that if they stole your cherries or killed the trees in your orchard by chewing off the bark around the trunks," Ty returned.

Just then the doe turned and headed deeper into the forest. One fawn paused, still watching, then whirled around, and, leaping over a fallen tree trunk, darted after its mother and sibling.

"Let's follow." Heather tapped her heels against Roxanna.

"Go for it." Ty snuggled up behind Heather, wrapping his arms around her waist. "But I doubt we'll catch them."

Heather grinned. With all the rank broncs Ty rode, he certainly didn't need his arms around her to stay on.

Roxie needed little encouragement as she extended her trot in pursuit.

Giggling, Ty and Heather struggled to keep straight on the mare's bouncing, soaked back. When Roxie passed under a low-hanging branch, they both leaned the same direction. Ty began to slip and tried to regain his seat. Heather squealed and lost her balance and they both toppled off.

Ty lit on his back in the dirt, and since his arms still encircled Heather, she landed on top. She experienced a fleeting sensation of hard muscles before protocol demanded she wiggle and squirm to his side. For the briefest second he'd held onto her. Laughing, they sat, knees touching, and peeked up through the grass at Roxie. The mare swung her head around as if to say, "What's your problem?"

"Are you okay?" Ty grinned.

"Yep. I lit on you, remember. The more accurate question is, are you okay?"

He rubbed his chest. "I'm pretty squashed, actually—probably never be the same."

"Oh!" Playfully she slugged him on the arm.

"Yeah. I'm . . . I'm just fine," he said slowly. His eyes found hers and held. For a moment all was quiet except for a chorus of birds in the trees above them and waves lapping against the shoreline.

Heather tried to glance away, but Ty's topaz-colored eyes kept their lock. His hand slipped under the long, brown hair at the back of Heather's neck and drew her closer. She leaned into him, her heart pounding. He wound her hair around his fingers just like . . . just like David did. David. She caught her breath. What a time to think about him.

Ty drew back. Then without further warning, he jumped up, grabbed Heather by the wrist, and pulled her to her feet.

"Never a horse that couldn't be rode, or a rider that couldn't be throwed," he joked.

"Two riders. That was graceful, wasn't it?"

Ty walked to where Roxie grazed. "Want a leg up?" he asked Heather.

She started forward, but stumbled a step.

"You're not hurt, are you?" Ty reached for her.

"No. My toe caught on something, sandals, you know." She pointed to her feet, and looking down, she noticed an object in the grass. "Is this yours, Ty?" She stooped and picked up a watch, still shiny beneath a coating of dirt.

As he took the watch, his hand brushed Heather's. She wanted to kick herself for thinking about David earlier.

"It's a little rich for my blood," Ty said.

Heather moved closer for a better look.

He rubbed the watch between his long fingers—nice fingers, she thought.

"I may be wrong," Ty said, "but this looks like a Rolex. I wonder whose it is. I guess it could be McCade's—you know the guy we bought this place from. I wish I could ask him."

"You don't know where he is?"

"Well, yeah. I do. . . . Unfortunately. He was in England for awhile, but he died."

"I'm sorry," she said.

"Me too."

"I guess it's yours for now then." Heather touched his arm. "At least until some other owner shows up—if and when."

He took her hand and slipped the watch over her fingers. "No, it's yours. You found it."

She held up her arm and the so-called Rolex slipped down around her elbow. "It's really not me." She held her hand over Ty's and the watch fell into his palm.

He dropped the Rolex into his T-shirt pocket. "We'll have to take it to town and find someone to look at it—see if they can tell us if its real or not, maybe even get it running again."

Heather liked the sound of the plural "we'll," she decided. "It's a plan."

Ty boosted Heather onto Roxie. Then he placed his hands on the mare's back and, with a jump, ended up behind Heather.

"I wish I could to that," she said, marveling at his strength and athletic ability.

"Long legs." He slapped the top of one of his.

He clucked to Roxie and they headed back through the forest. When they reached the first clearing where the three deer had been, Heather asked, "Do you feed the deer hay?"

"Nope. No need to feed them anything, not that we would anyway. They like grass better and, as you can see, there's plenty of it around, even in the winter. Why?"

"There's a bunch of hay over by that tree. See where the grass is tromped down?"

"Hmm. That's hay all right." Ty reached around Heather to guide Roxie closer. "Looks like there's been an animal here. Notice the smaller branches have been broken off."

"It was a horse. See?" She pointed at a pile of not-so-fresh manure. "Seems a strange place to leave a horse." She smiled. "I know. The Rolex belonged to the horse."

Ty chuckled. "Or maybe the Rolex and the horse belonged to the same person."

"But why would McCade keep a horse out here when he had all those stalls in the barn?" She twisted around to look at Ty.

"Maybe it wasn't McCade's."

"Maybe not, but who else? The bachelor?"

"You got me." Ty shrugged. "Guess it doesn't matter much, and I'll wager that watch isn't even a Rolex."

"Probably not." Heather faced forward again, then shivered. "You still cold?"

"A little." She cocked one brow. "Actually I'm cold, wet and bruised all in one outing. See if I ever go riding with you again."

"Oh, come on, you loved it."

"Did not."

"Did too. Say, do you want to go off again?" Ty took her by both shoulders and tipped her to one side.

Roxie tossed her head.

"No. No. I'll be good." She placed her hand over one of Ty's on her shoulder.

"That's my girl," he said.

And at that moment—if for only that moment—Heather realized, she wished she really was his girl.

CHAPTER
SIX

Katie slipped her arm through Ty's as he led the now sun-dried Roxie down the aisle in the barn. "Take us for a ride on the wave runners, okay?"

Horse heads extended over stall doors. One of the mares whinnied.

Ty squirmed from Katie's advances and turned Roxie into her stall. "You may be a lady of leisure, Kate, but Heather and I have things to do. Don't you have a play or something?"

Heather's hand rested on the latch to Image's stall. Her brows raised.

"That's tonight." Katie drew herself up to her full height, and molding her hairdo with her fingertips, took on the air of an aristocrat. "Until then, I guess I am a lady of leisure." She came out of characterization and continued, "and, and . . . you promised. Heather would like to go too, wouldn't you?"

Joining them, Heather wagged her finger at Katie. "Don't get me in the middle of this . . . wave runners, huh?" She peeked over her shoulder at Ty. "It does sound fun. How about if I help you with your work when we get back?"

Ty shook his head. "Okay, you two."

Katie batted her eyes. "Please."

Gazing heavenward, Ty threw his hands in the air. "I can't fight both of you, especially when I'd like to go too, but I'll take you up on that helping part, Heather. What do you know about computers?"

"Computers?" Heather wrinkled her nose. She figured Ty had meant help with the horses. "What kind?"

"Oh, I don't know. It's sorta tan and about this size." Ty formed a big cube with his hands.

Heather scratched her head.

"IBM, Mitsubishi, Zenith? You got me," Ty said.

Katie slapped him on the arm. "You know it's a Macintosh. He's not as stupid as he puts on, Heather." She paused, narrowed her eyes, then continued, "Well, maybe he is. He's been sitting at his desk, just staring at that computer for days."

"McCade left it," Ty explained. "I've been thinking about putting my billings on, but I only know a little word processing, not tables and stuff."

Heather smiled. She'd worked on a PC a lot at David's father's law office, and she'd recently finished a night class where she'd used a Macintosh and learned some programming. "I'll give it a try."

"It's a deal then. I'll finish up a few things here and meet you in, say, thirty minutes at the boat house." He'd already latched Roxie's door and headed down the aisle. "Kate, if you get there first, check the gas in the wave runners. Let's go see Wild Horse Island."

Katie brushed a lock of wayward hair off her forehead and favored Heather with an I-usually-get-my-way grin.

Back in the house, an important decision had to be made. Would Heather wear a bathing suit or cutoffs on the ride? Katie had already decided what she wanted to wear.

"I've got a suit you can use," Katie said, modeling an emerald blue one-piece. The french cut made her long, slender legs look sensational.

"Do you have one like they wore in the twenties, you know, heavy knit with long sleeves and legs that come to here?" Heather touched just above her ankle. Thoughts of wearing a suit in front of Ty had her breaking into a sweat.

"Like you need a suit like that. I have this one." Katie held up a black bikini. "And this one."

Heather reached for the second—a black and white one-piece, with legs similar to shorts, and a belt. It was actually something she'd choose for herself.

"Run in the bathroom and try it on," Katie said.

Turning from side to side, Heather studied herself in the mirror. She didn't look all that bad and she had a pair of black cutoffs and a white knit shirt she could wear over the top.

"I think you should just wear the suit," Katie said. "Give old Ty something to think about other than his horses." She gave Heather a once-over. "Actually, you'll probably give him a heart attack. Wear the cutoffs if you want."

The girls arrived at the boat house first. In fact, much to Heather's surprise, Katie had checked the gas in the wave runners, hooked their trailer to a small tractor and begun backing into the water before Ty, still dressed in jeans, arrived.

"Ty," Katie said, shaking her head. "You live by a lake now. People must think you've got gout or something. Go take your pants off, or at least whack the legs off those jeans."

"I have a suit." Ty straightened.

"You have a suit?" Katie asked. "Cool. Go put it on then. We'll wait. It won't hurt those pasty white legs of yours to get a little color."

"When did you say you had to leave for your play? The things I put up with. I'm only doing this because I was considering it anyway." Ty headed for the house, still mumbling to himself.

Heather and Katie had launched the wave runners before he returned, wearing navy blue swim trunks. Although several shades lighter than his darkly tanned arms, Heather quickly determined that Ty had no reason to hide those legs. She too, of necessity, had slipped out of her cutoffs and shirt and stood in the borrowed bathing suit, waist deep in the sparkling cool water, the side of a wave runner in each hand.

When Katie walked out of the boat house after parking the tractor and trailer, Ty pulled off his T-shirt, wadded it up and tossed it onto the lawn. Stepping back, he spread his arms wide and posed. "Satisfied?"

Heather didn't know about Katie, but she surely was. How could Ty look so lean in his clothes and be so broad and solid beneath? She felt goose bumps rise on her arms and decided it was not entirely from the chill of the water.

"Not bad. If you'd take off the boots, you might even look cute," Katie said, cocking her head. "Don't you think so, Heather? Heather?"

"What? Oh . . . a . . . uh-huh."

"Honestly Ty, cowboy boots with a swimming suit," Katie scolded.

Dutifully, Ty removed his boots and socks. "For your information, sister dear, I don't have anything else to wear on my feet." He put his socks in his boots and, picking up his shirt, placed everything in a neat pile next to the boat house.

"Poor baby," Katie said. "Okay, now. Here's the deal. Heather should ride with you, Ty. I get stressed with anyone behind me."

Heather rolled her eyes. Her friend was at it again, but did Heather care? No with a capital "N."

So it was settled. Katie would ride the two-man wave runner alone, and since, as she put it, Ty was an excellent driver, Heather would feel more relaxed riding behind him on the three-man wave runner.

Stealing another glance at Ty, Heather very much doubted she'd feel at all relaxed.

Ty held the wave runners close to shore while the girls climbed aboard. After Heather had pulled her knit shirt over her suit and slid back, he eased himself on in front of her.

The little boats were much more stable than Heather had supposed. Straddling them like a horse, the riders sat completely out of the water except for their bare feet. Heather tried to balance herself without holding on, but had to grab Ty during sharp turns.

"Why don't you just hang on here?" Ty placed her hands on either side of his waist, and although her fingers touching his bare skin seemed to burn, she held on.

Katie spun her machine into a tight turn, spraying a fan of water at them.

Heather squealed.

Ty took off after his sister, the wave runner practically leaping out of the water. Heather felt a freedom close to which she'd experienced only once before—last summer, when she'd ridden Image top speed across the vast fields at the Taggerts' former ranch. She noted that her arms now encircled Ty's middle and she clung to him like a shell on a turtle.

"Sorry." She loosened her grip and slid back on the wave runner seat.

"No complaints here."

Heather grinned. She'd been doing a lot of that lately.

As they traveled around Skidoo Bay, which was sheltered somewhat from the larger part of the lake by a peninsula of land called Finley Point, Heather marveled at the beauty of the Mission Mountains to the southeast and the huge peaks of Glacier National Park across the vast length of the lake to the north.

Homes, boat houses and docks edged the shoreline like lace on a huge blue cloth. The structures, earlier hidden from Heather's roadside view by forest, now emerged from the landscape, each as varied as the taste and bank account of its owner. Tiny log cabins and even an occasional trailer house bordered massive, stone mansions. Some homes sat on carefully manicured grounds, while others rose from undisturbed nature. The huge picture windows of many of the houses peered over jagged cliffs high above the water. Others viewed a pebbled beach only feet from the lake's edge.

Having studied a map of Flathead Lake during her drive through Montana, Heather had a general idea of its shape and size, but as they rounded the tip of Finley Point and sped past the tiny Bird Islands out into the lake's widest point, she exclaimed, "It's so big!"

Ty turned his head toward her. "It's pretty huge all right. I think it seems even larger, though, when you're riding something small like this."

"Maybe that's it." Heather shivered, feeling exposed and vulnerable. For some reason, thoughts of the Rolex watch and where she'd found it flashed through her mind. She slid her arms around Ty's waist again, glad she was with him instead of riding alone like Katie.

Several times Katie flew past them, taking the waves at top speed, sometimes going airborne between swells. Then she'd circle back by them for an instant before heading off again. Once she hit a wave straight on and the water splashed over her, drenching even her long red ponytail.

As they traveled closer to the center of the lake, the waves grew. Ty took them at an angle to keep spray to a minimum. Over her left shoulder Heather noticed a group of islands guarding the entrance to the more shallow Polson Bay, to her right the mammoth length of the much deeper Flathead Lake. Straight ahead a huge body of land rose out of the water like the back of an enormous dinosaur.

As they approached Wild Horse Island, Katie pulled up beside the other two. Heather stared at the land in front of them. Cliffs jutted from pine-covered mountains on the north end of the island, tapering into rolling green and brown hills dotted with sagebrush to the south.

"Are there really horses on it?" Heather asked as they circled the island at wakeless speed.

"Yep, and deer, bighorn sheep, ospreys, bald eagles, hawks and Canadian geese. I'm not sure exactly how many horses there are now, but I read that in 1983 the Fish and Game brought in three wild geldings from Wyoming as company for an old Arabian stallion that had been on the island for over twenty-five years."

"Twenty-five years? Where did he come from?" Heather squinted, studying the island.

"That's a long story." Ty brought the wave runner to a stop, and swinging his leg over the seat, he turned to face Heather.

Beside them, Katie shut off her machine.

"Wild Horse Island is a state park now," Ty said, "but for about seventy years it belonged to a series of individuals. One of those owners, I forget his name—actually, I believe he was the first to own the whole island—bought a bunch of mares and two stallions, one Arabian and one Thoroughbred. The Thoroughbred cost him over thirty thousand dollars and that was back in the forties and fifties."

Katie's wave runner bobbed closer and Ty, stretching his foot out, held her machine from hitting theirs. Katie immediately swung her legs over to secure her machine against Ty's. She leaned her elbow on her wave runner's handlebar. "Okay. Go on."

He rolled his eyes at Heather. "Apparently the horses and other wildlife on the island overgrazed the land. That next winter was one of the coldest in history. Inch-thick ice crusted over the snow. The animals were so desperate for food they ate sagebrush and trees."

Heather winced. "I don't think I want to hear this. Why didn't someone help them, bring them food or something?"

Ty's hand dropped onto Heather's knee. It surprised her so much she nearly jumped. Then, while Ty went on with his story, she just sat there enjoying the tingle of her skin beneath his touch.

"I guess the Polson Saddle Club did. 'Operation Hay Lift' they called it, but in spite of that, only two horses and a mule survived. I don't know where the mule came from; probably the same guy who brought the horses brought the mule. Apparently the Thoroughbred stallion didn't make it because I couldn't find any more about him after that. The mule died in 1982, leaving the old Arabian stallion alone on the island. That's why Fish and Game brought those three wild horses over, and I guess they liked the idea of having wild horses on Wild Horse Island."

"The Arabian's still alive? He must be ancient now," Katie said.

"No, he died in, I believe it was 1985, and one of the other horses put on the island in 1982 also died." Ty squeezed Heather's knee before removing his hand. "So several years ago, the local 4-H groups helped get three more wild horses from other states transplanted here, all geldings—one black, one buckskin and one pinto."

"How did they get them over?" Katie stretched out one long, suntanned leg, rotating her foot. "In a horse trailer on a barge," Ty answered.

Heather bumped her shoulder against Ty. "You sure know a lot about this island and you've only just moved to Flathead." She winked at Katie. "See, Ty's not dumb. Even though he can't remember a thing about computers, he doesn't forget anything when it comes to horses."

"He has a one-track mind." Katie nodded toward Heather. "Well, maybe a two-track."

"I got a book from the Polson library and read up," Ty said. "Wild Horse Island. Catchy name, don't you think?" He swung his legs around again, straddling the wave runner, and pushed theirs away from Katie's in preparation to leave.

"I'm glad you did." Heather slid closer to Ty. Her much smaller but browner legs brushed his and her heart leaped. "So did they get the name from the wild horses they brought here?"

"Actually, no."

Katie repositioned herself on the wave runner, ready to follow Ty and Heather. "There's more to this story, I can tell."

"As a matter of fact, there is," Ty said. "Probably one hundred years ago, Blackfoot raiders were making off with Kootenai

Indians' horses, so when the Kootenais spotted the Blackfeet coming into their territory, the Kootenais swam their horses into the lake and over to the island. After the Blackfeet left, the Kootenais went back to the island to fetch their horses. Well, this island's over two thousand acres, and there's lots of hiding places, especially for half-tamed horses, so the Indians didn't always find all their horses. Before long the horses they left behind turned wild again, so the Indians started calling this place 'Wild Horse Island.'"

"That explains it. Great story," Heather said.

Ty tapped the gas gauge with his finger. "We probably better get back. How's your gas, Katie?"

She blinked. "Isn't that a little personal?"

His hand came to his forehead and the tips of his ears turned red. "Okay, Kate, just for you, I'll rephrase the question. Does your machine have enough gasoline to get home?"

"Oh, is that what you meant?" She grinned at Heather. " I've got half a tank, thank you, and you?"

"The same," Ty said.

"We should go then."

"What a good idea." Ty's wave runner rumbled to a start.

"Wait for me," Katie cried and reached for the starter on her machine. She flooded the motor, but after several more tries, with and without the choke, her wave runner burst into action.

The three continued their journey around the island, making a large loop to include the privately-owned Cromwell Island, the second largest body of land in the lake, which was west of Wild Horse. Back near the larger island they searched the landscape for horses and other animals. They saw three deer, one eagle and numerous goats, but no horses.

"Look there," Heather said, surprised to see cabins scattered along the shoreline. Some appeared to be lived in, at least part-time. Others looked abandoned. On the east side, one broken-down cabin particularly caught her attention. Near it stood the remains of a large stone fireplace.

"I'll bet there's a story to that place," Heather yelled into Ty's ear.

He took the wave runner out of gear. "Believe it or not, I happen to know a little something about it."

Katie's wave runner floated to a stop beside them. "I sense another tale coming on."

"Even you might find this interesting, Katie dear," Ty said.

"As long as you don't ask me any more about my gas."

Shaking his head, Ty pointed at the old chimney. "That's what's left of Hiawatha Lodge, built in the early 1930s. The owner opened the place as a dude ranch and invited his wealthy friends from the East to vacation here. All went well until a particularly violent storm hit several years later. The man and his caretaker were trying to save the boats on the dock when a big wave swept them into the water. The caretaker made it to shore. The owner didn't."

"How sad," Heather said.

"The island's next owner," Ty continued "wanted to continue the dude ranch. He fixed up the lodge and added a large dock. He didn't have the eastern connections, though, and couldn't make a go of it. He ended up selling the property to that guy I already told you about, you know, the one who first owned the whole island and bought the thirty thousand dollar Thoroughbred and all the other horses.

"So where did the other cabins come from?" Katie asked. "You said Wild Horse is a state park."

"It is now, has been since 1978. The man who owned the island prior to 1978 sold off about forty-nine lots on the south and west shores, but only fourteen cabins were built."

"Hmm. Way out here. Where'd they get their electricity?" Heather asked.

"They didn't. There's no electricity on the island. They have generators."

"Wow. I guess we're pretty spoiled." For a moment Heather tried to picture what it would be like to be marooned on Wild Horse Island with no electricity. She rubbed her chin, thinking. If she were stranded with the right person, how bad could it be? She sighed. The question remained—who would she like that person to be?

So close to Ty, but almost engaged to David. Heather said little as they circled Melita, the other privately-owned island and neighbor to the south of Wild Horse, then ventured back across the open water to Skidoo Bay, the Taggert home, Kevin, Image and the impossible decisions that awaited her there.

CHAPTER SEVEN

When Heather walked into the barn the next morning, Image welcomed her with a whinny.

"Hi, big guy," she said. "Are you happy to see me or is it the grain bucket?" She held the blue pail up, tapping its plastic side.

He whinnied again.

Heather chuckled. "Just what I thought." The other day she'd cautioned Ty against feeding Image grain, but she had her own special recipe that conditioned her horse without providing extra pep.

Image followed her as she dumped her whole-oats concoction into his manger. While he ate she leaned against the corner of the stall, watching.

"I did good last night. You should have seen me," she told her horse. Thoughts of her time with Ty replayed in her mind.

Since Katie had returned to Bigfork for a performance, and Kevin, along with Ty's folks, had been involved in a serious cribbage game, Heather and Ty had been left to their own devices.

Heather smiled, remembering how they'd sat side by side in the downstairs family room and gazed into the computer monitor. Ty had looked and smelled freshly ironed. She'd always loved that hung-out-on-the-line-to-dry freshness about him. An unruly curl had fallen onto his forehead. In spite of all that, she'd managed to get his computer up and running and had put together a simple billing program that had made him happy. He'd placed his arm around the back of her chair, leaning close while he'd learned to operate the program.

Now, when Heather thought of David, Ty's face appeared in her mind. She shook her head and hurriedly selected a brush from a box outside the stall door. As she groomed Image, she hummed a George Strait melody, stopping short when she recalled the words to the song: "You always said you loved me. And I always believed you did. But now you say you're leaving . . ." She chewed her lip.

She retrieved Image's tack from the front of the horse trailer, bridled and saddled him, and led him to the training arena. Groaning, she struggled up onto his tall back, fit her feet into the stirrups and straightened her shoulders. She wore riding pants, boots, and a red tank top. Today it was back to business. She still had a show season to complete.

After several minutes of riding at a trot, Heather eased her horse into a canter, sometimes circling at each end of the arena or bending into figure eights. Image behaved remarkably well. Another trip around the ring and Heather slowed her horse to a walk.

The sound of voices drifted from the stable area. Heather couldn't make out exact words, but she heard laughter— feminine laughter. Ty laughed back.

Heather rounded the ring once more, thinking as she rode that she should have squirted down the arena. Dust filtered through the air. She coughed.

Heading toward the stable area entrance, she narrowed her eyes. Who was that? The girl walking with Ty was beautiful, slender and tall. As Ty led Sage, one of the ranch horses, into the arena, the girl hung so close, Heather marveled Ty could move at all.

"Heather," he said, "this is Allie Saunders, and this is . . ." He looked over his shoulder. "Where is he? Oh, there. This is Jason, Allie's little brother." The boy led Joker, another one of the geldings brought from the ranch. "They're here for lessons."

"Hi." Heather forced a smile. She couldn't stand the way Allie kept gawking at Ty.

The girl tore her gaze from him long enough to favor Heather with a quick hello and a cursory once-over, as if sizing up the competition and finding none. Then she turned to Ty. "Will you give me a leg up? I'm still stiff from our ride last week."

Heather's brow raised. Well, of course she was stiff. How could she help it in those jeans? They clung so tightly, they probably cut off the circulation, and what about that "ride last week"? It suddenly occurred to Heather that she'd been silly to think someone as handsome and sweet as Ty had been without female attention while she herself had been with David.

"Well, hello," Jason said, looking much like a Great Dane pup drooling over a thick steak named Heather. He appeared to be about fifteen and probably thought she was his age. He, like his sister, was much taller than Heather, and thin, only thin looked better on her than it did on him.

"Heather's my friend from Utah. She's here for a horse show," Ty went on.

The word "friend" was not lost on Heather.

"Sweet." Allie brushed a lock of light brown bangs from her eyes. Her hair, very short on the sides and much longer on top, was cut in a style Heather had never cared for. She took some pleasure in that.

"Horse show, really? Do you barrel race?" Jason stumbled over his big feet.

"Barrel race?" Heather tried not to smile. Anyone who knew horses would never mistake Image in his hunt seat saddle for a barrel racer, and she was not exactly dressed like she rode Western. Ty had his work cut out with these two. "No, Image is a show jumper."

"A slow jumper?" Allie asked.

"Show jumper." Heather accentuated each word. She turned to Ty, who checked Sage's cinch.

"Sorry we got it so dusty in here," Heather said. "Would you like me to squirt it down?" She wished she could squirt Allie down. Cool her off some.

"I think we'll be okay, but thanks." He patted Sage's shoulder.

"A jumper? Awesome." Jason grinned at Heather like he'd received a book on flirting and wanted to try his hand. "Are you going to . . . Are you going to take a lesson with us?" Jason repeated.

"Oh! What? I hadn't planned on it." To Heather's way of thinking, Ty stood way too close to Allie.

"Heather should be teaching the lesson." Ty boosted Allie onto Sage. "Do you want to stay, Heather, or shall I show you a good place to ride?"

"Do stay," Jason said.

Allie glared at her brother.

Ty adjusted the stirrups on Allie's Western saddle. She batted her big cow eyes at him until Heather felt her face go hot.

"I'll stay," Heather said.

The lesson began with all three riders walking their horses single file around the arena. Ty yelled instructions: "Hands down, Jason. Good, Heather. A little more leg, Allie."

The horses blew through their noses and tossed their heads. Image with his long legs passed the other geldings. Heather circled around several times, coming up behind. She really should have watered down the ring . . . and Allie.

Ty, Heather remembered, was a very knowledgeable and patient teacher. Allie was a more experienced rider than Jason, but she too had her problems. Many times Ty used Heather to illustrate what he tried to impress upon the brother and sister, and although Heather rode English and they Western, she was able to adapt her riding style to suit Ty's purpose.

All went fine at a walk. The trot presented a few problems for Jason, who nearly bounced off the saddle and continually reached for the horn. Allie did well until the canter when she failed to get Sage into the proper lead. Jason couldn't get Joker into a canter at all, which, considering the problem he'd experienced at the trot, was probably just as well.

Jason asked Heather one question after another while Allie concentrated on Ty—and concentrate she did. It seemed to Heather that Ty was overly attentive to Allie too, which made Heather's stomach tighten, and by the end of the lesson she felt like a wrung-out dishrag.

"Ty, I think I'll take that ride now, if you don't mind," Heather called, thinking escape favorable to double murder.

"Can I go too?" Jason asked.

Heather cleared her throat.

"I'd say that's up to Heather," Ty answered.

Jason turned his pitiful, pleading puppy eyes on her.

She'd have rather faced a hungry tiger. She'd grown weary of the boy's constant chatter and she hated the attention Ty and Allie showed each other, but remembering the tenderness of young feelings and how she herself had been hurt in the past, she couldn't bring herself to inflict any bruises.

"Sure, you can come if you want. I'll show you a neat route to the lake."

They rode through the forest, around the same area she and Ty had taken on Roxie. At a walk Jason handled Joker well, but then the gelding didn't need much handling. They discussed school and horses and Jason seemed surprised when she told him she'd graduated from high school a year ago. He would be a junior in the fall. They looked for the deer Heather told him about, but she didn't mention the hay by the tree where the horse had been tied. Again she wondered about that and the watch she guessed Ty hadn't taken to a jeweler yet.

Heather halfway enjoyed the ride. Jason was a sweet kid and Heather supposed he'd be cute when he grew up—his sister was, kind of. Actually, she was too cute and too grown up.

When Heather and Jason returned, Ty stood next to Allie's shiny red car, visiting with her through the open driver's side window.

"Looks like your sister's ready to go." Heather tried to keep the joy from her voice. "I'll put Joker away, if you want, so you won't keep her waiting."

"She's okay."

"Really. I insist. You've probably got lots to do—important places to go, people to see." She reined Image to a stop.

"No, I . . ." he began.

"Girls anxious for your call . . . a good-looking guy like yourself."

"Well, maybe." Grinning, he swung down from Joker.

Heather gritted her teeth and smiled at Allie as she rode past, taking both Joker and Image into the stable.

"What a piece of work I am, Image," she told him. "Ty was just being friendly yesterday. I'm nothing special. He's nice to everyone." She rubbed her hand along the gelding's glossy neck. "Ty has new interests, just like I do. Thank heavens I still have David."

At the sound of a car traveling up the lane, Heather poked her head outdoors to see what had become of Ty. He was busy fixing a pole that had come off one of the paddocks.

"Allie's pretty," Heather said as she drew near.

"Yes, she is." Ty kept working on the fence.

Heather would have felt better had he added "but not as pretty as you." Maybe he didn't think so—actually Heather didn't either. Well, one thing was certain, Heather had better hair. She figured even Ty would have to notice.

"How long has she been taking lessons?"

"Several months."

"So you went riding with her last week?"

"Would you hand me that hammer over there, Heather?" Ty sighted down the pole.

"So you went riding with her last week?" Heather repeated.

"Yeah."

"Did you have fun?"

"Yeah."

Blast him, he wasn't going to tell her a thing.

"Good." Heather sighed. "I'll start feeding."

"Thanks."

As Heather wandered back into the barn, she wondered what had become of her earlier happy feeling.

Katie charged into the barn. "I disappear for one minute and look what happens."

"What happened?" Straightening from her task of cleaning out Image's hooves, Heather turned to face her friend.

"Don't play coy with me." Katie pointed with an index finger, the other digits of her hand wrapped around a large red apple. "You know what I'm talking about."

Heather tossed the hoof pick into her tack box. "I do?"

"Yes. When I left day before yesterday, you and Ty were . . . shall we say, getting along. I stay in Bigfork two nights, two nights, and when I get back, he's in there," she nodded toward the house, "and you're out here. What's the deal?"

After meeting Allie the day before, Heather had kept to herself, or spent time with the adults. Ty had been working on the computer in his room, at least that's what Bea had said. "No deal. I'm with David. Ty's got Allie."

"Allie?"

"Yes, you know—tall, skinny, barracuda Allie." Heather selected a brush from the tack box and ran it along Image's sleek back.

"Ty doesn't like Allie." Katie bit into the apple. Image pricked his ears.

"I think he does." Being with Ty again had almost tempted Heather to question her feelings for David. Ty always had that effect on her. Like a virus. She'd best become immune, pronto. She frowned. David was far too neat a guy to take second place. He was wonderful, and she loved him.

"Well, shoot, Heather, how do you expect Ty to act? Here you are, practically engaged to another guy. He was probably trying to make you jealous." Katie wiped her mouth with the back of her hand. "Are you?"

"Am I what?"

"Jealous."

She was, darn it. She had no backbone. She readily admitted that. She and Kevin should probably just leave. Tonight she'd ask when they'd be heading to the next horse show. "Allie's not right for Ty, that's all." Heather continued brushing Image.

"I doubt Ty thinks David's right for you either." Katie took another bite of apple. Image turned his head.

"I doubt Ty thinks much about me at all since he has Allie."

"I give up." Katie stepped closer to Image. She held the unfinished apple out to him and watched him stretch his neck and reach with his lips before she fed him the apple. "But you know what?"

"What?" Thinking it was more information about Ty, Heather tried to keep her voice calm.

"You're going to brush a hole in that horse."

"Oh!" Heather jerked her hand away as if she had actually hurt Image. "It's pretty quiet around here this morning. You say Ty's in the house?"

"I don't know. He could've gone into town."

"He's with Allie," Heather stated.

"He is not."

"Bet he is."

"We'll just wait and see." Katie started for the door. "Come find me after you ride. We'll do something outrageous."

"Sounds good."

"Oh," Katie whirled back around. "Did you hear about the dead man they found in Yellow Bay?"

Heather sucked in her breath. "No."

"Looks like he drowned. Probably went to sleep or something and soared right off the road into the water, along with his truck and horse trailer. There wasn't even a guardrail up along that part of the highway where they figure he went in."

"Horse trailer? Was he hauling a horse?"

"Might have been. The trailer door was open and they found a broken halter and rope tied inside."

"So the horse may have gotten away." Heather didn't know the man, but any horse in trouble was a concern to her.

"Maybe."

"I wonder where it went." Heather ran her hand down Image's nose, imagining what it would be like for an innocent animal to be trapped in a sinking trailer. "Maybe he'll show up."

"He probably would have by now, if he was going to. The paper said they most likely went in sometime last summer. I guess they'll have to use dental records to identify the guy." Katie wrinkled her nose. "I'll bet he looked squishy."

Heather shivered. "Katie!"

"Sorry."

"So, how come they just found him? You said the truck and trailer went in last summer."

"That's the deepest part of the lake, around three hundred feet. A guy with one of those sophisticated sonar fish finder gadgets picked up on it. It didn't look like your average fish, I guess. They sent down divers." Katie paused. "Yuk! We've been swimming in that lake."

"Fortunately, it's big."

"Yeah, but . . . yuk!" She glanced at her watch. "Oops. Look at the time. Gotta go. Mom's waiting. Catch you later."

On her way out Katie passed by the stall of the cranky red stallion. She held her hands at the sides of her face, wiggled her fingers and stuck out her tongue. Rocky lay his ears back and lunged at her.

"Someone's having a bad day," Katie said.

"You shouldn't tease him."

"But it's so fun. Keeps my reflexes keen."

"You'll think 'keen' one day when he comes straight through that gate."

"It's a pretty strong gate." Katie rattled it. The horse snorted.

"Ty's waiting to see what that sorrel mare's foal is like. If it's mean like the others, Ty's gonna make an 'it' out of old Rocky here. That'll cool his jets."

"It certainly would mine," a voice said.

Both girls grinned at Kevin who'd walked into the barn.

Katie edged toward the door. "Later. Mom and I have a project."

In the approximately two years Heather had known her stepfather, she still marveled that no matter what he was doing or what time of day it was, Kevin always managed to look military tidy. Today he wore a blue polo shirt with tan slacks and loafers.

"I'm flying home tonight," he said.

Heather's mouth dropped open. "What? Why all of a sudden? Is Mom okay? Robby?" Robby was Heather's new half-brother and Kevin's only surviving, natural child.

"Don't worry. Everybody's fine. It's that real estate deal I've been working on. It's come to a head and they need me back, but I'm hoping your mother and Robby have missed me too." Kevin stopped beside the red stallion.

"But what about me . . . and Image?"

"You can stay another week or so, if you want. You've got time off work, right? Ty will take you to the Kalispell show and then I'll fly back after that and we'll hit Idaho Falls on the way home." He handed her Image's saddle that had been resting across the cinder block divider of the wash stall.

"I don't know if Ty can, or will." She took the saddle from Kevin and placed it on Image, but her thoughts were of Allie.

"I've already talked to him and he says it's no problem. In fact, he's going to enter Roxie in some classes and take her along." Kevin slipped off Image's halter, replacing it with a bridle.

Heather moistened her lips. "Ty really said he could go?"

"Uh huh. Are you okay with that?"

"I guess."

"Okay, I'll give your mother a call and tell her to expect me. I've really missed her."

"You know," Heather said with a tip of her head, "I'd feel more guilty about keeping you from Mom and Robby if this Montana trip hadn't been your idea."

Kevin walked over to Rocky and stood staring into the stall. "Kevin."

He paid no attention.

"Kevin," she said again, louder.

Still no answer.

She moved to his side, snapping her fingers in front of his face. "Is something bothering you?"

"No." He took an alfalfa cube out of his pocket and offered it to the stallion through the bars in the gate. "You know that I love you, don't you?"

Uh oh. Lectures that began with those words always put Heather on guard.

"Yes, Daddy dear, I know that you love me, and . . . and you're kinda cool yourself."

"And you know I never interfere . . ."

"That's not the way I remember it," she said, grinning. "You kinda always interfere."

The alfalfa cube nearly fell from his hand. Quickly he grasped it and favored Heather with a raised brow.

Ears pressed against his neck, the stallion approached. Kevin opened his hand and stood his ground. The ears came forward.

"I don't always, do I?" He watched Rocky. "She really knows how to hurt a guy, doesn't she, big fellow?" Kevin unlatched the stall gate and started inside.

Tossing his head, the horse backed, then reared. Kevin remained motionless.

"I'd watch out if I were you," Heather warned.

"She still cares about me even if I do interfere once in a while." Kevin spoke quietly as he stepped forward. "And she knows I only interfere when it's best for her."

Rocky continued backing until he was in the corner of the stall. Kevin moved closer, holding out the alfalfa cube in his palm. With retreat impossible, Rocky stretched his neck and quickly scooped the cube from Kevin's hand as if he hoped the man wouldn't notice.

"You did it. I don't believe it." She gave Kevin a thumbs-up sign. "Maybe there's hope for him yet . . . and you. I guess I'll have to admit, you usually do what's best for me—a lot of the time anyway, but like in this current situation, why do you think Ty's better for me than David?"

"It's not that I think Ty's better. I just want you to be sure David's the one." Kevin touched the stallion's nose, then turned and exited the stall.

"I'm sorry for saying you always interfere."

"Don't apologize." Kevin gave her a boost onto Image's back.

"No. Really. I'm sorry." Heather placed her hand on her stepfather's shoulder.

"I mean it, don't apologize . . . yet."

"Yet?" Her stomach twisted.

"I've got to run now." He smoothed Image's forelock, placing it beneath the browband of the bridle. "I see Ty set up some jumps in the arena. Why don't you work Image on staying consistent between obstacles. He had a problem with that at the last show, remember?"

Heather peered at him, her eyes narrowing. "Have you done something I'm going to regret?"

Kevin had no chance to answer. Katie bounded back into the barn. "Bachelor Number Two is here."

"What?" Heather gasped.

"Donald . . . Darby, whatever his name is—you know? That other guy. He's out there."

"David's here?" Heather whirled Image around to face her stepfather. She couldn't catch her breath. "Oh my gosh! What have you done?"

Kevin scratched his head. "Well, now you've got them together, you can compare."

She wanted to scream. "This isn't a horse auction, you know. The guys have some say. I'll probably lose them both." Letting the reins rest on Image's neck, she brought her hands to her cheeks. "Both! I've already lost Ty."

"You haven't lost Ty," Katie said, then retreated out of firing range.

Although Katie's statement caused a stirring somewhere in Heather's mind, she didn't say anything. Her attention centered on Kevin. "Have you been planning this all along?"

"Actually, no. It just occurred to me." He backed against Rocky's stall as if confronting the wild stallion was preferable to facing Heather.

"You invited David to come here and he agreed?"

Kevin nodded.

"What about Wells and Bea? Do they know? Where will David stay?"

Mouth twisting, Kevin scratched his head.

"Surely not here." She slipped from Image.

Her stepfather shrugged.

Heather massaged her temples with the tips of her fingers. "Ty won't be happy when he finds out."

"He already knows," Kevin said.

Her eyes widened. "Has everyone been told about this but me?"

"And me." Katie raised her hand.

"Let's see. Wells, Bea, Ty, David, me." Kevin counted on his fingers. "Yeah, pretty much everyone."

The red stallion edged closer to Kevin.

"Bite him, Rocky, will you?" Heather said.

Over the stall door, the horse sniffed Kevin's shoulder.

"I don't believe it." Heather shook her head. "I guess you two are buddies now."

Kevin held his arms wide. "Magnetic personality, you know, that and the fact I never interfere."

"Oh, yes. I keep forgetting that."

Katie cleared her throat.

Heather followed the redhead's gaze to where David stood—all six feet three inches of him—tanned and gorgeous. "David. Hi."

He smiled—a gleaming Tom Cruise, to-die-for smile.

Her heart fluttered and tingles shot up her neck. How could she have forgotten how much he meant to her?

"Hello, David," Kevin said. "How was your trip? Were you able to bring him?"

"Him who?" Heather said, almost afraid to ask in case Kevin had dragged up another boyfriend from her past. But where would he have found one?

David ran a hand through his dark hair. The locks sprang back into place. His hair never got messed up no matter what sport he played—and those eyes—sparkling blue as the lake on the other side of the house.

"Hi, Heather." David's voice was like warm honey. He walked over and dropped his arm possessively around her shoulders. He never had been, nor probably ever would be, timid in any situation. "I brought you Possum."

Heather glanced at Kevin. "Possum? Really?" They had earlier discussed bringing her favorite horse on this trip.

"It was supposed to be a surprise." Kevin loosened his shirt collar.

"Well, it was that. You're just full of surprises, aren't you?" Heather folded her arms.

"I know we'd decided against bringing Possum this time," Kevin's voice slowed, becoming businesslike. "But when I found out more about the Kalispell show, it sounded ideal for the old guy. I talked to David and he said he could use a little time away from the office. It sounded like the perfect solution." He turned to David. "I appreciate your bringing him. I don't know how else we could have gotten him here."

Kevin sounded so convincing, Heather almost believed him. Never able to stay mad at him long, she sighed. Even if Possum had been used as a pawn in Kevin's plan, she was excited to be reunited with her horse—her good buddy, her confidant, her easy ride.

Like an impatient filly pawing the ground, Katie cleared her throat again.

"Oh. Excuse me. David, this is Katie Taggert. Katie, David Cane." Heather emphasized his first name.

"Daniel, was it?" A playful sparkle danced in the redhead's eyes.

"David." Heather and Kevin said in unison.

Followed by David, Heather led Image back into his stall, where she replaced the bridle with a halter, securing the lead to the manger. "Thanks for bringing Possum to me," she told David. "How did you get him here?"

"I borrowed Sheila's truck and trailer. She said to tell you hello."

Heather felt her nostrils flare. Sheila—her onced-best friend who had tried to steal David. Was she at it again? Had she been spending time with him while Heather was away? Darn. Double darn. Heather touched David's arm and he smiled at her. What was her problem? She had no room to fault Sheila, considering her own feelings for Ty.

She checked the knot on Image's lead, patted him on the neck, then turned to David. "Let's get Possum. I'm sure he'll be anxious to stretch his legs and check to see if there's anyone around here to visit with."

When David and Heather came out of the barn, Kevin stood at the rear of the trailer unlatching the back door. Katie peered up at Possum whose head stuck out from the open side window of the trailer.

The gelding whinnied when he saw Heather.

Kevin backed the huge gray horse out of the trailer. Heather ran to Possum, throwing her arms around his strong neck.

David staggered like he'd been wounded. "You notice I didn't get a welcome like that."

"Well, silly. You're not a horse."

"In my next life, remind me to come back as one of your beasts," David said.

"We should all be so lucky," Kevin said.

Everyone turned at the sound of a truck engine.

Quickly Heather counted heads. Was it Bea and Wells . . . or was it . . . Her mouth went dry.

Climbing out of his vehicle, Ty walked toward them. He didn't smile. He didn't frown. In fact, Heather couldn't read his expression. She glanced back at David, then at Ty again. Wow! Matt Damon and Ben Affleck. Hunk bookends. Oh, dear.

CHAPTER NINE

"You must be David," Ty said, offering his hand. In his plaid shirt, jeans and silver-buckled belt, he looked every inch the cowboy. The extra height his boots added enabled him to study David eyeball to eyeball, his brown ones sizing up David's blues and vice versa.

"And you must be Tyler." David shook his hand, then placed his arm around Heather.

Energy seeped from her. David's arm rested warm and comforting on her shoulder, but one look at Ty's guarded expression made her consider the option of squirming away. "For the record, David, this is Tyler Taggert." She tried to keep her voice steady. "Ty, David Cane."

She glanced from one to the other. It was impossible not to notice how good-looking they both were. Alone, each was a definite head-turner, but together they were totally awesome— the dark and not so dark of handsome. Beads of perspiration broke out on Heather's forehead.

Katie and Kevin watched wide-eyed as if they expected another Mount St. Helen's. Actually, Heather would have much preferred an erupting volcano to the dead silence now lingering. She wished someone would say something—anything. Her own mind searched frantically, but nothing surfaced. Everyone stared at her. She felt like her nerves had popped out through her skin.

A horse in the barn whinnied and her knees nearly buckled. "I'd better take care of Possum." Heather frowned at Kevin as she took the gelding's lead rope. This was all her stepfather's fault.

Possum turned toward the barn with Heather in tow. The huge horse missed very few meals and the pressure on the rope measured the extent of his hunger.

Helping her hold him back, Ty joined Heather at Possum's head. "Now, that's a horse," he chuckled, staring up at the gelding's high withers. "He's huge. He doesn't look like your ordinary, garden variety jumper, does he? Nothing at all like Image."

Heather nodded. "That's for sure." The big gelding would have appeared more in character pulling a wagon or even a plow, but he was a capable, even excellent, jumper. He'd won Heather her first blue ribbon and was more importantly a faithful and loving friend. He was special too because his training had brought Heather's mother, Laura, and Kevin together. Little had she known then how much trouble Kevin could stir up.

"Let's go see if he likes the stall I figure we'll put him in." Ty peered over his shoulder. "Coming, Mr. Cane?"

David brushed horse hair off his slacks. "Of course, and the name's David."

"Why don't we get David settled first?" Kevin glanced at Katie. "Okay?"

A quick smile touched her lips. "What a good idea. Let's see, where shall we put him?"

"How about the room where I've been staying? Remember, I've got a plane to catch later today." Somehow, Kevin's lines sounded rehearsed.

Heather turned to Ty. "Looks like you'll have a new neighbor downstairs. Are you okay with that?"

"Sure he is, aren't you, Ty? Of course, if you'd rather, I can bunk with Heather and he can have my room." Katie's face was a mask of innocence.

Ty shook his head. "What's the big deal? Sure he can stay downstairs."

"Look, if there's a problem, I saw a motel . . ." David raised his hand to point.

Katie's eyes flashed. "Oh! Don't be silly! No one who comes to visit us ever stays in a motel."

Heather watched Katie and Kevin glance at each other.

"It's settled then." Kevin took a step toward the house. "I'll need someone to drop me at the airport later. How about it, David?"

"Sure," he answered, his eyes sharp and steady, "if Heather will come with me."

Kevin's shoulders rose and fell, and Katie shook her head.

Heather toyed with Possum's mane. "Okay." She needed time to thank David properly for bringing her horse and on the return trip from the airport, they'd be alone. "Just let me know when you're ready."

"Well, come along, David, I'll show you to your stall . . . uh . . . room." Katie giggled. "Just kidding."

"You had me worried for a second." David took a duffle and a small bag from the cab of the truck.

"Here, let me . . ." Kevin grabbed the small bag from David. "I'll help you settle in. It's a great room. Open the window at night and the sound of the waves will put you to sleep."

As he followed Katie and Kevin to the house, David called over his shoulder, "I won't be long."

"Don't you want to make sure Possum settles in?" Ty asked. "And what about Image?"

Heather felt like the rope in a tug-of-war. "Why don't you go with David and Kevin and I'll stay here and take care of all the horses." Her statement came out harsher than she planned.

Ty tipped his head. "A little touchy, are we?"

Touchy didn't even begin to hint at how she felt, but she knew she shouldn't take it out on Ty. "I'm sorry," she said. "I don't know what's wrong with me."

"You don't? Think about it, Heather." He took Possum's lead rope and led him into the barn, stopping in front of a stall he'd made double wide by opening the center panel. "Just your size, isn't it, fellow?" He turned the gelding into the enclosure.

Possum pawed the fresh sawdust, then lay down and rolled. Ty and Heather watched him until he stood, shook and stuck his head into the feeder. Heather heard him chomping as she started down the aisle toward Image.

Heather and Ty said little to each other as they finished caring for the horses. After filling Possum's water barrel, Ty aimed the hose at Heather. "Are you thinking about why you're so grumpy?"

"I'm thinking. I'm thinking," Heather squealed and dashed out of the barn.

Later that afternoon, at Kevin's suggestion, David, Ty, Katie and Heather all took her stepfather to the airport in Kalispell which, by way of Bigfork, was forty miles to the north. Since Katie had no performance at the playhouse that evening, she was able to tag along. Kevin's offer to treat them to dinner before his flight met with approval from everyone.

Wells and Bea, attending a town meeting that evening, offered to drive Ty's pickup so their Lexus would be available for the others.

"Nice car," Kevin said as he slid into the passenger side of the silver automobile. Ty drove while Katie and David sat in the back, on either side of Heather.

There were two routes to Kalispell. One crossed the more barren, higher populated west side of Flathead Lake; the other traversed the lavishly timbered east side, where the road in some places edged the shoreline. Katie suggested they take the east side, not only because of the view, but because that route took them closer to Bigfork, where they planned to eat.

"This is unbelievably beautiful." David, sitting behind Ty, peeked out the window. "Look at those trees and the lake—a water-skier's paradise."

"Do you ski?" Katie leaned around Heather.

"It's one of my passions, next to her, that is." He winked at Heather and she smiled. He could be such a heartbreaker. That grin, those bewitching blue eyes.

"Some of the guys at the playhouse ski too," Katie continued. "I've been trying to get one of them to teach me, but so far, no luck."

His arm around Heather, David turned his head to face Katie. "I don't know how long I'll be staying, but I could teach you. I've been trying to get this girl interested." His shoulder nudged Heather's. "Maybe she'd be more willing if you two learned together."

"Cool." Katie's brow lifted. Heather could almost see the cogs turning. What manner of intrigue ricocheted through the redhead's mind? Like a mother bear, she seemed intent on drawing David's attention away from Heather—leaving room for Ty?

"I can hardly wait," Heather said in an exaggerated tone. She had no desire to embarrass herself in front of David, let alone Ty.

"You might change your mind about skiing when you see our boat." Ty glanced in the rearview mirror. He seemed to be watching Heather.

"That bad, huh?" David laughed—a deep, rolling, contagious laugh. Heather couldn't help but smile.

"Remember Columbus's three boats—the *Nina*, the *Pinta* and the . . ."

"*Santa Maria*," Katie finished for him.

"No. The *Nina*, the *Pinta* and Old Rusty Bucket."

"Old Rusty Bucket?" Kevin glanced up from the sunglasses he'd been polishing with his handkerchief.

"Our boat," Ty said and adjusted the mirror.

David started to laugh again and coughed, his arm coming out from around Heather.

She pounded him on the back. "You all right?"

"Yeah," he said. "Maybe I could rent a boat. We have a MasterCraft at home. What I wouldn't give to have it here."

"I'll bet we could borrow Ted's. I'm training one of his horses." Ty glanced back over his shoulder. "Remember, Katie, that time he came over while I was working on Old Rusty Bucket and he told me we could borrow his sometime? I think it might be a ski boat."

"Oh, yeah. That was the day we first went swimming." She turned to Heather. "I'd just bought a new pink swimsuit, one piece, legs cut up to here." She pointed. "Nearly froze my tail off."

Ty braked as a deer ran across the road, disappearing into a cherry orchard. "Everyone have their seatbelts on?"

"Aye, aye, Captain." Katie saluted.

Seeing the deer reminded Heather of something. "Did you bring the watch, Ty?"

CHAPTER TEN

W hat watch?" Katie and David said together. Kevin shifted in his seat to look at them.

"The one Ty and I found the other day while we were riding." Heather traced the seam on the leather upholstery with her nail.

"You and Ty went riding?" David asked. His hand dropped onto her knee. Even though covered by jeans, her skin quivered at the warmth of his touch.

Katie's forehead wrinkled. "You didn't tell me about any watch."

"Me either," Kevin said, peering over top of his sunglasses.

Ty took the watch out of his pants pocket and tossed it over his shoulder. It lit in Heather's lap.

David reached for it. "You found a Rolex?"

"Is it a Rolex?" Heather asked, her fingers touching his as they studied it.

Katie leaned across her friend for a better look. "Rolexes are expensive, aren't they?"

"I'll say. Some more than others. My dad's cost about five thousand dollars." David rubbed his thumb over the crystal. "This looks just like a Rolex, a really expensive one."

"You're kidding." Ty gave the Lexus more throttle. They sped around a pickup carrying a wolf-type dog in the back.

"Let's see the watch." Kevin held out his hand.

"I'm surprised you don't have one," Heather said.

"Used to. It was a gift from my former wife. I sold it to help pay my attorney's fees after the divorce. You know how expensive attorneys can be." He tipped his head at David.

"Only the really good ones," he replied, grinning.

Kevin passed the watch to David. "It looks authentic, doesn't it? Don't Rolexes have serial numbers?"

"They're the only watches that do, and no two Rolexes have the same number. I remember the jeweler telling Dad that." David turned the watch over in his hand. "Right here, this is called the case." He pointed to the part of the watch that held all the workings—the part the crystal fit over. "See here at the 'six' end of the case where the band hooks on? Under there is a series of six or seven numbers preceded by a letter of the alphabet."

"Can you get the band off? Maybe we can find the number," Katie said, leaning into Heather.

On her opposite side, David also slid closer. "Only Rolex dealers have the correct tools to work on their watches."

"Is there a Rolex dealer in Kalispell?" Heather asked. "Hey. I'm getting squashed here."

"Oops, sorry." David straightened.

"I doubt it," Katie answered.

"But there's that old jewelry store on the corner of Washington and Fourth. I bet they'll know someone who can help us." Ty glanced around. "Katie, you're crowding Heather."

"I'm sorry." She touched Heather's hand and moved toward the window.

Heather sat back and stretched her arms wide, laying one across Katie, the other over David. "Ah. That's better."

All three laughed.

"They might send the watch to New York," Kevin said. "That's the Rolex headquarters in the U.S."

"I bet they do." David took hold of Heather's hand. "They'll be able to tell you the year the watch was made, when it was shipped from Switzerland to the U.S., which jewelry store sold it and to who."

"To whom," Katie said.

Heather giggled.

"Okay for you, little Miss English Major," David kidded.

Katie pulled a face. "Sorry. It just popped out."

"Things are always popping out of her mouth, kinda like gum balls from a broken machine," Ty said. "You get used to it sooner or later, so just ignore her."

Katie stuck out her tongue at Ty.

"So where did you find this watch?" Kevin asked.

Ty threw a wadded-up tissue at his sister. "In that forest area by the house."

"You found it there?" Kevin returned. "Wells and I were just talking about that piece of property last night. I asked him who owned it and if he thought they'd sell. Your dad said I'd have to stand at the end of a pretty long line and only end up disappointed."

"You were thinking of buying it?" Heather asked. What would David think about that? She glanced at her boyfriend—her current boyfriend. He stared at Kevin, seemingly intent on his answer.

"Oh, you know, I'm always on the lookout."

"Maybe it's the bachelor's watch," Katie said.

"I doubt it." Ty reached forward to turn down the music—an Alan Jackson tune. "We found it by a pile of hay where a horse had been tied."

"A horse? How do you know it was a horse? Step in the leftovers?" Katie asked.

Peeking over his shoulder, Ty shot her a pained look.

"Just about." Heather chuckled.

Katie combed her fingers through her hair, lifting strands of it from her forehead. "Well, how come nobody told me about this? It might be important."

"It was probably McCade who tied the horse out there," Ty said.

"McCade had a barn full of stalls," Katie returned.

"Maybe he had one more horse than he had stalls. I don't know, Kate," Ty said. "It's probably no big deal."

"It most certainly might be. Think about it. What would a hidden horse be doing with a Rolex watch?"

"That's what I wondered," Heather said.

"Just because you two solved a mystery last summer doesn't mean that something as simple as McCade losing his watch while tying up one of his horses is another one," Ty said.

"But what if it isn't his watch?" Heather asked.

"And if the watch is real . . ." Katie said.

"Hmm. It does give one cause to ponder." Kevin turned clear around in his seat and removed his sunglasses. "After last year, I don't know if I dare leave you, Heather. Will you please just show your horses and leave the mystery solving to the police?"

"I'll take care of her." David pulled her close.

She noticed Ty glance into the rearview mirror again. The car swerved slightly.

"I'm not going to need too much taking care of," she said. "I promise. Would you look at that. What a sight!"

The road rested on the hillside just above the shoreline. Not twenty feet below them, the full width of the lake stretched off in the distance, like shimmering blue taffeta amidst rolling green velvet.

"Big, isn't it?" Katie said.

"Is that an island way over there or part of the land?" David pointed.

Heather turned to look. "That's Wild Horse Island. We rode wave runners around it the other day."

"You and Katie?"

"Ty too," Heather said. "It's always good to have two machines in case one has problems."

"I see." David sniffed.

"We're pretty close to the water, aren't we?" Heather sat up straight.

"There wasn't even a guardrail along here until recently," Katie said. "That sure kept me from dozing while driving home from performances earlier this summer."

"I bet. It's keeping me from dozing now." Heather wondered if this was where the truck and horse trailer had gone off a year ago, but not wanting to bring gloom to the evening, she decided not to comment. Instead she said, "Look how green everything is— well, green and blue. An artist painting this scene would only need shades of green, blue and a dab of white for those puffy clouds."

"Darn. That reminds me," David said. "I left my camera in the truck. I can't believe how dumb that was."

Katie opened her mouth to speak.

"Don't say it." David held up his hand.

"Good luck keeping her quiet," Ty said. "Her jaw locks up if it isn't moving."

Katie leaned across Heather and punched Ty in the shoulder. "I've hardly said a word this whole time, have I, Heather?"

Heather shook her head. "I'm staying out of this."

David ran his tongue over his lips. "I still wish I'd brought my camera." Heather knew photography was one of his many hobbies. Actually, most everything interested him, with the possible exception of horses.

Katie leaned back in her seat, folding her arms across her chest. "I'm not saying another word." She tried to act perturbed, but both sides of her lips wiggled and she put a hand to her mouth, hiding her giggle.

"Just go ahead and jump right in anytime you feel the urge," David advised.

"She will," Heather and Ty echoed.

David laughed. He hadn't seemed this carefree and happy for a long time. He loved people and people loved him. He knew it and counted on it. Their impending engagement seemed far from his mind as he joked, asked questions and exchanged wisecracks with Katie, Ty and Kevin. Heather rubbed her cheek. Did David still care about her?

The thought of losing David saddened Heather and she vowed to treat him better, but what about Ty? Was he still in the running or had she blown it with him completely? Did she care? Was it possible to be in love with two guys at the same time?

She looked back and forth between the two, who were now engaged in a lively conversation about water-skiing. Anything was possible.

Katie glanced at Heather and, lifting her hands, rapidly opened and closed her fingers and thumbs, mocking the two talking boys. Katie shrugged and Heather giggled. The Lexus turned off the main highway.

The town of Bigfork, Montana had a winter population of around three thousand people, but a summer population of closer to five thousand, Katie explained. It overlooked its own quiet harbor where water lapped against the edge of some of the locals' properties. The town's center was a collection of galleries and shops which catered to tourists. The narrow street was lined with cars. In no apparent hurry, people wandered along the sometimes board sidewalks, in and out of shops where the storekeepers visited with them like long-lost friends. The Bigfork Summer Playhouse sat in the middle of all this.

"Well, here it is," Katie announced.

Once a wooden garage-type structure that seated around one hundred and fifty people, the old playhouse had recently been replaced by a larger cinder block building holding closer to five hundred, Katie told them. Its redwood front blended nicely with the overall rustic feel of its surroundings and masked its inner up-to-date technology.

Katie ushered them in, introducing her brother and friends to the owner/manager of the theater who had years before been a struggling actor in the old playhouse. He and his wife, a pianist who had accompanied in the early theater orchestra and still played in the current one, had turned the playhouse into a lucrative business. Many college students and actors from other theaters auditioned to perform in Bigfork during the summer, making Heather realize even more the importance of Katie's position here as a leading lady.

"I'm impressed," Heather said as she and Katie walked out to the front of the playhouse. The guys stayed behind for a bathroom break.

"Pretty cool place, huh?" Katie returned.

"I'll bet you meet some cute actors." Heather raised her brows.

"Some cuter than others."

"Sounds like there might be someone special." If only that were true, then there'd be someone to help take Katie's mind off matchmaking.

"No, I'm not like some unnamed person who has two."

"Two what?" David exited the theater.

"Two? Did she say two?" Heather narrowed her eyes at the other girl.

"Now I've lost my train of thought," Katie said, flipping her hair.

"Look what I have." David fanned three tickets. "Front row seats to your next performance, Katie. I got one for Ty too. He said he didn't have anyone to invite, so it will just be the three of us staring up at you."

Katie wrinkled her nose. "Those are hard to get. Most of the tickets are sold out way in advance. How'd you do it?"

"I don't know. My magnetic personality, I guess."

"Oh, sure," Katie returned.

David clapped his hand across his chest. "You don't think I have a magnetic personality?"

Katie shrugged. "I'm neutral. Ask Heather."

"I'd say you're guilty as charged." Heather slipped her arm through David's. When had he become such a fan of live theater?

"See, Katie. Heather thinks I have a magnetic personality. Actually," he spoke out of the corner of his mouth, "there was a cancellation. One of the actors' family couldn't come."

"Ah-ha. I thought so," Katie grinned. "Hey, look down here." She pointed.

A brick sidewalk and patio surrounded the front part of the theater. Names of patrons who had made donations to the building of the new theater were etched into the bricks.

"See. Here's Mom's name and Dad's," Katie said. "When Ty and I find someone to marry, Mom and Dad are going to buy us our own brick."

Kevin stepped up behind them. "Now that's incentive."

Ty followed. "I don't know. I think it'll take more than that." His eyes caught Heather's and held.

"You two finally through?" Katie asked. "I thought you fell in or something."

Shaking his head, Ty said, "I can't take her anywhere."

They all laughed.

"Where's this place you've been telling us about?" Kevin put on the jacket he held. "I'm starving."

"Quit your dawdling then," Katie said, "and follow me."

The Bigfork Inn, with its exposed beam ceiling, wooden walls, and stuffed animal heads, reminded Heather of a large Hansel and Gretel cottage.

A teenage girl with a figure that looked like she ran marathons or climbed mountains greeted them as they walked in. Her gaze scrutinized the five of them, but settled on Katie. "You were in the play the other night, weren't you? You played Kim."

Katie smiled and nodded.

"You did good."

"Thanks." A slight blush touched Katie's cheeks, a perfect highlight to her flawless makeup. "You liked the play then?"

"I'll say. I'm going to drag my boyfriend to it next week."

"You have to drag him?" Katie chuckled and hooked a lock of her thick red hair behind her ear. Dressed in a form-fitting beige pantsuit with chocolate brown western braid across the front, Katie looked just how an actress should for her public.

"Yeah, but he'll like it once he gets there."

"What's your name?" Katie said. "I'll look for you. I might be ushering that night before the performance."

"My name's Robin. You'd look for me? That would be so cool."

"Nice to meet you, Robin."

Ty cleared his throat.

"Well . . ." Katie said.

Robin grabbed some menus. "Come with me. I'll give you our most special table."

"Great. I'm starving," Ty said.

As Robin led them to the table, Heather noticed that many of the patrons turned to stare at them. They'd smile, then visit among themselves. They probably recognized Katie, or maybe they just admired the view.

David, dressed in charcoal trousers and a short-sleeved black mock turtleneck and Ty in a blue denim shirt with a leather collar and matching denim jeans were enough to turn any female's head and if they weren't, along came Kevin, dressed in a sports jacket and slacks. Of course the male viewing public had Katie and maybe, just maybe, Heather also caught an eye or two. Her new double pleated jeans with tiny vertical stripes made her look quite slender, especially when she wore them with her white, oversized-style shirt, and, like Katie, she'd taken extra time fixing her hair.

"Can I have your autograph?" Robin asked, as Katie, then David, Heather, Ty and Kevin seated themselves around a circular table topped with wildflowers in a glass jar.

Katie smiled and blushed again. "You want my autograph? Sure. I guess. Do you have something to write on?"

Patting her pockets, Robin came up empty. She finally grabbed a napkin from the next table and handed it to Katie. "Will this do?"

"I think so. Now, I guess we'll need a pen?"

Glancing from side to side, Robin patted her pockets again.

"Allow me." Kevin removed a mechanical pencil from the inside of his jacket, twisted the lead into writing position and handed it to Katie.

"Thanks." She touched the lead to the tip of her tongue and with a flourish wrote: "To Robin, Your friend, Katie Taggert" on the napkin. "There you go." She handed the napkin to Robin and returned the pencil to Kevin.

"This is so cool." Robin held the napkin to her heart and studied the others seated around the table. "Are they anyone? Kinda reminds me of *Bay Watch* or something."

"We're just fans, like you," David said.

Katie rolled her eyes.

A darkly tanned waitress in a sleeveless cotton dress, tied at the waist with a rope belt, cleared her throat.

"Okay," Robin said. "I'll let you order now."

"Nice to meet you." Katie waved.

Heather noticed her group was still center stage. She supposed the patrons thought they were couples and wondered which boy they would link her with. Then, expelling any doubt, David took her hand, leaving brother and sister to complete the second so-called "couple."

Back in the car, they headed for Kalispell. At the jewelry store, everyone stayed in the Lexus but Ty, who ran in with the watch. He returned about fifteen minutes later. "Like we thought, there aren't any Rolex dealers in Kalispell. These people said they'd find out where to send it and get back with me in a few days. Ty turned the key in the ignition. "Where to now? The airport?"

Looking at his Timex, Kevin said, "As much as I hate to leave this happy group, I'd better get going."

When Heather walked Kevin into the airport, Ty, Katie and David remained behind. Hugging her good-bye, Kevin said, "I'd like to stay and supervise, but you know I never interfere."

"I do, huh?" Heather tried not to smile. "Give Mom and Robby a squeeze for me." She narrowed her eyes. "It's a good thing you're leaving. You've complicated my life to the point where I've entertained thoughts of murder, mayhem, hiring a hit man . . ."

"Me? I've complicated your life?"

"Okay, maybe I helped a little."

"It will all work out." He touched her cheek.

Walking out of the airport, Heather noted that David sat in the passenger seat of the Lexus, up front with Ty. She climbed into the back, next to Katie, wondering if the redhead had anything to do with the seating arrangements.

Heather yawned once, then again. She was so exhausted from the mental turmoil of the day that she fell into a sound sleep on the way home, not even waking up until they pulled into the driveway.

In the front room, David kissed her good night just as Ty walked by on his way to the basement. "Wait up, Ty," David called. "I'll go down with you."

"Pleasant dreams, Heather," Ty said, catching her glance.

Even as tired as she was, Heather feared sleep would be out of the question that night.

CHAPTER
ELEVEN

Flinging the covers aside, Heather opened the window over her bed. The tangy scent of pine and dying campfires met her nose. She fluffed her pillow, plopped back down on the sheets and continued to toss and turn. Finally, in frustration, she climbed out of bed. Pulling a terry cloth robe over her shorty pajamas, she peeked out the bedroom door. Except for the ticking of the grandfather clock that stood at the top of the basement stairs, the house lay silent. Heather moved closer, glancing up. The hands on the clock read three-ten.

At home when she couldn't sleep, she headed for the stable. Here, though, the beauty and serenity of the lake beckoned. She'd visit the stable later, if sleep still eluded her.

On the cement dock, she dangled her feet in the silently calm water, clearing her head somewhat. She must have dozed at least once during the night because she could remember dreaming. It had seemed so vivid. She'd been walking with David in a lush green field. His arm encircled her waist. She felt happy and protected. Then out of nowhere, Ty appeared. She left David and went into Ty's waiting arms where she felt happy and protected. Then David reappeared and she went to him, then to Ty, then to David, and back and forth until at last Heather had pictured herself standing alone, arms outstretched, as both boys faded into the background. When she awoke, tears trailed down her cheeks. She hadn't been able to go back to sleep.

Running her hands through her hair, she pressed both palms against her forehead. The image of David and Ty leaving made her heart heavy.

Heather slipped out of her robe and dived into the water. The cold clutched her, but swimming blocked her thoughts for a moment. Her strokes lengthened. Water washed over her body.

Her breath came in gasps. She kept swimming—harder and harder, one arm, then the other. Kick. Again. Over and over and . . . Oh, no! Something was happening. Her foot twisted up. She couldn't straighten her leg.

She screamed in pain. Choked as her head sank beneath the water.

Thrashing with her arms and one good leg, she tried to force her head to the top. She took in a mouthful of water. Choked some more.

Spitting, she gasped a quick breath. Her face felt like ice.

Grabbing her leg, she tried to straighten her foot. So much pain.

She dropped beneath the surface again. Came up coughing. Not enough air. Head spun. Heart pounded.

Panic gripped her body. What had she been thinking? She clenched her teeth. If only her leg would quit cramping. She tried to see how far from shore she'd come. Which direction had she been swimming?

Like a video on fast forward, she thought about her mother and Kevin, her baby brother, even Possum and Image. How silly she'd been. There were so many more aspects to her life than choosing between David and Ty. Why couldn't she have both of them as friends for a while? She was still so young, so very, very young—much too young—to die.

Forget the pain. Look for the shore. Remember how the moon had lit the landscape when she'd first come down? Landscape? She couldn't even see the shore!

What was that? Something brushed passed her. She felt an arm around her middle, water flowing around her head as she began to move. Someone was pulling her. She tried to help swim, but her leg still ached.

Only when her foot touched the sandy lake bottom was she able to identify her rescuer. Ty—strong, steadfast Ty. He drew her into his arms and held her close. She clung to him, sobbing, standing on her one good leg.

"You little dummy. What do you think you're doing?" He spoke into her soaked hair, holding her close until her shaking subsided.

Standing enabled her to work the cramp out of her leg. "I couldn't sleep and the water looked so pretty. I guess I didn't think." She stared up at him, so handsome in the moonlight. "I don't know what would have happened if you hadn't been around. Why were you here, anyway?"

Ty backed away, retrieved her robe and wrapped her in it. It wasn't until then that Heather noticed her soaked shorty pajamas left little to the imagination. Ty pulled jeans over his wet shorts. He'd been pretty exposed himself. Heather should have been embarrassed, but she wasn't.

"I couldn't sleep either. Darn it, Heather, what are you doing to us?" He turned and started for the house. Then he whirled around, walked straight to Heather, pulled her to him, and kissed her.

"Next time you can't sleep, try warm milk. And by the way, tell David he owes me one." Then Ty broke into a jog and disappeared through the basement door.

Heather watched him go, too surprised to move. Finally, hugging her robe tightly around her, she crept back into the house. She changed into dry pajamas, wrapped an extra blanket around her shivering body and, with Ty's kiss still tingling on her lips, crawled into bed, grateful to be alive.

The next day in the barn, it was as if the night before had never happened.

"Hi, Heather." Ty held a hose over Image's water barrel. "I've set some jumps in the arena. We should get Possum working if you're going to show him with Image."

Had it not been for the fact that her leg still smarted when she stepped on it wrong, Heather would have thought last night had been a dream. "Yes sir, boss." She saluted. "Hello to you too."

He smiled and returned the salute. "Get to work."

The horse show in which Kevin had entered Image and recently seen fit to add Possum would take place in a week. Ty ran Heather through such a rigorous training schedule that day, she found herself missing Kevin. She knew her stepfather had left instructions for Ty, as Kevin had for her. When the training of horses was involved, especially when someone had placed complete trust in him, Ty switched into a no-nonsense mode. Heather had barely found time to say hello to David.

Not until the horses were stomping in their stalls ready for dinner did David finally come to the barn to see her. "Hold it right there." He lifted the camera, sighting through it. With those blue eyes and that square jaw, he should have stood in front of the camera, not behind.

"Don't even think about it." Heather raised her hand, blocking the view of the lens. After riding all day, she knew she looked far too thrashed for pictures. She removed Possum's halter, walked out of the stall and latched the door.

Draping his arm around her, he squeezed her shoulder. "What's that?" He stared at the top of her head. "Hold still." He pulled a piece of hay from her tresses. "Will you pose for me tomorrow? I need a beautiful model."

Heather blew her hair out of her eyes. "You better keep looking then."

David laughed. "Nope. I've found my girl." He pulled her into a hug.

She lay her head against his chest, avoiding the camera that hung around his neck. "I'm glad you have." A stab of guilt made her gasp. Was she really? Yeah, of course she was!

"And I've found the perfect place." Taking her chin in his hand, he tipped her face up to look at him.

"Where?" She cleared her throat.

"In that forest by the house. There's this little grove of trees . . ."

"That's where we found the Rolex," Heather said, straightening.

"Hey, David." Ty came down the aisle, pushing a wheelbarrow full of hay. "If you've got some time later, let's take a look at that boat McCade left."

A chorus of whinnies greeted Ty and his wheelbarrow.

"Old Rusty Bucket?" David asked.

"That's the one." Ty stole a quick glance at Heather. "Sometimes the old tub can be a real problem. Are you any good with engines?"

Reaching into the pocket of his perfectly fitting jeans, David pulled out a lens cap and clicked it into place. "I've been known to peek under a hood or two."

"But this is a boat." Ty's jeans fit pretty well too, darn well.

"No problem." Rarely did David admit to anything he couldn't do. But . . . he could do most anything. He pulled the strap of the camera over his head and attached the leather to the latch of one of the doors.

"Will it start?" Following Ty's lead, David lifted two flakes of hay from the wheelbarrow and dropped them into the feeder next in line.

David helping with the horses without being asked? Heather couldn't believe it.

Ty shook his head. "The motor won't even turn over."

Heather took hay to Possum, then fed the horses across and down from him.

"Is the battery dead or do you think it's seized up?" David tossed feed to another horse, almost completing the chore.

"I think it's probably a dead battery." Ty fed the last two horses, then parked the wheelbarrow at the end of the aisle.

David grabbed his camera and followed. "Before we even try to start it, we should probably flush out the carburetor and fuel lines. It's been sitting a long time, I'll bet."

"I know fuel leaves a varnish-like residue after a while," Ty said.

Rubbing the back of her neck, Heather watched the guys saunter out of the barn exchanging ideas, like two colts weaned in the same pasture. "I'll just finish up here," she called.

No answer.

Her hands moved to her hips.

After fixing the boat the next morning, the guys took to the lake. Heather stayed behind since she had to care for the horses. Well, she didn't have to, she'd just offered. She'd been a little surprised when Ty had agreed to her doing it.

The day after that, however, everything changed. Since Katie had some time off, the guys decided the girls should join them on the water. After Heather's recent experience, she had some misgivings. She'd been right to have them.

CHAPTER TWELVE

Put this on, Heather." Ty came up behind her and wrapped a life jacket around her bare shoulders. Even though the horse showing season had taken its toll on her suntan, at least with all the activity, she felt she looked trim in the black and white bathing suit Katie had lent her—not sleek like Katie, but Heather doubted she'd ever look that good. Katie had legs—what was the expression she'd heard Ty use to describe length—"as long as a well rope in dry season." Katie's legs were at least that long.

Heather slipped her arms through the holes in the jacket as Ty reached around her to fasten the front. She caught a whiff of his cologne. He smelled wonderful—like vanilla spice with a touch of pine.

"You never know when you might need one of these," he whispered into her ear.

Heather's face turned hot, but she managed a weak smile.

They all piled into Old Rusty Bucket, Ty in the driver's seat. David, camera in hand, sat next to him, with Katie and Heather behind. The guys had cleaned up the boat to the point where Heather thought they'd have to rename it. She saw no rust anywhere, and it was a pretty yellow gold color with six seats—two under a removable black top, two directly behind facing to the rear of the boat and two clear at the back.

"Ah. Would you listen to that engine purr? We're good, aren't we?" David said.

Katie twisted her long red hair into a bun at the top of her head and pulled on a baseball cap. "We'll let you know when we get back. Are you a good swimmer, Heather?"

Ty glanced around at her. "I used to think so," she said. "But they're not going to make us swim, are they?" she emphasized the last two words.

"Of course not," David said. "You question our skill, Miss Chambers, Miss Taggert?"

"Does your skill need questioning, Mr. Cane?" Katie responded.

"I've had no complaints about any of my skills, have I, Heather?"

"I refuse to answer on the grounds it may incriminate me." Her answer slipped out before she realized her statement might have a double meaning. Ty stared at her for a moment, then looked away.

At least the weather couldn't have been more perfect—warm, with just enough breeze to spread the wonderful freshness through the air. Purplish mountains and tall pines reflected in the clear, smooth lake. In spots Heather could see the bottom, perhaps twenty to thirty feet down.

"Look, Ty. It's Ted." Katie shielded her eyes from the morning sun with her upraised hand. "Wait until you meet this guy, Heather. He invented some kind of an exercise gadget and he's filthy rich. He's been really nice to Ty and me."

A blond man driving a sleek red and white ski boat pulled up alongside. He cut the engine. The wake from the boat rolled under Old Rusty Bucket.

Katie stood, lost her balance and flopped back down on the seat. "Don't have my sea legs yet."

Heather smiled.

"Hi, Ty, Katie." He grinned at Heather and David, including them in the greeting. "Hey, Ty, you have a lot better taste in horses than you do in boats."

"How you doing, Ted?" Ty eased the gearshift lever into neutral as if afraid the engine wouldn't start again if he shut it down. "We just took the old girl out of mothballs."

Like ducks on a pond—one old and battered, the other sleek and cocky—the boats edged toward one another. David jumped up and leaning over the edge, caught the side of Ted's boat to keep the two from bumping.

Heather joined him, holding the rear of their boat away from Ted's while David held the middle.

"Thanks," Ted said. He reminded Heather of Crocodile Dundee—a weathered nature-type man.

"Beautiful boat," David said. "My family has a MasterCraft too, but I've never seen one this color. Is it new?"

"Pretty new. You ski then?" Ted took a Hawaiian print shirt off the seat and slipped it on. His skin looked taut and leathery brown—too much time shirtless, Heather supposed.

"A little," David said.

"Truth is, Heather says he's some kind of a hotdog skier." Katie squirted suntan lotion into her hand from a squeeze bottle of Coppertone.

"That's slalom skier." Heather sat on the side of their boat, stretching her leg across to rest on the MasterCraft, holding it at bay.

"Oh! Heather says he's some kind of a slalom skier," Katie repeated, smoothing the lotion onto her arms.

"Tell you what. Follow me home, drop me off and take this boat," Ted said. "You won't be doing a whole lot of skiing behind that one."

"Ah, Ted, we can't take your boat." Ty wiggled around in his seat, kneeling on its cushion.

Ted ran a hand through his hair. "Sure you can."

"Tell you what," Katie grinned. "We'll trade you straight across . . . and throw in Ty."

Her brother grunted.

Laughing, Ted held up his hands. "Take the boat okay? I'm going out of town for a few days anyway. Just pull it onto your shore station." He eased into the driver's seat, reached for the key, then paused. "Of course, Ty, I'll expect extra time put in on my gelding."

"You got it." Ty grinned. "You'd get it anyway."

"I know." Ted started the engine.

David and Heather pushed Old Rusty Bucket away from the MasterCraft.

Ty put their boat in gear and, engine roaring, their little gold boat did its best to keep up with Ted's fancy red one.

They dropped Ted off on his impressive dock in front of his even more impressive house—actually mansion, complete with Greek columns. David followed the others in Ted's MasterCraft.

Ty put Old Rusty Bucket on its trailer and pulled it into the boat house with the small tractor Wells had recently purchased. Then Heather, Katie and Ty climbed into the MasterCraft.

"I'll be right back," David yelled, jogging toward the house. "I've got to get my gear."

"What gear?" Katie folded a towel lying on the boat seat. "We've got the skis and life jacket."

He held up a hand. "Just give me a minute."

Ty studied the MasterCraft's control panel. "It's got a CD player. Music anyone?"

David returned with an armload of "gear."

Katie laughed. "What's all this? Looks like you're going into space."

"Never mind."

He climbed into the boat.

Staring up at him now standing in black swim trunks, Heather had to admit she had all the respect in the world for his athletic club membership. He lifted weights several nights a week. Wow! And where did he get that dark, even suntan? Oh, yeah, water-skiing.

Ty backed the ski boat out of the dock area and headed out onto the lake. Heather watched droplets of water spray out on either side of the boat.

The MasterCraft slowed, then stopped. Ty edged out from behind the wheel to check the ski rope. He whipped off his T-shirt and Heather scolded herself for staring. Although she was sure Ty had never possessed an athletic club membership, lifting hay and wrestling broncs had produced their own muscular display and the sun had left a red trace across his chest and shoulders. Ty and David looked like an ad for Katie's Coppertone . . . before and after.

Katie scrutinized David. "You're putting on long underwear?"

"It's called fleece." He zipped into a gray long-sleeved, full-legged suit that really did look like long underwear.

"Geez. I sure hope you'll be warm enough." She stuck her hand in the lake. "It's not that cold." She flipped water on him. "See."

David lifted a brow. Heather knew he loved to kid almost as much as Katie. "It's not only for warmth. Here's a pop quiz for you, Miss Taggert. Why do you think Heather wears a hard hat when she jumps her horses?

Katie put a finger to her cheek as if thinking really hard. "Could it be to protect her head?"

"Correct. And that's one of the reasons . . ."

"Are you going to wear a helmet too?"

"Is she always like this?" David asked.

Ty nodded.

"I think it's so if he falls he'll have a little protection," Heather said. "He goes really fast and only uses one ski." She held up his specially designed Kidder water-ski. "Look. It's really pretty."

"Stay tuned, Miss Taggert," David said. "Remember, a picture is worth a hundred words."

"A thousand."

"Ah. You were listening." David wiggled into another, heavier full-body drysuit that went over the fleece. It had tight rubber-like material that fit closely around his wrists, ankles and neck. "Zip me, will you?" He turned his back to Katie.

A long, thick zipper extended from one shoulder tip to the other.

Katie drew away. "My hands are slippery from the lotion."

He winked at Heather. "How about it, hon?" He turned so she could help him. "Thanks." He strapped on a matching life jacket and climbed over the back of the boat. Standing on the teak ski platform at the back, he slid his feet into the boot-like neoprene bindings on the ski and eased into the water.

Ty threw him the rope, then idled the boat out in front.

"Hit it," David called and popped out of the water. He skied back and forth behind the boat traveling at such fast speeds that his weight shifted the rear of the boat in the direction he headed.

"Not bad," Katie said.

"Dang good," Ty said.

"Yeah," Heather said and grinned.

David put on an exhibition of water-skiing worthy of Cypress Gardens. His shoulder nearly touched the water as he cut back across the wake, and the rooster tail shooting up behind him reminded Heather of the fountains in front of the Bellagio Hotel in Las Vegas.

As it turned out, David didn't need his drysuit. He never fell. When he finally dropped off, Ty circled around to pick him up.

"Your turn, Ty," he called from the water. "Wanna use the dry suit?"

"Maybe just the jacket."

David climbed into the boat, handing his ski to Heather. Smiling, he touched her arm. "Unzip me?" He peeled off his dry suit and fleece.

"You're not even wet," Katie noted.

"Nope."

He turned to Ty. "What's your pleasure? Two skis, one, or do you want to try mine?"

Sucking in his breath, Ty strapped on David's wet ski jacket. "Cold."

"Should have used the suit." David glanced at Katie.

She sniffed.

"Let's start with these two," he said, showing David the pair of old skis he'd discovered in the boat house, "and I'll see if I can drop one. I doubt if I'll be able to, though."

"If you do and stay up, just rest your foot on the binding until you get your balance. Sometimes people try to get their foot in right away and usually go down." David threw the ski rope to Ty before crawling in behind the wheel.

With David turning around to shout directions, Ty skied across the bay and back using both skis. Although he didn't drop one, when he released the rope in front of their dock, a huge smile adorned his handsome face.

Heather and Katie cheered, as did David. He circled the MasterCraft to pick up Ty.

"Which one of you ladies wants to go first?" David asked.

The girls stared at each other, neither saying a word. Heather's heart thumped in her throat. Katie had said she'd skied a couple of times before, but Heather never had. She wished now she'd taken David up on his earlier invitations in Utah to go skiing, but she guessed she'd been too busy with Kevin and the horses.

"I'll go," Katie said finally. She popped up on the second try, fell only once and looked great in her bright blue bikini, even while wearing the life vest.

When it was Heather's turn, she was so nervous she could hardly breathe. Had it not been for the life jacket Ty had given her, Heather would have panicked when she inched into the water. She struggled so hard to put on the water-skis that David jumped in to help. He held her straight in the water, saying, "Get your tips out of the water, bend your knees and pretend you're being pulled out of a chair." It sounded quite simple.

Heather leaned back against David's strong chest, feeling confident in the water near him. All at once, the rope tightened in her hands. She shot forward, out of her skis and onto her belly. For a moment she peered through a veil of water as her head plowed along, leaving an awesome wake, she was sure. The boat dragged her for what seemed like miles before the rope pulled out of her hands.

"You're supposed to let go when you fall," Katie said as they circled around.

Heather couldn't help but smile, knowing she must have looked totally stupid. Now she was more determined than afraid. She wasn't going to let this darn thing get the best of her. Very few sports did.

"Now you tell me." Heather rolled her eyes.

"Are you okay?" Ty cut the gas on the boat to bob beside her.

"I don't know. My pride hurts pretty bad." Her body in the life vest rose and fell with the roll of the boat wake.

Ty smiled. "How does that jacket work?"

"A-Okay." Bending her leg, Heather slipped her foot into the ski binding. She leaned back and held the tips of her skis out of the water. "Look, Daddy," she said in a little girl voice, "I can put on my skis all by myself."

Nodding his approval, Ty said, "Okay. I'll go pick up David and bring you back the rope."

"Deal."

Alone in the vast lake, she shivered. How deep was it here? Where had that body been discovered? On the verge of a scream, she turned herself in the water. Where was the boat? Oh, there it was, heading back now. Calm down. You're all right.

They tossed her the rope. This time when she tried skiing, she leaned back too far and fell flat on her back causing a huge splash. Oh, my gosh. David was taking pictures! Darn him. Talk about humiliation.

"David! Cut it out!"

"You don't want to preserve this moment?"

"Let's put it this way. You take a picture, you die."

She tried several more times, only ending with bigger splashes and no success. Did she really want to ski? Her arms ached. Again the boat idled out in front of her. The rope pulled in her hands.

"Ty?" Katie called. "Was it in this bay where they last spotted the Flathead monster?"

Pushing her feet against the skis with all her diminishing strength, Heather rose out of the water. She tipped to one side then the other, but, gritting her teeth, she finally acquired her balance. Amid cheers from everyone in the boat, she stayed up all the way back to the dock.

Hooray. She'd actually skied. She felt like she had when Possum finally conquered the triple bar. She handed the skis to David, then quickly climbed into the boat. "Flathead monster? Did you just say that to get me up?" Heather remembered last summer when Katie had thought a neighboring ranch house was haunted, and although it turned out not to be, there had been good reason for her concern.

"There is a monster, isn't there, Ty?" Katie passed Heather a towel.

Ty shrugged and turned around in his seat to face them. "I don't know. Maybe. Actually I was reading an article the other day. It said there's been about seventy documented sightings of a Flathead monster during the last hundred years." He pointed at Katie. "My mistake was showing Katie the article. We've been on monster alert ever since."

"Oh, we have not. Hey, it wasn't me who saw it just last year over by Wild Horse Island."

The boat rocked and Heather stumbled against David. "Last year?" David asked. "Someone saw the monster last year?" He steadied her, holding her close for a minute.

Heather glanced over at Ty, then patted David on the chest and moved away. She plopped down in the seat next to Katie. "And we've just been in this lake?" Heather shivered as she thought about the other night. Maybe the monster had been lurking beneath her in the dark depths. Maybe drowning wouldn't have been her worst fate.

"I guess if there's a monster it's not all that mean. No one's ever reported any attacks. In fact it seems quite shy—swims off pretty quick after it's been sighted."

"What? Is it a big fish?" David took his seat beside Ty and picked up his camera.

"Some people think it's a huge sturgeon that entered the lake before there were dams, or one that evolved from when all this was Glacial Lake Missoula, thousands of years ago."

"Huh. Could be, I guess." David rubbed his jaw like he always did when pondering something. "I'd surely love to get a picture of that."

Ty slid from behind the wheel to coil the ski rope. "You and hundreds of other people."

"I'll bet." Sighting through his camera lens, David scanned the shoreline.

"Almost twenty years ago, around 1985, a father and son tried to get a picture of something they saw in Yellow Bay. It was huge—as long as a telephone pole and twice as big around, with smooth, coal black skin. Its head looked like a serpent's and it had four or five humps sticking out of the water. At first it moved real slow, then took off like a streak, stopping to look back before it dived into the water. By the time they got hold of their camera, the creature had disappeared. They said they saw it another time a couple of years later—again no picture."

"They needed you with them," Katie told David.

"Yeah." Heather peeked over the edge of the MasterCraft. She could see a long way down. A trout about ten inches long swam under the boat. "Yellow Bay? Is that where they found the man's body?"

"Yeah, I believe it is," Ty said.

Katie jumped up. "Maybe the monster ate the horse that was missing from the dead man's trailer."

Ty sighed. "Like I said, there's never been a report of the monster attacking anything or anybody, and maybe there isn't even a monster."

"What did all those people see then?" Katie's chin lifted.

"Well, the article said some of the sightings turned out to be a log, a shadow, and once it was a flock of tightly packed swimming ducks. Another time it turned out to be a horse swimming in the lake."

"That wouldn't have been you and Roxie, would it, Ty?" Heather raised her brows.

Ty smiled. "Nope. The horse sighting happened before we came here. Come to think of it, though, they did say the monster from about a year ago had a horse-like head, but the creature was about fifteen feet long." His shoulders lifted. "I guess a serpent head in the dark would look like a horse head." He paused. "I'm starting to sound like Katie."

"See," she said.

"So you still dare ski in this water?" Heather asked.

"Well, when most of us ski we don't spend as much time in the water as you do." David put his arm around her and pulled her to him.

Heather let her mouth drop open like she couldn't believe he'd say such a thing.

Everyone laughed.

Ty maneuvered the MasterCraft into the docking area and David helped him guide it onto the shore station. "Flip that switch, will you, Heather?"

"Right here?"

"Yep."

A motor sounded and the boat lifted out of the water.

"It looked like a horse head?" Heather asked.

"That's what the article said," Ty answered.

Hmm. Dead man, missing horse, a monster with an equine-like head. It was all too weird.

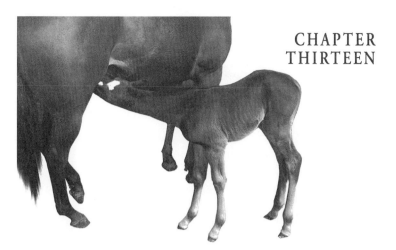

When the grandfather clock in the adjoining front room struck three, Heather shot upright in bed. Another sleepless night. If this didn't stop, she'd look like she carried luggage under her eyes.

Every time she'd tried to fall sleep, she'd picture the Flathead monster, its head a clone of Red Rock's. Ty's red stallion from the barn—the Flathead monster—not much of a stretch.

Whispering waves in the lake below her open window beckoned, but Ty's words from last night, "Next time you can't sleep, try warm milk," echoed through her brain. Okay. Maybe not warm milk, but something.

She pulled on her terry cloth robe, and with slippers flip-flopping, wandered into the kitchen. The scent of baking bread filtered through the room. Bea must have set the timer on her bread maker so there'd be fresh bread in the morning again.

Selecting a glass from the cupboard, Heather turned on the tap and leisurely stared out the window. Her glass overflowed as light in the barn drew her attention. Was something wrong with Image? Possum? Surely Ty would have awakened her. Maybe it wasn't Ty. Could it be Wells or Katie? She gulped the water, placed the glass in the sink and scurried back to her room. She tugged on jeans, pulled a sweatshirt over her head and shoved her feet into white tennis shoes.

On her way out the door, she grabbed a flashlight from a shelf in the hall. The illumination in the barn drew her at a brisk walk. A branch snapped. She whirled, directing her light. Was it the wind in the trees, or . . . the Flathead monster?

Her hand shook. She gripped the flashlight tighter, forcing herself to think. The monster, if there was one, would be in the lake not the trees. But what about a bear or cougar? She broke into a run and was out of breath when she reached the barn.

Heather hurried to her gelding's double stall where she saw Ty through the panel of bars comprising the upper portion of the stall wall. "Where's Image?" she asked.

A sorrel mare, the one McCade had left behind, stood in the center of the enclosure. Sweat darkened her neck. She swung her nose around to touch one of her bulging sides.

"I moved him." Ty opened the stall door and motioned her in. "I'm glad you're here. I need your help."

"What's wrong?" Six inches of fresh sawdust on the ground buried Heather's shoes as she stepped inside.

Closing the stall door, Ty latched it. "Have you ever delivered a foal?"

"No! Deliver?" Heather took in a quick breath. "I thought mares handled these things themselves."

"One of the foal's legs is back. We're gonna have to help."

Heather tried to swallow, but couldn't. She coughed instead. "I don't know, Ty. I've never . . ." She studied the mare—the sagging belly and wide, pitiful eyes. "What do you want me to do?"

"Hold her down so I can get in there and find the other leg."

"Hold her down?" Heather felt her eyes widen. "Do you think I can?"

"You'll have to, unless you'd rather go in after the baby."

"Go in after . . . Oh, no. I'll hold her."

"She'll lay down again soon. Then, if you keep her neck on the ground, I think she'll stay."

"Okaaay." Heather stepped closer. "Poor thing. Look. She's scared to death. Do you know what you're doing?"

"Yeah. I think so."

"You don't sound so sure."

"I've delivered calves before, never a colt."

"Great." She touched Ty's arm. "Shall I run get your dad or call the vet?"

"No time. We've got to get that colt out soon or the mare will start pushing so hard I won't be able to get my hand in to find the other leg."

The mare circled. With a deep groan, she eased onto the sawdust.

Ty knelt by the mare's back, stroking her sweat-soaked neck. "Come here, Heather." He grabbed her arm and pulled her to the ground beside him. "If she starts to get up, lay hard across her neck. If you can't keep her steady, get out of the way and we'll go to plan B."

"What's plan B?"

"Darned if I know."

"You're not inspiring much confidence here."

"Sorry."

Heather stroked the mare's neck. "Whoa, girl. We're going to take care of you. You're gonna have a beautiful baby."

Ty moved to the mare's hindquarters. He slipped off his jacket and rolled up his shirt sleeve. "One leg's out about sixteen inches.

No sign of the other. As soon as this contraction's over I'll see if I can get my hand in and find that second leg."

The mare groaned. White shone around her eyes.

"Okay, I'm going for it. Easy girl. Dang, where's that leg?" He leaned down farther until his head rested on the horse's hip. "There's the shoulder. Oh, shoot. Another contraction." Ty sat up and stripped off his shirt.

The mare strained then relaxed.

"Okay, it's now or never." Ty dropped down.

Heather rubbed the mare's neck. "Easy, lady. Let us help you."

"It's way in there. Oh, there's the knee. If I can just get my fingers under . . . Whoa, girl. I need longer arms. I'll have to push the little one back."

The mare struggled to lift her head. Heart rising to her throat, Heather leaned across the mare's neck.

"Got it. Now if I can ease . . . Okay, the knee's forward. Now for the hoof. Okay, okay, there it is. Now I'll bring both legs out together. There we go. Okay, lady. Go ahead and push." He sounded triumphant.

Ty rose higher on his knees, his hands, chest and one arm covered with a watery red substance. Heather wondered if he was cold. She was shivering.

The mare tensed. "We're almost there. Okay. Good girl. Once more. There's the nose. Come here, Heather, you gotta see this."

Heather eased off the mare's neck, stood and quietly moved to the back of the exhausted animal. "Oh, my gosh. Look at that."

Except for its front legs and the tip of its nose, the colt lay still enclosed in its membrane sack, its sides heaving.

"Is it okay?" Heather asked.

Ty pulled the sack off the colt's head and, taking his discarded shirt, wiped out its nostrils. Then he pulled the remaining sack off the colt.

The mare struggled to her feet and turned to lick her baby's face. The two exchanged greetings in a horse language of squeaks and half nickers. The new mother continued to clean the colt with her tongue, all the while talking to it.

The baby struggled to stand, its long legs wobbling, then tumbled over. Ty and Heather laughed in spite of themselves.

Walking to the faucet in the aisle, Ty washed his hands and arms. He returned to the stall and retrieved his jacket from the sawdust-covered ground. He took a bottle of iodine from the corner of the stall and dipped the colt's dangling umbilical cord in it. Then he poured on more. Placing one arm around the baby's chest and the other around its hindquarters, Ty lifted the foal up, holding it secure until its legs stopped shaking.

He stood back next to Heather and watched as the little animal found its first breakfast beneath its mom's hind leg.

Raising the foal's tail, Ty said, "Looks like we'll be using a pink halter. We've got ourselves a beautiful little red filly."

"I wonder if she's going to be ornery like her dad?" Heather thought about the Flathead monster with Red Rock's head.

"I hope not, but all his other colts seem to be. I'd better start eating my spinach."

"Spinach?" Heather asked.

"For strength, you know, like Popeye."

"Better buy a case."

They turned to watch the foal. Heather heard loud sucking sounds and smiled. When the filly finished she had a white milk mustache that matched the white markings on her dainty face.

Tears sprang to Heather's eyes without warning. She tried to blink them off her lashes.

Ty put his arm around her. They stood close for several minutes, watching the new life they'd helped bring into the world. Then Ty gave her shoulder a final squeeze and stooped to pick up his soiled shirt and the bottle of iodine. "She'll be fine now. We might as well see if we can get some sleep tonight." He glanced at his watch. "Three twenty-five. If we're lucky we can still nab three or four hours. I'll race you to the house."

"Race? How about amble, maybe stroll, more likely limp. I'm far too tired to race." She closed her eyes. Tired now, sure, but would she be able to sleep once she got back to bed?

"How about we saunter?"

"Deal." Heather retrieved the flashlight she'd left by the door to the stall. As they *sauntered* outside, she switched it on.

The stillness of the Montana nights continually surprised her. Only the rustle of the leaves in the trees, the distant lapping of the waves against the shore and the brush of their footsteps over the graveled road met her ears. The breeze, fresh with pine scent, blew her sweat-dampened hair back from her face.

"Thanks for helping, Heather."

"Oh, no problem. It was kinda special."

"Yeah," he said.

"Beautiful filly."

"She is, isn't she? Let's hope she has a decent disposition. I don't know if I can take another one with Rocky's temperament."

"I hear you," Heather said.

They reached the door to the house and Ty opened it. The smell of Bea's homemade bread wafted past their noses. Together they walked through the kitchen and dining room into the front room. They stood near the grandfather clock while it chimed twice to signify the half hour.

"Good night, Heather, or should I say good morning?"

Before she realized what she was doing, she slipped her arms around Ty's waist and hugged him. It seemed only natural after what they'd shared. She felt his arms encircle her and his heart beat against her cheek. They stood quietly for a moment before she stepped back. "Good morning, Ty," she said and fled to her room.

She lay in bed and listened to the clock mark three forty-five and four. Ty had said something about moving Image. Was the gelding okay in a different stall? Apprehension gnawed at her. Since she couldn't sleep anyway, she might as well go check on both her horses and peek in on the new baby. Dragging herself out of the bed, she pulled on the same sweatshirt and jeans and headed for the barn. Her eyes stung from exhaustion. Since she'd brought the flashlight again, she decided not to turn on the barn light and alert Ty if for any reason he couldn't sleep and happened to glance out there.

Remembering where the mare's old stall was, she checked that one first. Sure enough, Ty had just swapped stalls, putting the mare in Image's stall and Image in the mare's. Her gelding snorted when she turned the light on him, but, of course, he was just fine. Across the alley in his stall, Possum barely opened his eyes when she checked on him. Both horses were just trying to rest like most normal creatures. So was the filly. She lay in a pile of fresh sawdust, with her mom standing over her.

Heather let herself in, turned off the flashlight and crept forward. Hardly moving, the mare merely glanced at her. As Heather lowered herself into the sawdust, the foal stretched and flopped her head into Heather's lap.

Yawning, Heather lay next to the foal and stroked the velvet face. Heather would just rest a moment before venturing back into the house. The filly made tiny snoring sounds and snuggled her warm body close. The mare stood protectively overhead. Fresh-smelling sawdust cradled Heather and the foal. Silence blanketed the barn.

The next thing Heather became aware of was a puff of warm air across her face. She forced her eyes open to the light of a new morning and focused on a big, broad nose nearly touching hers. The mare. Heather struggled to sit up, reaching out to stroke the horse's cheek. "Best sleep I've had all week. Morning, Cinnamon. Is that what Ty called you? Where's your baby?"

Peeking out from behind her mother's back leg, the foal nickered.

"Oh, there you are." Heather leaned against the stall wall. She held a hand out to the filly. "You're such a pretty girl." The foal really was beautiful—a dark red chestnut, the exact color of her sire, straight, fine-boned legs and a delicate head with a wide white strip from her nostrils pointing up to a perfect diamond between large, expressive eyes.

Heather turned as the door to the stall slid open. Mouth ajar, Ty performed one of the best double takes she'd ever witnessed.

He recovered quickly. "Mom's inside stirring up breakfast, or if you'd rather, I'll just throw you a flake of hay."

"I was checking the horses." Heather jumped to her feet.

"I can see that." Ty reached out to pick sawdust from her hair.

"I couldn't sleep."

"Hmm. Chronic problem lately. What's wrong, I wonder. Good thing you didn't decide to snuggle up next to Rocky."

Heather grimaced. "I select my roommates more carefully."

His brow raised. "Glad to hear it. This is preferable to a midnight swim."

"Less rescuing, anyway." Her cheeks burned.

His eyes held hers. "So," he said.

"So." Heather cleared her throat. "What's up with you today?"

"I think David and I are going water-skiing. We only have Ted's boat until tonight. You can come too if you want."

The foal eased close to Heather, stretching its neck to sniff the girl's leg.

"I'll pass," Heather said. "Better spend some time riding." She touched the filly's face. "And some time with you, little sweetie." She scratched behind the foal's ears. "Have you decided what you're going to name her?"

Ty took a long breath. "I've been thinking Jasmine, maybe."

"That's pretty."

"It's the name Mom gave my first horse, a beautiful white pony Dad brought home from the auction." Ty reached his hand out to the filly. "I was only five that year and I thought Christmas had come early—my own horse." He shook his head. "Meanest little devil you ever did see. Bucked me off nine times before I finally rode her. Of course, I never told my folks that." He chuckled. "Mom was reading a book back then about an elegant lady named Jasmine with hair so blonde it was almost white."

Jasmine sniffed Ty's hand.

"Don't tell me . . ." Heather began.

"Yep, my pony was named after the heroine in Mom's book." Ty touched Jasmine's nose. She tossed her head and backed up against her mother.

"Just like you." Heather bit her lip to keep from smiling at the filly's reaction. "Katie told me how the kids in your family got your names."

"Yeah. Mom reads a lot. I guess I can be grateful she wasn't reading a book with a hero named . . . Felix or something when I was born."

Heather laughed. "I like your name and Jasmine's perfect for the filly."

"I think so. Actually, my little white Jasmine's been dead for about ten years, but she deserves to have someone named after her. She really taught me a lot." Ty glanced at the filly.

"Your pony taught you a lot?"

"Uh-huh, since Jasmine the First, it's never bothered me much to ride any horse, no matter how rank." He massaged the back of his neck.

"Hello, little Jasmine." Heather knelt down, holding out her hand.

Jasmine took a hesitant step forward and sniffed the tips of Heather's fingers.

Ty started for the door. "So you're going to work your horses instead of going with David and me?"

She wished he would have sounded more disappointed. "Yeah. I guess that's why Kevin left me in Montana." Heather touched Jasmine's cheek.

"Oh. I wanted to ask." Ty stopped. "You know that program you designed for me to do my bills?"

"The one that took me all evening to put together?" She accentuated the words "all" and "evening." Heather loved being able to do something he couldn't, at least for the time being.

Ty headed back for the filly. With a snort, she backed away. He cornered her and, like the night before, placed one arm around the filly's chest, the other around her rump to hold her. "Yep, the one that took you all evening."

"What about it?" She grinned, pleased that Jasmine tried to get away from Ty, but came to her. Soon he'd win the foal over. Heather had no doubt about that.

"It's gone." He moved his hand to Jasmine's back, then stroked down her hind legs.

"What do you mean it's gone?"

"The screen's blank. Everything's gone."

"Where did it go?" It was fun giving him a bad time.

"I don't know." He released the foal, who squeezed underneath her mom's belly. "Last night when I got in I . . ."

Heather gestured with a pointed finger. "Ah-ha. You worked last night after we got in. I guess I'm not the only one who couldn't sleep."

He pulled a face. "Last night when I got in I did some bills and when I tried to save, the computer crashed."

"Really." She chewed her lip, thinking. "Hopefully I got everything backed up on that disk you found in the desk. There was some other stuff on the drive too."

"That must have been McCade's. The only thing I had on it was our billing program. In case you haven't noticed, I don't have much computer savvy."

"I've noticed." She giggled. "I'll take a look at it later, but we can get David to help if we need to. He's the real computer geek. I'll bet he even brought his laptop with him on this trip. He never goes anywhere without it—camera in one hand, laptop in the other."

"You probably won't have time tonight," Ty said. "We're going to Bigfork, remember?"

Heather tapped the heel of her hand on her forehead. "That's right. Katie's performance. You'd think I could remember that." She glanced at Ty when he didn't respond. His hand rested on the stall door latch and he stared across the aisle. "Earth to Ty."

"I was thinking about computers."

"Good topic, even for you."

"I told McCade I didn't know anything about them, but he insisted I keep the one in the house and made me promise I'd learn to use it. Even in his last letter to me he mentioned it would be easier to write to him if I'd use the computer."

"He probably couldn't read your writing." She elbowed him in the ribs. "Seriously though, it would have been easier. I'll teach you word processing if you want, or David can. What happened to McCade? How come he died?" She followed Ty out of the stall. "You sound as if you really liked him."

"I did. It was cancer. He never even told me he had it. That must be why he was in such a hurry to get us settled here." He shut the stall door, then stood there studying it.

"What?"

"When the attorney came to notify me of McCade's death, he, of course, had some legal matters we needed to discuss about this property. But also, he said that one of the last things McCade wanted him to do was ask me if I'd learned to use the computer." Ty laughed. "McCade was like that, he'd find something to kid me about and wouldn't let go of it. I guess this computer thing was a standing joke between us, but now I'll never know the punchline."

CHAPTER FOURTEEN

"Will you all please welcome Heather Chambers and David Cane from Springville, Utah, to the front row," Katie yelled. "Also my brother, Tyler Taggert, from Polson, Montana." Pursuant to a long-standing custom at the Bigfork Summer Playhouse, all arriving front-row guests were announced and greeted, which to Heather's way of thinking made sitting on that row far less desirable. She smiled and tried to act pleased though, as Katie—already in costume for the evening's performance—made her friends and brother turn to face the cheering audience who grinned down at them from their more lofty stadium-type seating.

Ty's face colored, but David favored the onlookers with one of his easy, dazzling smiles before plopping into the chair between Ty and Heather.

"Here's a program." Katie handed one to David. "That will be five dollars, sir."

"Five dollars?" He winked at Heather. "What if it's not worth five dollars?"

"Trust me. It's worth it." She held out her hand for the money.

David dug in his pants pocket for his wallet where Heather knew he always carried plenty of cash. Slowly, he removed three one-dollar bills then reached into his other pocket and withdrew a fistful of change. "Let's see. That's one, two, three. Three fifty, three seventy-five, four."

By the time he'd counted out the rest of the five dollars—the last twenty cents in pennies one by one—Katie's foot was tapping.

"Thank you, sir." In a flurry of starched petticoats covered by a fifties-style full skirt, Katie bounced up the stairs to complete her night's ushering duties before she headed backstage to perform in the evening's play, *Bye Bye Birdie.*

Ty high-fived David. "Good one."

Heather shook her head and tried to act perturbed for Katie's sake. "May I see the program?"

"Do you have five dollars?" David grinned.

Heather leaned across him and grabbed her prize. "Thanks for sharing," she said sweetly. "So, David," Ty said. "Do you think I should try to slalom tomorrow even though we'll have to use our old boat?"

"You bet. No problem." David shifted in his chair to fully face Ty.

With the back of David's head toward her, Heather flipped through the pages of the program. She soon found Katie's picture and bio. "Wow! Look at this." She held the picture up for the guys' inspection. The glamour shot made Katie look years older. In the photo, the redhead gazed down demurely over the tip of her shoulder, her long red hair curling away from her delicate face then tumbling down her back.

"Ooh. Let me see." David took the program for a closer look. "Pretty hot, I'd say." He passed the picture to Ty.

"Doesn't look a thing like her," he said.

"Sure it does." Heather giggled.

David handed the program back to Heather. She pointed at a different photo on the same page. "Now this guy's cute."

"Where?" both boys said.

Heather held up the program.

David cocked his head. "If you like that type."

"What's not to like?" She ran her finger across the page.

"Looks like a momma's boy," Ty said.

She rolled her eyes.

"So, which foot do I put forward on the ski?" Ty asked David.

"Which foot do you kick a football with?"

"The right, I think. It's been a long time since I've kicked a football."

"So tomorrow you'll stand on the right leg and lift your left ski out of the water. Once you feel solid on your right leg with your left leg up, you can go ahead and drop that left ski. We'll loosen the binding beforehand so it will slip off real easy . . ."

Yawning, Heather glanced up at the theater's cinder block walls. Groups of long plaques hung in rows of four or five on metal slats along each side of the five hundred-seat theater. Each decorative plaque listed all the plays performed in that particular year from 1965 to the present. Beneath the plaques, stairs ran from the entrance doors, near the top circular row of seats, to the darkened stage fifty rows beneath. Apparently tonight's first scene would take place in the McAfees' cozy front room with its draped windows and raised entryway.

". . . pretty big wake," David was saying. He leaned back in his seat but remained focused on Ty. "A person's tendency is to come out of their cut and jump the wake instead of holding the edge of the ski all the way through, like they would if it were smaller."

Heather sighed and centered her sights on Katie, who continued to show people to their seats, her red ponytail swishing back and forth as she walked. Ty was right—made up in her theatrical makeup, she looked less like the young girl Heather knew and more like the professional actress in the program.

Extracting smiles, giggles and even a few hugs, Katie spoke animatedly to everyone she encountered, probably making each of them feel as if they were her personal friends. She sold more programs than any of the other actors and actresses who were ushering.

"When's it supposed to start?" Heather asked David, who turned away from his conversation with Ty long enough to stare at her blankly.

"What? Oh, yeah. Katie should be good in the part," David answered.

"That's it." Heather stood. "Move over. I'm sitting between you two so you won't visit all through the play."

"Okay." He got up and stepped to the side so Heather could have his seat. Then he sat, put his arm across the back of her seat, leaned around her and said to Ty, "A lot of engineering goes into a ski boat. A MasterCraft has a flat bottom while your little yellow boat has a "V" bottom . . ."

"Last chance. I only have two programs left." A cute blonde actress, dressed in a shirtwaist dress with lots of petticoats like Katie's, stood nearby. "Anyone who buys one gets a kiss from . . . from Katie." The blonde gestured toward the redhead. Katie's mouth fell open but she smiled, waved and fluttered her eyelashes.

David shifted in his seat.

Heather grabbed his arm. "You already have a program."

"I was just scratching my nose." He smiled.

She held onto him. "I'll do it. Where does it itch?"

"I think you scared it out of me."

Heather nudged him.

Ty's leg touched hers.

"Okay," the blonde said as a stocky man of about thirty bought a program. Katie scurried over and planted a kiss on his cheek. The crowd laughed.

Lights dimmed. The actors and actresses waved as they moved to a passageway leading behind stage.

"Too late," Heather kidded.

"I wasn't going to buy one." David pulled her close. "I only want kisses from one girl."

Heather grinned, but felt her stomach tighten—probably just her guilty conscience booting up.

The curtains closed and Heather straightened in preparation for the show to begin, but out walked a handsome dark-haired guy dressed in regular street clothes. Perhaps recognizing him from years past, the crowd applauded wildly. Now Heather remembered. She'd seen his picture in the program. Tonight's director had been with the Playhouse for ten years, seven of those years doubling as an actor.

"Good evening," he said. "Welcome to the Bigfork Summer Playhouse and tonight's presentation of *Bye Bye Birdie*." He went on to talk about the fire exits, the scholarship program, the special guests . . . "and Katie's brother, Ty, and her friends from Utah are here on the front row." He pointed.

David grinned.

Smiling, Heather nodded. "I feel sufficiently welcomed," she whispered to Ty out of the corner of her mouth.

"I'll say," he said.

". . . and those of you with small children, thank you for introducing them to live theater. But should they cause a disturbance, please take them out of state . . ." Everyone laughed.

"No . . ." He held his note card up in front of his nose. "No, out of the auditorium, to the foyer where we have monitors set up so you won't miss even a tiny part of the performance."

Heather turned to her left and grinned at David, then to her right to grin at Ty. She'd glanced back and forth so much she felt as if she were watching a tennis match.

"And these small dark boxes on the stage floor," the director went on, gesturing. "Please don't sit on them, empty your purse on them, spit on them . . ." The audience laughed again. ". . . or the people wearing the small infrared hearing devices will hunt you down and . . . kill you." He smiled. No wonder Katie enjoyed performing with this fun group of talented people.

The performance began in "Albert's" office where he'd just learned that Conrad Birdie, an Elvis Presley-type character, had been inducted into the army. Now Conrad would be unable to sing "Mumbo Jumbo Gooey Gumbo," the title song Albert had written for a movie Conrad had planned to do. But the ever resourceful Rosie, Albert's secretary, talked Ed Sullivan into booking Conrad on his program where the singer would say good-bye to the nation's population of young women by kissing one symbolic girl and, of course, he'd sing Albert's song, "One Last Kiss," on the show and make Albert an immediate success.

Katie played Kim McAfee, the girl chosen to receive Conrad's "one last kiss." When the redhead came on stage to sing "How Lovely to Be a Woman," David took a deep breath. Katie really did look cute and when she sang, Heather couldn't believe what a wonderful voice the girl had. The choreography started with Katie dressed in a bright yellow blouse, an orange skirt and dainty slip-on shoes and ended with her changing beneath a bulky blue sweater into jeans, tennis shoes and a baseball cap. The crowd showed its approval by whistling and applauding.

The song that really attracted Heather's attention, though, was a later one where Kim, Katie's character, tried to convince her boyfriend, Hugo, that kissing Conrad Birdie would mean nothing to her. The song "One Boy, One Special Boy" had Heather squirming. It must have affected Ty too because he bumped his leg against hers a couple of times when David wasn't looking. Actually, David wasn't looking a lot. His gaze never left Katie.

At the end of the performance, the redhead received a standing ovation, led by David, Ty and Heather. David clapped louder than Ty and herself, and whistled too. Heather hadn't realized he enjoyed live theater so much.

They waited in their seats, as Katie had suggested, while everyone else filed out of the auditorium.

"I'll be right back," David said, standing. "My camera's in the car. Maybe I can get some pictures." He disappeared out the door with the last of the audience.

Ty nudged Heather. "How ya doing?"

"Huh?" She'd been thinking about Ty . . . and David, and Katie's song. "I'm good." Her voice went hoarse and she had to clear her throat. "How about you?" She searched his eyes.

"I'm good, too." He held her gaze.

"Got it." David bounded down the stairs to rejoin them.

"Our man on the job." Heather touched his arm.

Now dressed in cutoffs and a sweatshirt, Katie swooped to center stage. "Thank you, ladies and gentlemen, thank you." She bowed and bowed and blew kisses. "No autographs, please."

"It's getting kinda deep in here," Ty said, standing.

Heather and David jumped up and moved to lean against the front of the stage.

"You were fabulous," Heather said. "I didn't know you could sing like that."

"You really were great," David said. "I've never seen *Bye Bye Birdie* performed better. You're right up there with Ann-Margret."

"Who? Oh yeah, well . . ." Katie batted her eyes. "Ann-Margret. We're buds."

David held up his camera. "How about some pictures?"

"Sure," Katie said. "Can we get a couple with Gavin too? Come here, Gavin. There's some people I want you to meet."

The tall, good-looking guy, who'd put on one heck of a good show gyrating his way through a lively rendition of "One Last Kiss," walked onto the stage. His black, slicked-back hair glistened under the lights. As Conrad Birdie, he'd left many of the girls in the audience screaming whenever he'd made an appearance. Of course, sandwiched between two hunks of her own, Heather had been immune.

Katie made introductions.

Gavin, now wearing baggy jeans and a T-shirt, stuck out his hand. "I've heard so much about all of you I feel like I know you."

"We loved your performance," Heather said, absently fanning herself with the program. "Are you going to make acting a profession? You sure are good."

"I've been thinking about it, but my folks want me to get a real job," Gavin said. "I'm going to college right now at Wayne State in Detroit. We'll see what happens."

"Detroit, huh?" David said. "Montana must be a big change for you."

"All this peace and quiet." Ty grinned and with an outstretched arm, gestured around the auditorium.

"Yeah, really," Gavin said. "But you have excitement here too—missing racehorses, dead bodies in the lake."

"Missing racehorses? Here?" Ty asked.

"Yes. I was talking to the sheriff today at the boat dock. He told me they'd identified the body found in the lake last week. The man had been transporting a famous racehorse when he and the horse disappeared last year."

"Freedom's Choice?" Ty and Heather asked together.

"Yeah. That's the one." Gavin sat on the edge of the stage.

"You didn't tell me that." Katie plopped down beside him.

"I was going to. No time," Gavin said.

"This gets stranger and stranger," Ty rubbed his chin.

"I'll say," Heather said.

"Okay." David focused through his camera lens. "Everyone crowd together. Then I want a shot of Katie and Gavin; Heather, Katie and Gavin; Ty, Katie and Gavin; and one of just Katie."

After all the pictures were taken and visiting completed, Ty, Heather and David left Katie, who'd opted to stay in Bigfork that night, and started for home. Ty drove. Heather fell asleep against David's shoulder.

Bea met them as they drove into the driveway. "Ty, the Sheriff and an FBI agent were here to see you tonight. They'll be back first thing in the morning."

CHAPTER FIFTEEN

"Hello. I'm Special Agent John Campbell, with the FBI and this is Dale Tuttle, Polson PD."

"I know Officer Tuttle. Hi, Dale," Ty said. He pushed the screen door open to let the two men in. "I heard you wanted to talk to me."

Heather stood in the adjoining bedroom, out of sight. She listened at the slightly open door. Footsteps thumped across the tile entrance, softening as they reached the carpet.

"Have a seat," Ty said.

Someone turned off the television, probably Wells.

"Beautiful place," the deeper of the two visitors' voices said. Heather decided that voice belonged to the FBI agent.

"These are my parents, Agent Campbell." Ty cleared his throat. "Wells and Bea Taggert."

Now farther away, the voices became somewhat muffled. Heather strained her ears.

"We m . . . la . . . night." What was that? Bea was really hard to hear.

"Oh. That's right. You met last night." Ty's words came through clearer.

Chairs creaked as people sat.

"What can I do for you?" Ty asked.

"I understand you found a Rolex watch," the deep voice said.

"I did. But how do you know?"

"We know everything."

Everyone laughed. Agent Campbell must have been smiling.

"I'll bet you do." This from Wells. Heather would recognize his voice anywhere.

"Rolex watches have serial numbers," the FBI agent explained. "Anytime someone turns a Rolex in to be fixed, cleaned— anything, the jeweler is supposed to send the numbers in to the Rolex headquarters in New York. There they run a check on the registered owner of the watch. If the owner's name differs from the person who brought the watch in, the jeweler is alerted."

"I told the man it wasn't my watch—that I found it. I didn't even know if it was real. He called the FBI?" Heather pictured Ty shaking his head, incredulous that anyone would not believe him.

"In an ordinary case, we wouldn't be involved. As it turns out this may be an ITSP."

"ITSP?" Wells asked.

"That's Interstate Transportation of Stolen Property," a new voice chimed in. Officer Tuttle had come alive.

"The watch was stolen and transported to another state?" Bea spoke louder now.

"No. The horse."

"What horse?" Ty asked.

Heather edged closer to the open space between the wall in her bedroom and the edge of the door. She squinted as if that would improve her hearing.

"I'm not explaining this very well." Agent Campbell coughed, then tried again. "The watch Tyler found belonged to a man named Anthony Grange."

"Call me Ty.

"Fair enough. Does the name 'Anthony Grange' mean anything to you?" Agent Campbell asked.

"Can't say that it does. Should it?"

"Do you follow horse racing?"

"Some."

"Last year a famous racehorse disappeared . . ." Agent Campbell started to say.

"You don't mean Freedom's Choice, do you?"

"You are familiar with him then."

"Yes. Most Quarter Horse people are."

"Anthony Grange was the last person known to have possession of that horse," Agent Campbell said. "We just identified his body."

"The horse's?"

"No, Anthony Grange's."

"Anthony Grange's?"

"Did you hear about that guy we fished out of Yellow Bay a piece back?" Officer Tuttle entered the conversation again. Bea and Wells remained quiet. Heather figured husband and wife were staring at each other wondering what to say. Her own eyes felt bugged out from the news.

"Yeah. Someone mentioned something about it . . . Don't tell me! It was Anthony Grange?"

"One and the same." There was a slapping sound. Officer Tuttle must have brought his hands down on his knees.

"You're kidding." Ty's voice shot up an octave. "I found a dead man's watch, the same dead man who last year disappeared with

Freedom's Choice, one of the greatest racing Quarter Horses of all time?"

"It would appear so." The deeper voice again.

When Heather heard the last statement, she flung her hand across her mouth. Her elbow knocked the door shut.

All talking stopped. Then the door to the bedroom opened and Ty peeked in. "You can join us, Heather, if you want. You probably know as much about this stuff as I do."

Having been caught spying, heat rose in her face, but she followed Ty into the room.

"This is my friend from Utah, Heather Chambers," Ty said. "Agent Campbell and Dale . . . uh, Officer Tuttle."

Both men stood, then sat when Heather found a place on the couch next to Bea and Wells.

"I'm sorry about that." She motioned toward the bedroom. "I . . . I have no excuse."

"That's okay," Agent Campbell said. "We do stir up a certain amount of curiosity at times."

Heather stared at the man. Dressed in a dark suit, he appeared more kindly than she figured an FBI agent would be and his wavy white hair made him look very distinguished.

"Something wrong?" he asked.

"I'm sorry. It's just that . . . that you look too gentle to be an FBI agent." More like someone churchy, a priest or a mortician, she thought.

He reached into his coat pocket and retrieved what appeared to be a folded leather wallet with a gold badge secured to the outside. He flipped it open to reveal his picture, signature and writing on the inside. "FBI," he said.

"Cool," Heather sat back in her seat. "Please go on."

"The horse's owner . . ." Agent Campbell took a small notebook out of his jacket and flipped through its pages. "Let's see. His name is Matthew Randall. He reported the stallion and Anthony Grange missing a little less than a year ago. Mr. Grange was supposed to transport the animal to California for the Redland Memorial, some kind of a match race Mr. Randall and some other Quarter Horse breeders had planned. It was in all the newspapers. When Mr. Grange never showed up, Mr. Randall reported the stallion and Mr. Grange missing and after several months collected ten million dollars from the insurance policy he carried on the horse."

Wells whistled. "Ten million dollars?"

"Yes. For death or theft of the horse," Agent Campell said. "He didn't know if Grange had stolen the horse or met with foul play somewhere on his way to California."

"It wouldn't have made much sense for someone to steal that stallion," Ty said. "He could never have been raced or sire any colts that could be registered without people finding out."

"So maybe he didn't swipe the stallion," Officer Tuttle said, "and I guess it could have been an accident. Grange might have fallen asleep and driven off the road. There is that deal about the VIN number, but that could have been smashed during the crash."

Officer Tuttle looked just how Heather would have pictured a small town police officer. Young, blond, a little too short and skinny to support the heavy police belt he wore around his waist, from which dangled handcuffs, a ring of keys, a flashlight, a two-way radio, a night stick, his gun and extra ammunition clips.

"Then there's the watch," Agent Campbell said. "We need to talk about where you found it."

"Hello," David said as he came up the stairs from the basement. "Sorry to bother you. I'll just hurry on through."

"You may as well join us." Bea slid closer to Wells. "Is that okay, officers?"

"No problem. Are there more?" Glancing from side to side, Agent Campbell stood from his chair.

"I think that's it," Wells said. "Unless our daughter Katie shows up. She's not here right now and she's going to be mad as a bear with a sore tail when she finds out what she's missed." He tipped his head at David. "This is David Cane, also a friend from Utah."

"His father's an attorney," Bea added.

"I couldn't help overhearing." David squeezed in on the couch next to Heather. "If you don't mind my asking, how did you put all this together? You've got a missing person—there must be thousands, a lost horse—probably lots of those, a dead body found in an entirely different state than where the person was last seen, and a Rolex watch registered to someone other than who turned it in."

"Leads and hits," Agent Campbell said, dropping back into his chair. His jacket gaped open and Heather noted that he also carried a gun on his belt, handcuffs and a cell phone.

David frowned. "Leads and hits?"

Agent Campbell straightened his jacket. "Have you ever heard of the National Crime Information Center?"

"I've heard police officers at my work say they are going to run an NCIC on something," David said.

"That's right. Anything retrievable is entered into NCIC—fingerprints, vehicle identification numbers, missing person names. When Matthew Randall reported Anthony Grange and the stallion missing, everything known about them would have been entered into the NCIC. Then when the body turned up last week, fingerprints would have been taken, the VIN number of the truck, even the name of the horse would have been entered into the NCIC. Isn't that right, Officer Tuttle?"

"Yes. We did have a little trouble with the fingerprints, him being in the water for a year and all. And both license plates, one on the truck and one on the trailer, were missing. We couldn't tell anything about the VIN either because that part of the truck under the bottom of the windshield had been completely demolished."

"Bear in mind too," Agent Campbell continued, "that although the FBI have two hundred million fingerprints on file, we, of course, don't have fingerprints from everyone, only if a person has served in the military, applied for a government job, or been arrested. Correct me if I'm wrong, Officer Tuttle. I think when we finally got a hit on the vehicle, we identified the body through dental records and not fingerprints."

"That's right. Since we couldn't locate the VIN on the vehicle, we contacted some of your FBI people." Officer Tuttle turned to David. "Manufacturers send the FBI listings of where to find confidential vehicle identification numbers on all vehicles."

Heather was impressed. She'd already placed Agent Campbell right up there with Jack Ryan.

The FBI agent cleared his throat. "So then you ran an NCIC on that number and came up with a hit."

"Right. After we identified the missing vehicle that Anthony Grange had been driving, we checked his dental records. They matched the body," Officer Tuttle glanced back at Ty. "Then we were notified about the Rolex, which brings me to why we're here. Where did you find the watch?"

Ty leaned back, tapping his fingertips on the arms of his chair. "I can show you where we found it."

"Great," Agent Campbell said.

"What about Freedom's Choice?" Heather leaned forward.

"No sign of the horse. He could have been disposed of before the truck went into the lake." Agent Campbell gestured with both palms up. "He could be at the bottom of the lake. We have no leads on him."

Heather and Ty stared at each other.

"We might know something," Ty said.

CHAPTER
SIXTEEN

Like troops following their sergeant, they all filed out of the house trailing the FBI agent—Ty, Heather, David, Wells, Bea and Officer Tuttle. It seemed no one wanted to miss the possibility of excitement.

A gentle breeze spread the aroma of Bea's carefully tended roses and Wells's freshly cut grass. A deer darted across the lawn and into the forest.

"That dang little devil's been stealing cherries again." Wells picked up a rock and threw it in the doe's direction. "I don't mind her eating off the ground. It's when she snacks off the trees that I get grumpy."

Glancing at Agent Campbell, Bea reddened. "Now, Wells. Don't go getting all riled up. There's plenty to go around."

"You didn't say that the other day when she ate all the roses off your favorite bush." Wells grinned down at her.

"No, I didn't, but that was an entirely different matter. Cherries are for eating. Roses are for . . . for looking."

Heather hid a smile behind her hand. "She's right, you know, Wells."

"Okaaay," Ty said. "Do you want to see where we found the watch first, Agent Campbell, or take a look at the horse?"

Bea touched Ty's arm. "Tell me again who the horse is."

"Red Rock looks a lot like Freedom's Choice," Ty said as he covered her hand with his own, "the horse who won the All American Futurity three years ago."

"In record time." Wells bent to pluck a cherry branch from the lawn, shaking his fist toward the forest. "Some say he's the fastest horse in history."

"Faster than Secretariat?" David asked, bringing up the rear.

"Probably faster at the quarter mile," Ty said.

"Wow, David. I'm impressed." Heather turned to smile at him. "You've heard of Secretariat."

"I read sports." His eyebrows lowered indignantly. "Everyone knows about Secretariat."

Officer Tuttle opened his mouth, but remained silent.

"Well, maybe not everybody," he continued. "But that's not all." He held up his index finger. "I read another article about Freedom's Choice just last year. It talked about him having some kind of problem with his feet, or was it his eyes?"

"Which was it, his feet or his eyes?" Ty asked.

David stopped walking. "Hmm. I can't remember for sure. I only read it that one time."

"Where?" Heather asked.

"I think I was in my dorm at college."

"No. Where did you read it? In a magazine? A newspaper?"

"I can't remember for sure. It might have been on the Internet."

"I've never heard anything about his having problems," Ty said.

"Me either," Heather added.

"It could have been someone trying to put the word out so people would bet on that California horse in the match race."

Wells rubbed his chin. "Then when Freedom's Choice won, everyone savvy enough to bet on him would have cleaned up."

"That's a thought. Happens all the time." Agent Campbell stopped by his black Chevrolet parked in the Taggert driveway. "I think I'd like to see the horse first. I understand the insurance investigators conducted an all-out search for Freedom's Choice through a dozen states a year ago. It's hard to believe he may be right here in your barn." He took a file folder off the back seat, moved aside his briefcase, then peeked under a coat. "I thought I brought my camera. I'd like to document everything we find today."

David puffed out his chest. "I have cameras."

"Digital or film?"

"Both."

"Great. If we use the digital camera, we could unload the pictures online to the FBI." Agent Campbell closed the door to his car and clicked the electronic key gadget.

"Ty's computer doesn't work, remember?" Heather said.

"I have a laptop," David and Agent Campbell said at the same time.

"I'll have to make you an assistant." Agent Campbell shuffled papers in the folder.

Officer Tuttle tugged at his belt that had slipped down on his hips. He sighed softly.

"You might think I'm crazy." Ty started walking to the barn. "But if it's not Freedom's Choice, it's his twin. Heather picked up on the similarity right away, didn't you?"

"He sure looks like Freedom's Choice."

"Does Freedom's Choice have a twin?" Officer Tuttle hurried to catch up.

Ty chuckled and winked at Heather. "No, but if he did, he'd look just like the horse in the barn."

Officer Tuttle tried to pull his belt a notch tighter, but there were no more holes. "If you wondered about your horse, shouldn't you have reported it?"

"Lots of horses look the same. How likely was it that a famous stallion the whole world seems to be searching for would be in my stable? He wasn't even supposed to be in Montana." Ty took a deep breath. "Now, though, with Grange's body being found just across the lake, I have to rethink this whole thing."

"Cherries anyone?" Wells plucked a handful of huge deep red fruit from the tree near the barn.

"You're not going to throw rocks at us, are you?" Bea said.

"Okay, okay. I won't chase the doe away anymore." He held his hand out to Agent Campbell.

"It's a smart man who knows when he's beat." The agent took some cherries.

"Amen." Ty slid the door to the stable open and gestured everyone in. "I've got some suspenders you could use, Dale."

"What? Oh. Very funny, Ty." Officer Tuttle dropped his hands to his sides.

"Have some cherries, Dale," Wells said. "They'll put some weight on those bones."

"Really?" Heather handed her cherries to David.

Possum whinnied as they entered the barn.

"We'll be there in a minute," Heather told her horse.

The red stallion Ty called Red Rock or Rocky flattened his ears as everyone stopped in front of his stall.

Agent Campbell opened his file and withdrew a glossy eight by ten showing a side view of Freedom's Choice. He held it up so he could view the picture and the stallion at the same time.

"Wow. This really could be the same horse. Even the tiny white mark on his forehead is the same."

"Weird, isn't it?" Heather peeked at the photograph the FBI agent held in his hand.

"May I see him closer?" Agent Campbell asked.

"I'll get a halter." Ty started down the aisle. "You won't want to go in there while he's loose."

"Why not?" Officer Tuttle stepped to Heather's side.

"He's an ornery bugger," Wells reported.

Bea grimaced. "Wells. Your language."

He seemed not to hear. "Several of the horse people around here who have new colts sired by him tell me the colts are ornery too." He nodded to Bea.

"Jasmine's not mean," Heather said.

Ty returned with the halter. "You wouldn't notice if she were. According to you, that filly is plumb near perfect."

"Well, she is, and she's the sweetest foal I've ever seen."

"From what you've said, she's the only foal you've ever spent time with." Ty slid the latch to the door.

"Well, she's still the sweetest." Heather lifted her chin.

"It says nothing in the report about Freedom's Choice being unusually mean." Agent Campbell shuffled through the papers in the file.

"Is that right?" Ty slipped in through the door. "Maybe something happened after he disappeared to make him mean."

"Where did you get him?" Agent Campbell asked.

Ty shrugged. "He was here when we bought the place."

"When was that?"

"In November." Wells guarded the stall door. "He and that mare down there, Jasmine's mother, were the only horses the previous owner didn't sell. He told Ty they were his favorites and he didn't want some stranger having them."

"So where is this former owner? How come he didn't take them with him?" Agent Campbell took a pen out of his shirt pocket.

"He moved to England for several months and then his attorney came to visit Ty and told him McCade had died," Wells said.

"McCade never mentioned he had cancer," Ty said.

"McCade?"

"McCade Saxton." Ty walked toward the stallion who whirled around, preparing to kick.

Agent Campbell wrote the name in his notebook.

"Looks like you'll need this." Wells handed Ty the whip which had been leaning against the aisle wall.

Ty cracked it in the air, then tapped the stallion on the rump. "Turn and face me." He tapped the stallion again a little harder.

Slowly the big red animal swung around.

"That's a boy," Ty said, holding out his hand.

Once Ty had the stallion haltered, he lowered his head and followed Ty out the door. "He's almost decent when he's caught."

Walking to the horse, Agent Campbell said, "I guess the only way we'll know for sure is if we DNA test him."

"I'll bet Freedom's Choice was DNA tested while he was racing," Ty said. "The American Quarter Horse Association should have samples. I can't believe it. What if they match?"

"Oh my gosh, Ty." Heather clasped her hands in front of her. "You would have owned a famous racehorse."

Ty scratched his head. "Here's a question for you police-type people. If this guy here turns out to be Freedom's Choice, who owns him? Would he go back to his prior owner or would the insurance company own him?"

"Would Ty have any claim?" David asked.

"I think since the insurance company put up the ten million dollars, they would have the greater claim." Agent Campbell reached out to touch the stallion's neck. "I'm sure attorneys could keep the matter in court for years. Let's get the test results back first. I see no reason to involve anyone else unless we have to."

"What about Jasmine? She'd still be yours, wouldn't she, Ty?" Heather asked.

David put his arm around her. "Let's not worry about that just now, okay?"

"They can't take her away. Maybe we could get your dad to help."

"We don't even know if that'll be a problem," Ty said.

"I'll be right back," said Agent Campbell.

"Ty, this is so weird. If he's Freedom's Choice, how did he get here?" Heather asked. "What happened to Anthony Grange? Do you think? . . ."

"What? That McCade had something to do with all this?" Ty said.

"He left a lot of unanswered questions," David said.

"Yeah, but if you'd met him, you'd know he wasn't capable of doing anything wrong."

"Everyone is capable if they're pushed," Wells said. "But let's not go jumping to conclusions."

"Okay. I've got an evidence bag," Agent Campbell said as he joined them again. "I guess we could check to see if he has a lip tattoo, but I'd just as soon stay away from his mouth."

Wells backed away. "Good thinking."

"I'll just pull a couple of hairs out of his mane, or Officer Tuttle, would you like to do it?"

"Me?" His young face brightened.

"Sure. Make sure to get the root. Hold him for Officer Tuttle, will you, Ty?"

The stallion tossed his head, but did nothing more threatening when Officer Tuttle pulled out a strand of mane.

The officer placed the hair into a plastic bag that looked like something you'd put a sandwich in. Then Agent Campbell taped it closed with white tape showing red lettering that said "Evidence, Federal Bureau of Investigation, Washington, D.C."

"Thanks, Ty," Agent Campbell said. "Maybe we'd better get a mane sample from your filly too and have David take some pictures. Then, will you show Officer Tuttle and me where you found the watch?"

I want details." Katie tucked her long red hair behind her ears. "They actually think that red devil is Freedom's Choice?"

Heather led Image from his stall. "They think it's possible. They took DNA samples from him, from Jasmine, too."

"Jasmine? Why?"

"I guess just to help get to the bottom of things. Of course, if Ty can prove that Freedom's Choice is Jasmine's father, she'll be a lot more valuable."

"But then Freedom's Choice's owner might have claim on Jasmine." Katie followed Heather and Image down the aisle.

"I guess that's what's worrying Ty." Heather turned into the saddling area of the barn, securing Image's lead rope to a hook in the wall boards.

Katie plopped down on a bale of hay in the corner of the enclosure. "I can't believe I missed all the excitement. So an actual FBI agent came along with Dale Tuttle?"

"You know Officer Tuttle?"

"Oh sure. The skinny guy."

Heather giggled. "You know those big belts police officers wear that hold all their stuff?"

Katie nodded.

"His kept slipping. Ty said he had some suspenders Dale could use."

"You're kidding." Katie laughed, wrapping her arms around her middle. "I wish I could have seen that—skinny little Dale Tuttle with an FBI agent."

"You know, it was sweet, though," Heather said, ducking under Image's neck. "Toward the end of the visit, Agent Campbell was kinda mothering Officer Tuttle. Agent Campbell explained how to get the DNA samples, bag them and prepare them to send. Then when Ty showed the officers where we found the watch, they both walked the area together, stooping down, searching through the grass."

"Did they find anything interesting?" Katie asked.

"Not really. They were curious about that pile of hay next to a tree with broken branches and chewed bark. They felt like Ty and I did—that there had definitely been a horse tied there."

"What horse? Freedom's Choice, if he is Freedom's Choice, was in the barn." Katie brought her long tanned legs up to prop her chin on her knees.

"You got me. None of us could figure out anything about the horse." Heather took Image's saddle from the tack room and, walking back to the gelding, placed it on his back.

"So you said the watch belonged to an Anthony Grange, and that he was the last person known to have Freedom's Choice?" Katie rubbed the front of her legs.

"Uh-huh." Heather reached under Image's belly to grasp the saddle's girth. "Maybe Anthony Grange lost his watch when he was tying up Freedom's Choice. But why would he tie him up out there instead of in the barn? What's more, how did Grange's body get in the lake?"

"Don't they feel it was an accident? That Grange fell asleep or something?" Katie asked.

Image lay his ears back as Heather tightened the girth. "Maybe, except I think they're wondering if the license plates on the truck and trailer were actually lost in the lake. Then there's the window that was damaged right where the VIN number was supposed to be."

"Weird." Katie's nose wrinkled.

"I think they might be wondering if Ty's friend, McCade Saxton, was somehow involved. But Ty says if they knew McCade, they would never ask such a question. I've about worn my head out thinking." Heather's hands went to her hips. "I can't come up with answers. I just decided not to worry about it anymore. I'll fret about the horse show tomorrow instead."

"That's tomorrow?" Katie asked.

"Can you believe it?"

Katie stood, brushing hay from the back of her shorts. "Is Ty taking you?"

"Yes, Ty and David." Heather slipped the bridle onto Image's head.

"That should be interesting."

Heather nodded. "Tell me about it. David can sometimes get underfoot at horse shows."

Rubbing the corner of her eye with the tip of a finger, Katie said, "You could always leave him here for me to tend and then you and Ty . . ."

"Still trying to play Cupid?" Heather held up her hand to display David's ring.

"Would it do any good?" This from Katie.

"Ty doesn't like me anymore."

"Who says?"

"I can tell." Heather buckled the throat latch on Image's bridle.

"I think you need your radar checked."

"My radar's fine."

Katie combed her fingers through the thick hair at the back of her neck. "Can't blame me for trying."

"What?"

"Never mind." She looked away.

Heather studied her for a moment. "You doing anything right now?"

"Why do you ask?" Katie's head snapped around.

Pinching the bridge of her nose, Heather said, "Because I want to know if you're doing anything right now."

"Oh." She smiled. "What do you have in mind?"

"Will you ride Possum while I jump Image? Then we'll switch horses. That way they'll both get exercised and we can talk."

"About Ty?"

Heather squinted at Katie. "Do you, or do you not, want me to help you study your lines for the Bigfork Review?"

"Okay, but tell Image not to buck me off. I haven't ridden much this summer."

"It's like riding a bike. It comes back to you."

"Is Ty taking Roxie tomorrow?" Katie asked.

"He said he was. I think he's going to enter her in some halter classes, maybe a Western Pleasure class or two. She should do well."

"Ty's a great trainer, don't you think?"

"He sure is," Heather answered.

"He's cute too, huh?"

"Katie!"

"Okay. Okay." She turned a nearby bucket over so she could stand on it and put her foot into the stirrup of Possum's saddle, swinging on. "You and your tall horses. They're tall like Ty."

"And David?" Heather studied Katie.

"David is tall, isn't he?"

Heather felt her brows raise.

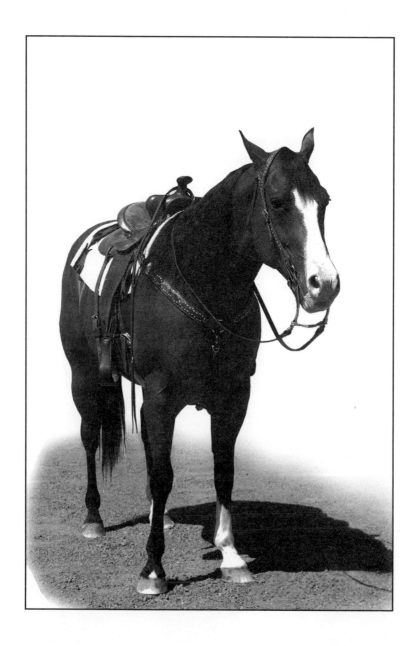

CHAPTER
EIGHTEEN

Headed for Kalispell ten days after she'd arrived at the Taggerts, Heather sat in Kevin's pickup between Ty, who drove, and David, who pointed out picture-taking possibilities on this beautiful, cloudless morning. "Wow," she said.

Both guys turned to stare at her. "Wow what?" David asked.

"Here we are heading to a horse show with Image, Possum and Roxie when Ty might be stabling one of the nation's most famous racehorses in his barn." Heather straddled the raised section in the middle of the floor. Every time Ty shifted, his arm brushed her leg and her heart switched into overdrive. She shivered.

"You cold?" Ty asked.

In Utah during the last part of June, the air conditioning would have been blasting, but here in Montana they hadn't even turned it on. The temperature outside hovered around seventy-eight degrees.

"Oh, no," Heather said quickly. "I'm just thinking about . . . about Freedom's Choice." She smiled to herself. Good recovery.

Ty focused his attention on the road again. "I still have a hard time believing it could be him."

"And you might own a Freedom's Choice filly," Heather added.

"She's such a sweetheart—so different from the others the stallion's sired." Ty adjusted the rearview mirror.

David playfully leaned against Heather as Ty took a curve.

"Are the others all stud colts?" Giggling, Heather punched David's solid belly.

He feigned a cough. "Hey! Take it easy on us fellows."

Heather gestured with open palms up. "I only meant, stud colts are more aggressive than fillies."

"I believe there's one filly." Ty kept his eyes on the road. "She's ornery too."

"Jasmine's special. I keep telling you that." Heather wagged a finger at him.

"Yes, you do." Ty turned on the radio, touching buttons until he found a station that seemed to satisfy him. "Okay?"

David nodded to the beat of a Garth Brooks tune. "That's good. Oh, I talked to Dad about your little horse," he continued in his serious voice. "He said he's not up on horse law and he'd have to do some research, but he thinks since you had no knowledge of the mare you now own being bred to the purported Freedom's Choice, you might be okay on the ownership issue."

Ty stared at David, mouth ajar. "Do you always talk like that around your house?"

Heather nodded. "Yeah. He does. His dad does too. I think he means you'll probably get to keep Jasmine, but we'll have to wait and see for sure."

"Thanks for looking into it, David," Ty said.

"Dad's going to call after his clerks have researched the matter fully. He'll make sure your interests are taken into consideration."

"That means he'll fight for you," Heather said.

A smile twitched across Ty's face. "I figured."

She scratched her head. "I've been thinking. If the stallion in the barn is Freedom's Choice, where is Red Rock's Last Chance, McCade's stallion?"

"Good question," Ty said. "I've been wondering the same thing myself."

"Maybe there isn't a Red Rock's Last Chance." David ran his fingers around the collar of his shirt.

It occurred to Heather that all three of them were dressed in blue jeans and white knit shirts. They matched, at least they would until she and Ty changed into their clothes for the show ring. Heather smiled to herself remembering how Ty had finally surrendered and allowed Katie and her to pick out what he'd wear in the Western Pleasure class today—a colorful shirt of rust, yellow and brown, tan jeans, and suede chaps. The darker brown of his boots, silver buckled belt and matching Stetson tied the whole outfit together nicely.

"But I've got registration papers for him," Ty said.

"Maybe they're forged. Maybe Freedom's Choice is Red Rock, or Rocky as you call him," David said.

Ty shook his head. "I don't know. The registration looks pretty authentic."

"Does the description on the papers for Red Rock match what Freedom's Choice looks like?" Heather asked.

"Yeah. The papers say a chestnut stallion, who'd now be five years old, with just that one little white mark on his head." Ty checked the rearview mirror again.

"Sounds like Freedom's Choice, all right," Heather said. "Maybe he was the horse tied to the tree in the forest so no one would see him."

David held up a finger. "Maybe Freedom's Choice got eaten by the Flathead monster, or maybe it was Rocky that did."

"Oh!" Heather said. "You could have gone all day without saying that."

Ty smacked his lips. "I guess we'll find out soon enough when the FBI gets the results on the DNA test."

"I hope." Heather moved her legs back on either side of the gearshift. "Well, enough of this. Let's talk about something else. My brain's about to cramp."

"So, Heather," David took her hand. " I guess you and I get to horse around again today."

Stealing a quick glance at Ty, Heather said, "You, me, Image and Possum."

"Oh, yeah. You always have to bring those guys, don't you?"

"You love it, you know you do."

"No," he said. "Ty loves it. I put up with it because I love you." He stared at her solemnly, then grinned. "That and I'll be able to take pictures. In case you've been worrying, I brought my camera."

"What a surprise." Heather leaned back. "I'm so relieved."

"Better get it loaded then. Here we are." Ty looked at his watch. "We don't have much time, though. It's eleven forty-five and Heather's jumping class starts at one. Good thing you're riding old pros."

They pulled off the graveled road into a freshly cut alfalfa field where horses from a row of other trailers were already being unloaded. About a hundred feet away stood the old wooden grandstands, several corrals and numerous panel paddocks. Heather and Ty chose to operate out of the horse trailer.

Image whinnied and pulled at his lead shank as Heather led him from the trailer, but quieted quickly when his buddy and girlfriend joined him.

David snapped photos of Roxie tied to the trailer between Possum and Image. "Hmm. Two boys and a girl. Who does that remind you of?"

"I have no idea." Heather favored him with a blank stare.

Putting the camera aside momentarily, he helped her with Possum and Image while she ducked into the dressing room at the front of the trailer to change.

Heather's show ring clothes consisted of traditional English riding attire—tan breeches, a fitted navy English jacket, black boots and riding helmet. She took a moment to finger the necklace she'd worn under the shirt she now replaced with a white, high-necked blouse. This morning she'd slipped the silver key from Ty's necklace onto David's chain which already held the running horse charm.

Why she'd done that, she could only guess. Was it that now she could feel close to both boys?

The jumping class in Kalispell was the smallest Heather had ever entered—only seven jumpers total. Why had Kevin scheduled it? Oh, yeah. Shaking her head, she remembered. Of course, but then Kevin "never interfered."

Actually, the class turned out to be a blast. Image took the course like it was a romp in the pasture, never even breaking a sweat. Possum also completed a perfect round, but his was more stressful since something on the sidelines distracted him and Heather had to tap him with her quirt to remind him of the competition.

Her geldings ended up tied for first place, which would have called for a jump-off, but Heather gave the first place to Image since those points would go toward his overall state championship.

When Heather rode Image and led Possum into the show ring the crowd was as generous with their applause as David was with his photographs. In fact, several other photographers joined him.

Head up, ears pricked, Possum seemed undisturbed by his second place and posed more beautifully for the pictures than Image, who had a difficult time standing still.

The other five competitors were equally complimentary and a lady of about thirty, astride a huge Clydesdale/Thoroughbred cross, rode along with them as they returned to the trailer, where David took more photos.

The Warmblood gelding was enormous, making Heather feel like she rode ponies. A few more years' experience and the big bay would be a real competitor.

"Give me your address and I'll send you some pictures," David told the woman before she waved and rode off, her third place ribbon secured to her horse's bridle.

After unsaddling her geldings, Heather put halters on them, tying the lead ropes to the outside of the trailer. "I think they'll be okay here." Heather patted Possum's shoulder. "He'll look out for Image. Let's go watch Ty and Roxie in that Western Pleasure class."

Normally, Heather wouldn't have left the horses unattended, but here everyone seemed casual and friendly, like family. Actually she and David would be able to see the horses from the bleachers. Today the rodeo grounds doubled as a show ring—a show ring that rested in the midst of lush green fields under an endless sky.

Perhaps sensing more photo opportunities, David followed without complaint. They stopped near the entrance gate at the end of the oval-shaped arena. Heather saw Roxie and Ty in the ring. The mare's saddle blanket matched the colors in Ty's shirt and she carried a floral tooled western saddle with silver double corner plates and silver conchos.

"There's a Kodak moment for you." Heather pointed. Far more popular in Montana than jumping, the Western Pleasure class consisted of thirty-five horses. The stands, which reminded Heather of the bleachers at her former high school, were almost full. This competition promised to be tough. "I'll bet Ty would love some pictures of Roxie in the ring. Isn't she gorgeous?"

"Who?" David asked. His camera was pointed in a different direction.

Heather turned to see what had caught his attention. "Oh my gosh. That's Allie, one of Ty's students. Great looking mare. I wonder where she got her?"

"From that guy in Bozeman Ty told her to call." The voice came from a tall, lanky kid who Heather recognized as Allie's brother.

"Hi, Heather," he said. "Is this your boyfriend?"

His presence as well as his question caught Heather off guard. "This is . . . uh . . ."

"David Cane." David stuck out his hand.

"I'm Chad Phillips, Allie's brother." He pointed toward the bay mare that cantered along carrying—by some people's standards—a very attractive girl dressed predominately in maroon. Allie was tall and skinny as a Holocaust survivor. The black, silver-accented saddle matched the mare's mane and tail. No doubt about it, the pair was eye-catching. "Heather and I went riding the other day," Chad went on. "I practiced my best flirting, but I figured she already had a boyfriend."

David laughed. "That would be me."

"Put her there." Chad held up his hand for a high-five. "Allie will be happy about that. She figured Ty was Heather's boyfriend. Wait until I tell her."

Heather felt her eyes growing so large she thought they might roll out on the ground. "Maybe we'd better go check on Image and Possum, David. We've been gone awhile."

Stretching to his full height, David said, "They're fine. I can see them."

Actually, Heather could too. Their long manes fluttered slightly in the breeze and the afternoon sunlight glistened upon their backs. The geldings stood quietly, heads close together, like they shared a secret conversation. "Okay, we'll wait a bit."

The horses in the ring slowed to a walk. Heather watched them silently for a moment. Ty rode behind Allie. Their mounts seemed to have their minds squarely on business. Each carried its head quietly at the appropriate height straight out from its body, and on a loose rein. Heather knew what Image would have done had she given him his head. But this was a pleasure class. She'd probably never be able to enter Image in this type of an event. Now, Possum, he'd be fine if she could keep him from staring into the audience, ensuring that all eyes were on him—the big ham.

"Entries 144, 310, 401, 177 . . ."—the announcer read off twenty numbers—"are excused from the ring."

Heather, David and Chad stepped aside to let the horses pass through the gate. Ty's and Allie's numbers had not been called. They were still in the competition with thirteen other riders. Darn. Why hadn't they called Allie's number? One look at the bay answered her question. The mare was flawless. When Allie put her into a gait, her speed never varied. Although Roxie missed a lead change once right in front of the judge, each of the bay's was perfect.

"Come in and line up, please," the announcer said.

Ty and Allie positioned their horses next to each other and Heather felt heat flood to her face.

"This has been a difficult class to judge," the announcer said. "Unfortunately, we can't send blue ribbons home with all of you, so we're going to have to narrow this group down again. Will entries 211, 139, 481 . . ."—he named off a total of ten numbers, 481 being Ty's—"exit the ring, and thank you. This has been a beautiful competition."

Smiling, Ty said something to Allie before he reined Roxie around and rode out of the arena. When he saw Heather, David and Chad, he waved and trotted his mare over to them.

"I'm sorry, Ty," Heather said. "You and Roxie did great."

"Hey. Don't feel bad." Ty slipped off Roxie. "I'm so happy with this little filly I could burst. I never thought she'd behave so well. She's just a baby after all and this is her first time out—no where else to go but up." He smiled at Chad. "Hi. Your sister's doing great. I love that mare. I bet old Vince charged her a bundle."

The young boy cupped his hand to the side of his mouth and leaned toward Ty. "Allie said we can't talk about it, especially to Dad. I think she had to get the money from her trust account."

"Ouch. Hope I didn't cause any trouble." Ty brought Roxie closer so she stood next to him. "I just heard about that mare being for sale—she won at Nationals last year, you know—and I figured since I could never afford her, someone I knew ought to have her."

Heather cleared her throat.

"I thought about Kevin first, Heather. I really did." He stroked Roxie's neck. "But that mare isn't a jumper, never will be. She's exactly what Allie needs, though. A seasoned horse like that will teach her everything she needs to learn. They'll be hard to beat. Snap a picture of her, will you, David?"

"I'm on it," he said, smiling broadly—a little too broadly Heather thought.

Four people and one horse stood in a row peeking through the web-wire fence. Two sorrels, one palomino, one black and Allie's bay remained in the ring.

"What's that mare's name?" Heather gestured toward the bay. "She's a pretty thing."

"Let's see." Ty tapped his finger on his chin. "Her registered name is Diamond Jubilee."

"Allie calls her Babe," Chad said.

The horses, ridden by three girls and two boys, loped around the ring, their beauty enhanced by their riders' show ring finery—blues, browns, reds and golds set off with the glittering silver and hand-tooled leather of the bridles and saddles. The horses' coats gleamed like satin. Their freshly washed and conditioned manes and tails shimmered. Their hooves sparkled with the coats of clear polish that had been brushed onto them.

"Jog," the announcer said.

With the slightest touch to the reins, all five horses slowed to a jog.

"Look at Babe's cadence." Ty pointed. "One, two, one, two. She's not off a split second."

"Cadence?" David lowered the camera.

"That's the way her feet hit the ground." Heather rested her hands on the cross-wires of the fence. "Each foot falls precisely where it should at each gait. Notice that at the jog—that's sorta like a trot, Western style—the left rear hoof and the right front hoof hit the ground at exactly the same time, then the right rear hoof and the left front hoof hit the ground together a moment later. That's a two-beat cadence."

"Hmm," David said. "Look. That sorrel horse's feet don't hit together. Its cadence is off." He puffed out his chest.

Ty nodded and Heather laughed.

"And see," Ty's eyes twinkled, "Babe's pole is level with her withers and her nose is slightly in front of the vertical."

David glanced at Heather who said, "That means the top of her head is level with the top of her shoulder and if you drew a line down her face that was exactly straight up and down, her nose would stick out slightly in front of that."

"I figured." David straightened.

They all laughed, even Chad, who had no way of knowing the extent of the joke.

Roxie tossed her head.

"What I don't understand," Ty nodded at Heather, "is how you know all this Western stuff."

Chad sniffed. "Heather's smart."

"I know, but a lot of smart people would have no idea what Heather was talking about." Ty raised a questioning brow.

"I watch videos," she said softly.

"Are you Tyler Taggert?" a voice asked.

All turned to stare. The voice came from an elderly man of about seventy with wavy gray hair and a thick gray mustache.

"Yes. What can I do for you?"

"Nice filly." He patted Roxie's shoulder. "You bought McCade Saxton's place, I hear."

"My family did."

"Shame about McCade. Ugly way to go," the man continued.

"Yeah. Cancer's the pits," Ty said. Heather could tell by his reserved answers that he wondered who this man was.

"Ain't that the truth. Nice fellow, McCade." The stranger wasn't giving many clues.

"He was good to me." Ty too remained cautious.

"I met him a couple years ago and saw him at some Quarter Horse functions after that." The man shrugged. "He seemed a little odd that day I dropped in on him, the last time I ever saw him, but other than that he was a straight-up guy. What did he do with that red stallion, the one he called Red Rock?"

"I still have him. McCade . . . uh, Mr. Saxton sold all his horses except Red Rock and a sorrel mare in foal by him. He said they were his favorites and he didn't want them to go to just anyone."

"I'd have bought that stallion." The man flicked dirt off his jacket sleeve. "He looks just like that racehorse, Freedom's Choice."

Ty's brow raised. "Yeah. When did you last see McCade's stallion?"

"About a year ago, that day McCade acted so funny." He stroked Roxie again. "I haven't been able to find a stallion I like better. I've got a mare I want to breed to Red Rock next spring, if it's okay with you."

Drawing their attention back to the arena, the announcer said, "Fifth place goes to Bimini Midnight Star, owned and ridden by McKenzie Williams."

Allie sat motionless on Babe as the fourth and third places were announced. When the second place name was called, knowing she'd won first, Allie fell forward in the saddle and threw her arms around Babe's shoulders.

"Yay, Allie," Ty cheered. David, Chad and Heather joined in, Heather a little less enthusiastically than the males in the group.

When Allie came out of the ring, she leaped off Babe and threw her arms around Ty. "Did you see us win?" she asked. "I'd never have been able to do it without you."

Heather rolled her eyes. *I'd never have been able to do it without you*, Heather mimicked to herself. Her fists clenched.

David put his arm around Heather's waist, drawing her close.

"Sure you would have." Ty backed away slightly. "Allie, you remember Heather and this is her friend from Utah, David Cane."

"Hi, David." Allie grinned. She favored Heather with a quick nod.

"And this is . . ." Ty tipped his head toward the man. "I'm sorry, I didn't catch your name."

"Alex Saunders at your service."

"Mr. Saunders wants to breed his mare to Rocky."

"Ooh." Allie's nostrils flared. "Good luck."

"Ma'am?" Mr. Saunders cocked his head.

"I should warn you," Ty said. "With Rocky's disposition, some of his colts turn out pretty ornery. I've even thought of having him gelded."

"You're putting me on." The man grinned. "You can't mean Red Rock. He's the best-natured stallion this side of Kingdom Come."

CHAPTER NINETEEN

Alex Saunders had no sooner spit out the words that left Ty speechless than an attractive gray-haired lady in a lavender pantsuit called to him, "Come on, dear. We'll be late."

"I'll get with you later, Ty, about my mare," he said and scurried off after the woman and another classy couple of similar age and wardrobe.

"But . . ." Ty said to the man's back.

Heather returned her attention to Chad, who favored her with frivolous remarks and puppy dog glances. David snapped pictures of Allie sitting on Babe. They hadn't moved far from the show ring. Spectators still congratulated the grinning girl. Some of the people also recognized Heather from the earlier class and had kind things to say.

Ty stroked Roxie's shoulder, then led her forward a step. He paused, chewed his bottom lip and stared at the ground. Finally, he shook his head and led his mare over to where David had lined Heather and Chad up on either side of Allie and Babe. "This should do it," David said.

"Oh, just a few more." Allie adjusted her vest. "Will you take some photos of Ty and me?"

Handing Roxie's reins to Heather, Ty stood dutifully next to Babe. Then he said, "One more, Allie, and we'll let you and Chad go. I know you have to prepare for your ladies-to-ride class and we should be heading home. I'll see you Wednesday for lessons, although . . ." he gestured toward the blue ribbon attached to Babe's bridle, "maybe you should be teaching me."

Her face glowed. "Oh, Ty," she purred. "Of course I'll be there Wednesday. I could never teach you anything about riding . . ." she lowered her eyelids, "but maybe other things."

He lifted his hat, rubbing his forehead with the back of his hand. "Wednesday at nine, okay? We'll try Babe on the barrels."

"Will you be there, Heather?" Chad peered around the tall bay.

Heather blinked. "Oh, uh, I don't know, maybe."

Ty slapped Babe on the rump, starting the mare off. "See you, Allie. See you, Chad."

Some of the competitors, like Heather and Ty who'd come for only a class or two, hadn't bothered to reserve a stall. Others rented space for their horses in the 20-stall metal barn not far from the show ring and grandstands. Of course, Babe had a stall in the barn.

When Allie, her horse and brother disappeared into the stabling area, Ty and Heather started toward the trailer.

"Hold it." David held up his hand. "Before you two change into civvies, I want pictures."

"Why am I not surprised?" Heather sighed.

"I think Heather has an admirer," David said, blowing dust from the lens of his camera.

Ty's head swiveled around. "Who?"

David's brows arched. "Chad, of course."

"Oh, yeah, Chad." Ty clucked to Roxie and walked forward.

"Okaaaay," David said. "I want some pictures of you alone, Heather, and a couple of you riding Image. Then I want Ty riding his horse, what's her name, oh yeah, Roxie, and some of you two together—kind of an East versus West thing. It'll be cool."

Heather swatted at a horsefly that had settled on her arm. Other flies tried to land on the horses, but earlier she'd sprayed the animals with insect repellent. "I guess that means I'll have to saddle Image again, or Possum."

"Image is the most photogenic," David said.

"Possum will be insulted." Heather wrinkled her nose.

"I'll get some of him too." David took her arm, tugging her along. "Come on, I'll help saddle."

She lagged behind. "You must really want those pictures."

"Yep. I have a cool idea."

"Uh oh," Ty said.

"Trust me on this. You'll be impressed."

Walking from hard-packed dirt to short-cropped alfalfa, they arrived at the trailer where David helped Heather and Ty saddle her geldings.

"Let's go over there." David pointed to the corner of a field, not far from where they'd parked, to a small grassy area. A pole fence rested along one side, balanced on the other by three pine trees of varying size. "Perfect," he said when they arrived. "Ty, you hold the horses, and Heather, lean against that fence. Now rest one arm on the top rail. Hold it. Good."

Heather felt like an imposter as David walked around her, snapping pictures from all angles, as if she were a fashion model. He took a few shots of her riding Possum, then had her mount Image and they went through the whole routine again. He snapped several shots of Ty sitting astride Roxie in full Western regalia.

"Good," David said. "Now, stand your horses next to each other, right in the corner there. Good. Now let me take a few more."

Heather glanced at her watch.

"I saw that." David peeked over the top of his camera. "Be good or I'll have Allie pose for me again, maybe even Chad."

Heather growled.

Ty chuckled.

Staring at them for a moment, David rubbed his chin. "Now switch horses."

"Switch horses?" Heather's hand went to her hip. "And saddles and bridles?"

"No, just you and Ty switch horses."

"You want me dressed English, riding a horse with Western tack and Ty, dressed Western riding a horse with English tack?"

"Yep."

"That'll look funny."

"Do I have to get Allie?"

Heather rolled her eyes but climbed off Image as Ty dismounted from Roxie. Then each mounted the other's horse.

David sighted through the camera and a big smile spread across his face. "Oh, yeah. This is awesome."

He took pictures with the digital camera until he exceeded its storage capacity then switched to his thirty-five millimeter Nikon and shot two rolls. "That should do it. And yes, Heather, you may be excused now. Thanks for your patience, Ty."

"What about my patience?" Heather asked.

"Patience isn't exactly your strong suit," David said.

Ty smiled.

She pulled a face and swung off Roxie, immediately shedding her jacket and helmet. "I feel better now." She glanced at Ty. "You've been kinda quiet. Everything all right?"

"I'm still thinking about what Mr. Saunders said about Rocky." He led Roxie toward the trailer. Heather followed, leading Image. David brought up the rear with Possum.

"That's right." Heather tied Image to the trailer, then took Possum from David. "Can you believe it? No way could he think Red Rock . . . uh . . . Rocky is gentle."

"Maybe I've been working the stallion wrong." Ty uncinched Roxie's saddle.

"You know that isn't true." Heather ran the irons up the stirrup leathers on each side of Image's saddle. "You handle Rocky the only way you can. You're wonderful with horses. Look what you did for Image last year."

"I don't know." Shaking his head, Ty put Roxie's saddle in the trailer's tack room.

"I think there are two stallions." At long last, David eased his cameras into their cases.

Heather scratched her head. "It almost sounds like it, doesn't it? But where's the other stallion? If Mr. Saunders saw the nice stallion, who he thought was Red Rock, and we have the mean stallion, is he Freedom's Choice?"

"Or is the nice stallion Freedom's Choice and Mr. Saunders saw him at our barn where Red Rock should've been and now we have the mean Red Rock back?" Ty led Roxie into the trailer. "If you guys come to the barn in the morning and I'm riding in tiny circles and babbling to myself, you'll know this whole thing's driven me over the edge."

"I'm about to join you." Heather uncinched Image's saddle.

"Maybe the FBI report will help you decide who's who." David lifted the saddle from Image's back.

"We can hope anyway," Ty said.

As soon as the three horses were loaded into the trailer and the tack was put away, David, Ty and Heather climbed into the cab of the truck. Ty and Heather hadn't changed back into their jeans but had rid themselves of the show ring extras—hats, jackets, chaps and such.

The ride home that evening promised to be quiet by this group's standards. They needed Katie to liven up their conversation, but she was entertaining at Bigfork.

As they traveled, Heather thought about Freedom's Choice. She supposed Ty did too. David stared out the window, probably pondering further photo opportunities.

They arrived home and had the horses in their stalls by nine. The three friends were sauntering up the pathway from the barn when Bea called from the porch, "Ty, Agent Campbell's on the phone."

"I'll be right there." He glanced at Heather and cocked a brow.

They all sprinted for the house. Ty took the phone from his mother. "This is Ty."

Heather studied his face as it passed from anxious to completely blank. "You're absolutely sure," he said into the phone. "I don't know what to think either. Okay, I'll get back with you. Thanks for calling."

"What?" Heather said.

Ty stared into space. "He said that the stallion in the barn is not Freedom's Choice."

"Okay," David said. "We'd sort of figured that."

"There's more, isn't there?" Heather asked.

"The stallion in the barn is not Jasmine's father." Ty dropped into a chair as if his legs could no longer hold him.

Heather held her breath.

"Jasmine's father is Freedom's Choice."

CHAPTER TWENTY

Taking full advantage of the sun, Heather and Katie stretched their legs, propping them up on the side of Old Rusty Bucket. Ty drove the ancient boat. David sat up front with him, leaving Heather and Katie their choice of seats either behind the boys or at the rear of the boat on either side of the covered motor. The girls selected the latter. Better rays, which during June in Montana were sometimes a rarity.

Katie removed a claw clip from the hem of her shorts, wound her long hair into a twist and secured it behind her head. "This is great. I needed a day off. Sorry I missed the horse show on Saturday."

"I think we all deserve down time. Ty and I were talking about that last night, or maybe it was Monday." Heather waved her hand. "Doesn't matter." Actually they'd been discussing Freedom's Choice and Jasmine until Heather feared a brain drain. "I can't think about it anymore," she'd told him.

They'd gone on to plan this boat ride. Bea had even helped them pack a picnic in a fancy wooden basket, with lids that lifted up on the top of either side. Although Heather pictured sandwiches, chips, a can of pop, maybe a piece of fruit, under Bea's direction, the menu included fried chicken, potato salad, bits of watermelon and cantaloupe cut up bite size in a large plastic bowl, homemade cookies and a jug of lemonade.

"Listen to that motor." David clapped Ty on the shoulder. "We *are* good, aren't we?"

The motor did sound better since David and Ty had worked on it again.

Heather squirmed in her seat. The one-piece bathing suit beneath her cutoffs and knit shirt pulled when she sat. They'd all decided to wear suits underneath, even though Heather doubted either she or Ty would shed their clothes. It was a maybe for David and a most certainly for Katie.

"Would you pass me that tanning lotion?" The redhead pointed to the bottle stashed in the cup holder on the engine cover. "Thanks," she said and, right on schedule, slipped out of her shorts and top. Heather smiled to herself.

"Do we have enough life jackets?" Ty turned in his seat. "I'd hate to get picked up. Seeing this beautiful piece of machinery, a ranger just might be tempted to check on us." He grinned.

"We don't have to put them on, do we?" Katie rubbed lotion on her long legs.

"They just have to be in the boat." David knelt down, tugging two life jackets out from under the bow. "One, two and then there's my ski vest. That's three, and, oh, Ty, your seat cushion has straps on it. That would count. We're okay."

"Okay. Where to?" Ty pushed the gas lever forward and the boat putted off. "Any requests?"

"How about Wild Horse Island? Is that too far?" Heather pulled her hair into a ponytail and secured it with a rubber band from her pocket.

Glancing at each other, the guys shrugged. "We should be all right," Ty said.

"Too bad we can't borrow Ted's boat again." Katie passed the tanning lotion to Heather, who rubbed some on.

"I'll say." David removed his shirt, but left his jeans on. Heather could see the waistband of his swimming trunks peeking above the top of his Levi's.

They headed out of Skidoo Bay toward the main body of the lake. The slight roll of the waves caused a tickle in Heather's stomach and she giggled. Drawing a deep breath, she tried to decipher what the air smelled like. She cocked her head. Nothing really, just fresh. Here, she could almost forget that people had ever infringed on nature's beauty.

Off in the distance, the peaks of Glacier Park poked their chiseled heads into a clear sky, light cerulean at the horizon, darker as it rose into a wash of cobalt. The mountains farthest in the distance also appeared blue, more so than the enormous sky. As the ranges drew closer they grew darker—grayish, purplish— until the deep green of the forest burst out at the base of the closest mountains. The vast clear lake, ultramarine of its own accord, reflected the colors from above and around. Heather closed her eyes, marveling at the myriad of blues in God's palette.

They circled Wild Horse Island twice, spotting two deer and three goats. David took pictures with his ever-present camera. They swam. They skied, sort of. Old Rusty Bucket's motor could barely lift Ty and David out of the water. In the shelter of a cove, they lunched on Bea's lovingly prepared picnic. They dropped anchor farther out in the lake, replaced what clothes they'd earlier removed, and napped, David and Ty on the bow with the life jackets under their heads, Heather and Katie on the seats with folded towels for pillows.

When water splashed over Heather's leg, she gasped and sat up. The blue of earlier hours had metamorphosed into shades of angry gray. Whitecaps disrupted the surface of the lake. How could it turn from bath water gentleness into this raging menace in what seemed only minutes? David and Ty leaped into the boat.

"Hey!" Katie stumbled as she tried to stand. "What happened to the sun?"

"We'd better head home." Ty slid into the driver's seat while David pulled anchor. The boat rose and fell in the purplish gray waves that barreled straight at them from across the length of the giant lake. Heather fell back in her seat. Water sprayed over her as waves hit the rear of the boat.

"Anchor's up," David yelled. "Go, Ty. Heather and Katie, move up front." He held a hand out to each of the girls, steadying them as they stumbled forward.

Ty turned the key in the ignition. It whined for a moment before leaping to life. "If we head into the waves at an angle, we won't take on so much water," Ty called.

"Good idea." David yelled.

Now sharing a seat, Heather and Katie huddled under a beach towel. Wind tore the clip from Katie's hair and whipped her locks across her face.

"I don't know, Ty," David called. "Maybe we should find a place to tie up and sit this storm out on the island."

Heather watched as a bank of black clouds boiled up, covering the last remnants of blue sky. Raindrops pelted her legs.

"You're right," Ty yelled over the howling wind. "Did you bring your cell phone? Mom and Dad will be worried."

"No. I thought I had it in my camera case, but now I remember I took it out to call my folks last night." David slipped the case under the shelter of the bow.

"If we can make it to the other side of the island, we'll be protected a little, maybe find someplace to anchor." Ty turned the boat slightly, angling its nose into a whitecap.

The wave that came at them appeared higher than the sides of the boat. Heather stared as the wall of water drew closer and closer, threatening to swallow them whole. Drawing a quick breath, she remembered the panic of her midnight swim just before Ty had rescued her—her burning lungs, the desperate thrashing of her arms and legs. She glanced at him, his set jaw, hand easing forward on the gas lever. Her heart pounded. What could he do? He was as helpless as she and the others.

Lifting Old Rusty Bucket higher and higher, the swell held the boat in midair for a moment, then plunged it into the trough of another oncoming wave. Water splashed over the sides, soaking the four of them even more than the rain now coming in a steady pour.

The boat's motor sputtered and stopped. Katie gasped. All three stared at Ty. He brought the throttle back to neutral and turned the key. It sputtered again and whined, almost kicked over, but stopped dead. Waves spun the boat to the side. Water showered the four of them. Ty tried the key again and again. The last time the engine wouldn't even turn over. "Dang. There must be water in the gas and I think the battery's gone. What now? Any suggestions?"

Clinging to the side of the boat, David studied their position. "If only we were farther out. We're going to hit that island, no doubt about it." He bit his lip. "And it's not gonna be pretty."

Heather came out of the seat she shared with Katie, lost her balance and fell. David helped her up. "Put this on." He draped a life jacket around her shoulders.

"We only have three." Heather remembered that even though Ty had not worn a life jacket the night he'd saved her, the lake had been calm.

David guided her arms through the jacket and fastened the buckles. He grabbed another life preserver off the floor. "Here, Katie." He wrapped her in it.

She slipped her arms through the holes and David did up the buckles. "What about you?" Katie asked.

"And Ty?" Heather fought for balance as another wave drenched the boat.

"We're good swimmers." David grabbed the picnic basket and started rummaging through it. He dumped paper plates, silverware and glasses out of cellophane sacks.

"You hungry?" Katie said.

"My camera. I need to keep it dry." He slipped it into a ziplock bag, secured it, found another, secured it and finally used a third.

Ty stood. "It's no use. Do we jump and try to make it to the island on our own, or take our chances riding the boat in?"

David pushed his hand through his wet hair. "I don't think we have any choice but to jump. If the boat hits those cliffs, we'll be history."

"We're going to jump?" Katie cried.

Heather shivered, remembering Ty's story of the man who'd wanted to use Wild Horse as a dude ranch. While trying to save boats on the dock, he'd died during a violent storm. And . . . what about . . . what about the Flathead monster? She'd forgotten about it until now. Wasn't its most recent sighting near Wild Horse Island? Her knuckles turned white as she clung to the side of the seat.

Still kneeling, David stuffed the camera, now sealed in three cellophane bags, into the picnic basket.

"Our lives are at risk and you're worried about a camera?" Katie peeked out from under dripping hair.

"It cost ten thousand dollars and I've never had time to insure it." David rearranged napkins and a tablecloth around the camera.

Katie dropped to her knees. "I'll help. Will it fit in this bowl?"

Surprisingly, it did. They worked the covered, camera-filled plastic bowl down into the wooden picnic basket.

Ty edged his way to the back of the boat. "Here's your vest, David. Better put it on."

"No, you use it, Ty." David stood. "I'll hang onto the seat cushion . . . like they tell us to do on the airlines."

"It's your vest, David. You wear it. I'll take the seat cushion."

"Will one of you please put it on? We're getting close." Heather clenched her teeth to keep them from chattering. Like the huge dinosaur she'd likened it to, the island loomed up at them.

David shoved the vest at Ty. "You heard her. Put it on!"

Slowly, Ty slipped into the ski vest. His fingers rested on the buckles. "You sure?"

"I'll be fine." David uncoiled the ski rope. "You don't happen to have a knife, do you?"

Water dripped off Ty's nose. His forehead wrinkled. "There's one on the key chain." He leaned over the back of the seat and retrieved the useless key. "Will this do?"

"I need some rope to keep track of my camera. Do you think this basket will float?" Opening the knife, he sliced off a length of rope.

"Only one way to find out." He helped David tie the rope to the handle of the basket before reaching over and grabbing the seat cushion.

Heather watched breakers crash into the island, then claw at the rocks before rejoining the oncoming waves. That's where they'd be in minutes . . . if they were lucky. A lump caught in her throat. She felt around the neck of her shirt for the chain of her necklace—the one that held David's silver horse charm and Ty's key, then gripped Katie's hand.

"You guys ready?" Ty handed the seat cushion to David.

Slipping his arm through the straps, he nodded to Ty. "We'd better jump from this side of the boat. The wind will blow it faster than it blows us, so we won't get run over."

"Let's stick together in the water," Ty said. "Should we all jump at once?"

Katie broke into a sob and hugged Ty. Heather hugged David, then the girls traded boys and hugged some more.

"Let's go." Ty took his sister's hand and led her to the back of the boat. They climbed onto the motor cover, then before the wind could tear them away, they leaped into the whirling swells.

Bobbing to the top, Katie squealed. Soon Ty appeared, swimming close to his sister.

"Come on in, the water's fine!" Ty choked as water filled his mouth. He spit and beckoned to them.

David tied the rope that was attached to the picnic basket to the strap of the seat cushion and almost fell when he leaned over the side to place the basket in the water. It floated on the waves like a tiny Noah's Ark.

"You ready?" David helped Heather onto the engine cover.

She nodded. "Coming?"

He kicked off his shoes. "Right behind you."

Heather held her nose and leaped into the water. She'd expected it to be freezing, but after the wind and rain, it seemed warm. Glancing up, she watched as David jumped in, his arms wrapped around the cushion. Soon he was beside her. His kicking legs brushed hers. "This way," he said. They swam toward Ty and Katie.

As predicted, the boat floated toward the island faster than they did. Soon it was about ten feet from them, bouncing helplessly on the waves. It was a valiant ship heading to its demise. A pang of sorrow struck Heather's heart and she looked away. Silly. She'd better worry about herself and the others, not some old boat.

With the life jacket securely around her, Heather rode the waves and had only a little trouble keeping her head out of the water enough to breathe. Of course, rain still came down in torrents. There wasn't a dry spot around unless it was inside the picnic basket with David's camera. He held onto the ski rope even though it was still tied to the cushion, which David adjusted under his chest.

Heather wished there'd been a vest for him to wear. It must have taken a lot of strength to keep the cushion in place.

Each wave brought them closer to shore. The boat had almost hit the swells nearest the island. Heather's legs ached from kicking and she could hardly move her arms. Regardless of the landing, she'd be glad to be on Wild Horse Island. It was darker now. She couldn't tell if it was from the storm or approaching night.

The breakers had the boat in their grip now. With a terrible scraping, they threw Old Rusty Bucket onto the rocks, then dragged it out again, only to have another wave toss it end over end onto the jagged shore. It caught there, upside down on some boulders. They'd surely made the right decision when they'd decided to jump—a decision that had hopefully saved their lives.

David swam closer. "Won't be long now," he yelled. "Let's try to get over there."

Heather made out the tops of Ty's and Katie's heads in the water.

"The shore looks friendlier," David continued.

Friendlier than what? Big rocks versus small rocks, fallen dead trees versus live standing ones. An enormous pine with partially bared roots tipped precariously over the edge of the rocky shoreline. The lake wasn't likely to set them down easy, but David was right. It looked as if mud covered some of the boulders on the shoreline Ty and Katie swam for.

Heather kicked with renewed vigor. Thank heavens the waves headed toward the island rather than farther into the lake. It had become increasingly difficult to keep from taking in gulps of water.

As they worked their way toward Katie and Ty, David pulled the picnic basket along. The mind does funny things when pushed to the limit and, instead of crying at their predicament, watching David's ark bounce along on the waves made Heather giggle. In fact, when they finally got in place near Ty and Katie, the wind caught the basket and carried it out in front of them like a beacon leading them to safety. Well, maybe not safety . . . exactly. The waves battered the shoreline with amazing power and the logs and debris the lake had captured during its tantrum exploded against the banks. The huge pine, tilting toward the water, lifted and fell in the wind gusts.

They swam with the waves. Heather prayed the lake would dump them in some amiable spot where they'd be able to find something to hold onto to keep from being drawn back out.

A little ahead, Ty and Katie half swam, half crawled through the breakers onto the shore. Katie cried out as her legs scraped against boulders. She clung to a downed tree branch until Ty, who'd found his footing, helped her up onto the land. Then he paced the water's edge watching as David and Heather approached. When David's camera in the picnic basket crashed onto land, Ty grabbed it. The camera had survived.

David waved and let go of the cushion which was attached by the ski rope to the basket. They were so close now, he could just swim the rest of the way.

"Look out!" Ty yelled.

There was a sudden cracking roar. Heather gulped water and gasped for air. Thrashing around, she struggled to bring her head to the surface.

Was that Katie screaming? What was she saying?

"Heather! David!" Katie ran along the shoreline, ignoring the water's assault. "Heather! Thank heavens. Can you see David?"

Rubbing her eyes, Heather felt water running off her face. No, not water. It was red. Something sharp as porcupine quills poked her face, making it sting. What was it? Where did? . . .

Waves pummeled the branches of the giant pine tree that must have fallen into the water on top of them. Ty stripped off his vest and leaped into the oncoming waves.

Heather fought her way around the huge tree to where she'd last seen David, her throat so tight she could barely breathe.

D avid!" Heather twisted around, frantically searching for some sight of him. Waves rolled over her. Kicking and sputtering, she battled back to the surface.

Still secured by a tangle of roots that had not been underwashed, the fallen evergreen pointed into the oncoming waves like a huge spear, rising and falling at the command of the water.

"Here!" David clung to a limb in the higher branches of the floating tree. "I can't move my . . ."

Although water pounded against him, he held strong, but didn't seem to be doing much else.

Heather summoned strength that failed to respond. She made little headway against the white-crested waves.

Stronger and more streamlined without a ski jacket, Ty propelled past her.

The screeching and cracking of the tree's remaining roots signaled their distress. The lake's onslaught would soon tear the ancient pine away, smashing it against the shore, along with anything else in its path.

Heather inched toward David only to be pushed farther away by yards. She kept her gaze steady on Ty's head and shoulders as he struggled closer and closer. "David!" Ty called. Heather heard no answer and, even worse, saw no movement.

Eyes clouded with tears and lake water, Heather watched as Ty grabbed onto David's tree, using it to pull himself along. One of the branches snapped in Ty's hand and he seized another.

With a final yank, Ty reached David. Now both her guys clung to the same precarious refuge. Heather's pulse pounded as she noticed that instead of piercing the waves head-on, the tree now angled in toward shore.

"Hurry, Ty," Heather yelled. "The tree's shifting."

"He won't let go!"

"What?"

"Maybe I can pull his fingers loose."

Finally, like they'd been expelled from a clog in a pipe, the waves flung both boys away from the fallen tree.

His hand beneath David's chin, Ty pulled the limp floating figure along, at last reaching Heather. She grabbed the front of David's shirt to help keep him afloat. Now swimming in the direction of the waves, they bobbed along fairly fast.

"Is he . . . is he alive?" Heather's voice shook. A big purplish lump puffed out on David's forehead.

Ty breathed hard. "I found a pulse in his neck."

"Thank heavens." She prayed David wasn't hurt as bad as he looked.

Katie darted back and forth along the shore. Heather searched for a place where the rocks wouldn't beat them into monster bait. She kicked harder. She hadn't thought about the Flathead monster until now. That's all they needed.

"Over here," Katie yelled.

Peering through a filter of splashing water, Heather spied an opening in the shoreline where two outcroppings of rock tapered into a deep ravine. Here the craggy boulders parted, leaving smaller, rounder rocks on this portion of the island.

Grasping David tighter, Heather and Ty let themselves be carried along by the waves, working their way, as much as they could, to where Katie paced.

Heather tried to stand as the current drew them in, but another swell smacked her and knocked her to her knees. She cried out as a jagged boulder gashed her ankle.

"Come on," Katie yelled. "The tree!" She jumped into the water, leaping the smaller waves as they crashed into her.

Ty found his footing and dragged David through the swells. Katie and Heather joined him, and with the three steadying each other, they pulled him onto land.

The huge carcass of the Ponderosa Pine ripped free from its rocky base and, answering the call of the waves, rolled toward them sideways like a lance dropped in a giant jousting match.

"Come on!" Ty yelled.

Two girls on one arm, Ty on the other, they dragged David up the bank. Heather stumbled, pulling Katie and David into a heap on top of her. Ty threw his body over all three as the tree smashed against the rocky shoreline with such force that its trunk split in half.

Water and wood exploded into the air, pelting the group with woody shards. A piece embedded itself deep in Ty's shoulder. Lightning cracked the sky.

Reaching around, Ty pulled the large splinter from his shoulder. Blood colored his torn shirt for a moment, but the torrential rain washed the red away.

"Are you okay?" Heather cried.

"Yeah. We've got to find David shelter." Ty knelt behind his injured friend. Pushing him into a sitting position, he grasped

David around the chest and lifted. "Each of you grab a leg and help me." David's head tipped forward limply.

"Is he breathing? Does he need CPR?" Katie searched for a pulse on David's neck.

Still holding onto David, Ty began to drag him. "He drifts in and out, but he was talking to me in the lake, well, sorta— sounded kinda goofy."

Heather shot Ty a worried glance. "He's got that huge bump on his head."

Thunder rumbled above. Although it was still light enough to see, dark clouds made estimating the time of day impossible. Heather guessed it to be around eight. They'd surely be missed by now, but the storm would keep anyone from searching for them.

"Come on, you guys, let's find him some shelter, at least get him away from the water." Ty stared at the sky. "See the lightning?"

Heather and Katie each reached for one of David's legs.

"Oh my gosh," Katie cried and pointed. "Look."

From the knee down, David's jeans were soaked with blood and the toes of his foot faced sideways.

Katie and Heather gasped.

Ty lowered David to the ground. Taking the boat keys from his pocket, he opened the knife that was attached. He cut a hole in David's jeans that reddened by the second, then ripped the opening larger. "Geez!"

Blood gushed from the six-inch gash along the front of David's shin that almost hid the bone that poked out from it . . . almost, but not quite.

"We've got to get him out of the storm—get him warm." Ty carefully straightened David's leg. "Katie, give me your shirt."

"What?"

"You've got a suit on under." With a beckoning hand, he motioned for her to move faster. "It's white and sorta clean."

"It's as clean as we've got." Katie struggled out of her wet knit top and passed it to Ty.

He folded the garment and placed it over David's wound. Removing his own shirt, he tied it over Katie's. "Okay, let's move."

Rain pelted them without mercy.

David groaned.

Katie's fingers dug into Heather's arm. She choked back a sob. Don't fall apart, Heather told herself. Stay strong. Don't think about how pale David looked . . . how hopeless their situation was.

"Try to carry both legs together." Ty took his position at David's head. "Kinda make a cradle for his legs with your arms."

A muscle in Heather's side cramped as they lifted David, carefully moving him inland away from the waves and the downed tree that had almost claimed him.

Blood trickled down Ty's back from the puncture in his shoulder.

Heather's throat burned. With a prayer in her heart, she scanned the landscape, searching for anything that could pass for shelter.

Lightning streaked the sky, illuminating what appeared to be a large anvil-shaped outcropping of rock with a hollowed-out dark space beneath the overhang. A cave?

"Over there," Heather croaked. Stones and twigs cut into her bare feet.

"Glad you have eagle eyes," Ty said.

They lay David in a three-sided rock enclosure. The dry part was only about six feet by eight, but large enough to provide him some shelter, and the floor was dirt-packed, not rocky.

Ty knelt by his friend. "We've got to elevate his leg." He glanced from side to side, his gaze settling on Heather. "Let me have your life jacket, okay?"

Quickly she undid the buckles and slipped out of it, shivering since, though soaked, the jacket had blocked the wind.

"Thanks." Ty placed it beneath David's leg. "Okay, who wants to press here." He held the heel of his hand on David's groin. Katie and Heather glanced at each other.

"You better do it, Heather," Katie said, crimson coloring her cheeks."

"It's to help stop the bleeding." Ty shook his head.

Heather moved to Ty's side and placed her hand where his had been. "How do you know all this first aid stuff?"

"Classes," he said, "and experience with animals on the ranch."

"You'll be a great vet someday." She smiled, then turned back to David. "Gosh, he needs a hospital. If only this storm would let up."

"I know. Until then, though, we're all he has." Ty wrapped his shirt tighter around David's leg.

"Scary thought." Heather moved off her knees to sit closer to David. She kept her hand pressed to his upper leg. "Is the bleeding slowing any?"

"A little, maybe. It doesn't seem to be coming through the shirt as much." Ty glanced up at Katie. "Will you run down and find the other life jackets . . . oh, and the picnic basket. Maybe there's something in there we can use—napkins, that tablecloth."

"David's camera . . ." Katie grimaced.

Heather's mouth twitched. "Knowing David, he'd love a picture of all this."

"Wish he could take it himself." Katie hugged her arms around her middle and swallowed hard.

"I hear you." Her feet were freezing. Heather positioned one on top of the other.

Ty cleared his throat and stood. "I sure could use those jackets."

"I'll be back." Katie headed off through the downpour. Mud streaked the long legs that only hours before had been bathed in Coppertone SPF4 tanning lotion.

Ty shook his head. "I really don't know where to start. We need blankets, bandages, painkiller . . ."

"Let's think." Heather ran her fingers through her wet hair, pushing it out of her eyes. "Surely there are things here we can use. What would MacGyver do?"

"Who?"

Lightning slashed the sky. Rain puddled in front of their cave and trickled down one of the inside walls.

"He's a guy on TV reruns. He makes things out of practically nothing."

As quickly as she could with bare feet, Katie scurried back with the other jackets, the seat cushion David had used in the lake, and the picnic basket. "Here you go, master, sir."

Patting the top of her head, Ty told Katie thanks and took the jackets and seat cushion from her. He put one of the life jackets under David's leg, down by his heel, and the cushion under his head. Ty rummaged through the basket, taking out the large plastic bowl and removing the camera. "Looks like it made it." He placed the camera in the driest corner of the cave. "Kate, one more errand. I'll need some water. Will you run down and fill this container? We'll see if we can clean him up a bit. Ourselves too. Who has injuries?"

Katie rubbed the bottom of her foot against the calf of the other leg. "I'm pretty much in one piece." She shrugged. "My makeup lady is going to have a fit, though. I don't think Kim is supposed to look like she's tangled with tigers."

"Let's hope you'll be back in time for your next performance." Ty touched the toes on David's injured leg. "Ooh! Cold. That's not good." He loosened the makeshift bandage.

"Hopefully we'll have David back in time for whatever he's going to be late for too." Katie grabbed the plastic bowl and started off on her next errand.

"I'll second that," Heather said.

"How about you?" Ty asked her. "Any injuries?"

Heather had a cut on her ankle and scratches all over her legs. She touched a sore spot on the top of her head. Apparently, the blood that had spilled down her face earlier had clotted in her hair. No red came off on her fingers. "Nothing worth mentioning. You do, though. Your back."

"I'll live." He shook his head. "I wonder when David will wake up."

"He's going to be in so much pain," Heather said, changing hands against David's leg. "You said he was talking to you in the lake?"

"Yeah. Crazy like, but talking. We better get him fixed up as much as we can before he comes to. And we've got to get him warm. We need a fire. Wish we had matches." He took a quick intake of breath. "There were matches in the boat, in a pocket right next to driver's seat."

"Do you think they're still there—and dry?"

"Might be. They were in an old prescription bottle." He paused for a moment, then continued. "Remember that bright red tote bag Mom made me put in the boat the first day we took Old Rusty Bucket out?"

"Yes. I'll bet there's something in there we can use, or why else would she have brought it to us?" For the first time since they'd arrived on the island, Heather felt a tiny trickle of hope seep through her.

"I'm going to take a look—see if it's still there and if I can get to it."

Heather grabbed hold of Ty's leg. "Be careful. The boat's turned over and caught on those rocks."

"Maybe I can wiggle under."

"I hate the sound of that. Don't take any chances." She let go of him.

"Careful is my middle name." He started down toward the beach.

"Yeah, sure." Heather squeezed her eyes shut for a moment, then gathering strength, turned her attention to David. She studied the bump on his forehead. Had it grown larger? She took a deep breath. His face was so very pale. Never had she seen him so helpless and vulnerable. Why wouldn't this stupid storm stop?

Katie came back with the plastic bowl full of water. "How is he?"

"Still the same."

"Where's Ty going?"

"To the boat. He said there might still be matches in a pocket near the driver's seat."

"Matches would be good, also parkas, sleeping bags, a doctor, especially a doctor." Katie touched David's cheek. "He's freezing."

"Why don't you lay down by him and see if you can warm him up?" Heather said.

"You want me to?"

"Unless you'd rather put pressure on this artery."

"I'll lay by him." Katie dropped to the ground.

Peering out through the storm into the darkness, Heather said, "At least we're out of the rain. Wish Ty would get back."

"Maybe I should go check." Katie propped herself up on one elbow.

"Maybe we both should," Heather said.

"Maybe you both should what?" Ty came up out of a gully.

"About time you got back." Katie struggled to her feet.

"I was only gone a few minutes." He carried a large tote bag, which looked damp but not dripping.

"Sure seemed longer." Heather shivered.

"Look what I have." Ty pulled a small plastic container out of his pocket and shook it. "Matches, and I think they're dry."

Heather steepled her fingers under her chin, peering skyward. "Thank you, God."

Katie nodded. "I guess we're not going to freeze to death after all."

"And look what else." Ty knelt, unzipped the tote bag and pulled out an old Army blanket and several towels. "They're still mostly dry. And . . ." He held up a finger. "Bless Mom's heart. Take a gander at this."

"A first aid kit." Standing, Heather reached for the blue plastic pop-open container.

Katie took the blanket from Ty and laid it across David. "Mom's got intuition, big time." Prying the top off the prescription bottle, Ty dumped out a couple of matches. "We better get a fire started. Katie . . ."

"I sense another errand coming." Arms flexed, she posed like a body builder.

"Will you find something to start a fire with? Look under overhanging ledges and beneath dense undergrowth. Heather and I will see to David's leg, unless you'd rather do the doctoring."

Leaning back, Katie held up both hands. "That's okay. I'm not much in the medical department and . . . and I guess I don't want to see . . . oh, never mind."

Heather glanced at Katie, who tucked the blanket around David's sides, then quickly turned away. Taking a deep breath, she headed up an incline into the pines.

Ty turned to Heather. "Let's see what we have in here." He took the kit from her and opened it.

"How did you get this stuff?" she asked. "I thought Old Rusty Bucket was smashed against the rocks."

"The back of it is, but the front's being held by some boulders. I just crawled up under and helped myself. Look. We've got roll bandages, antiseptic, these little square things."

"So we won't be sailing out of here anytime soon?"

"Not likely." Ty removed the shirts wrapped around David's injury, slipping his own drenched garment back on.

"Too bad about your boat," Heather knelt by Ty "Ooh. That looks bad."

"At least the bleeding's stopped."

"Be thankful for small favors, huh?"

"We could use more."

Ty washed off as much blood as he could, pulled down gently on David's ankle to straighten the protruding bone, and redressed the wound with clean bandages from the first aid kit.

Heather wrapped the tablecloth from the picnic basket around David's leg, then she and Ty splinted his bad leg to his good one using roll bandages and part of the ski rope. David moaned some during the procedure but never fully regained consciousness.

"That should do for now. He'll need surgery, I'm afraid," Ty said. "Come morning, if the storm's over, the folks will probably have everyone, with the exception of the League of Senior Citizens, out searching for us."

Katie returned with an armful of branches, twigs and wood chips and positioned them on the ground. With the help of paper napkins from the picnic basket, she soon had a fire crackling just inside the cave.

"Good job, Katie." Heather gave her a thumbs-up.

"Summer camp." Katie blew on the tops of her fingernails, polishing them against her collar bone. She stole a look at David. "How is he?"

Heather touched his hand. "Still freezing."

"Let's get that wet shirt off him." Ty worked David into a sitting position and they pulled off the soaked shirt. Heather wrapped him in a dry towel and they lay him down again, covering him with the blanket.

Ty held a towel out for Heather. "You better do the same. You've got a suit on under don't you?"

"Yes." Turning around, she pulled off her knit shirt and backed into the towel.

He draped it around her, his hands momentarily resting on her shoulders. "Snuggle up next to him and see if you can warm him with your body heat. We don't want him to go into shock."

He handed his sister a towel. "You too, Katie."

"Me?"

"He's got two sides and I'll be darned if I'm going to cuddle up next to him."

"Chicken," Heather said.

"Darn right," Ty said. "Great fire, Katie. I'm impressed."

"As well you should be." She pulled a towel around herself, sat on the ground and following Heather's lead, curled up next to David.

"That shouldn't be too hard." Ty almost seemed disappointed that the girls had acted so promptly. "I'd think you two would consider him a pretty good-looking guy."

Katie put her arm over David's middle and peered up at Ty out of the corner of her eyes. "He is. Don't you think so?"

"Guys can't tell about other guys."

"Rest assured." Katie winked at Heather. "He is."

Wondering if David would ever notice how handsome Ty was, Heather smiled.

Just then David groaned. "My leg . . . oh . . . ouch." He tried to sit up, but both girls held on to him. His head rolled from one side to the other. A thin smile touched his lips. "All right," he said and drifted off again.

"Nothing wrong with his mind, anyway." Ty bent to pick up more wood. "Ouch."

Heather jumped up. "Your shoulder. I'd better have a look."

"I'll be okay." He tossed the branch on the fire.

Heather moved closer. "Take off that wet shirt."

"Excuse me?" He turned to face her.

"Take off your shirt." She reached to unbutton it. The towel around her fell open. She bent to place it over David.

"What ya got in mind?" Ty asked.

She slugged him on the arm. "This is strictly medicinal."

"Okay. Okay." His eyes dropped from her face and his brow raised.

She glanced down to where his gaze had settled.

Light from the fire flickered off the shiny surface of her necklace.

She brought her hand to her throat. Normally she didn't wear her necklace where Ty or David could see, especially now that the chain carried both charms, but clad in only a bathing suit, there'd been no place to hide it.

"I like your necklace," Ty said, his eyes soft.

"You do?" She fingered the charms . . . no, she fingered one charm. Only Ty's silver key remained there on the chain. Where was David's horse charm? Had it been lost in the lake? A sliver of sorrow jabbed her.

"Thanks." Heather smiled up at Ty. Then taking him by the upper arms, she turned him around. "Sit."

"Arf, arf," he said and did as instructed.

Later that night Heather awoke, shivering. Although she and Katie were still snuggled next to David, the fire had burned low. She rubbed her arms.

The rain had finally stopped. She still heard waves beating against the shoreline, but they sounded less threatening.

Ty slept with his back against the cave wall. Before they'd bedded down for the night they'd dried what clothes they could on a limb propped up next to the fire. Ty had reclaimed his shirt as had Heather and Katie. They'd tried to wash it off, but David's blood still stained Katie's.

Heather added wood to the fire and checked David's forehead. Thank heavens he still had no fever. Every once in a while during the night he'd awakened, mumbled something unintelligible, then drifted off again.

She prayed they'd be found the next morning and be able to get him to the hospital. Nestling into her spot next to him, she closed her eyes. They must have all been exhausted from their ordeal in the lake. How else could they sleep so soundly on the hard, cold ground?

What was that? Heather thought she heard a sound, something different from the usual island sounds—wind whipping through the trees, waves beating the shore. A click—a horse's hoof striking a rock. It couldn't be.

There it was again. Yes, and another sound like a horse blowing air through its nostrils. No mistaking that.

She strained her eyes into the darkness. Nothing. She lay back. Surely, her ears played tricks on her. She cuddled close to David.

A horse whinnied, she was certain. He stood by the fire, the flames reflecting off his red coat. Red coat? What was Ty's stallion Rocky doing here?

Or was it Rocky?

CHAPTER
TWENTY-THREE

Heather's eyes flicked open. The fire had burned to embers again, but signaling dawn's approach, a gold-tinged eastern sky haloed the tops of the Mission Mountains. She sat up, laying her towel over Katie and David. Both still slept as did Ty, who now lay stretched out on the ground, his bare feet protruding from torn jeans. Although gray clouds still streaked the sky, the whitecaps on the lake had disappeared.

The horse! She'd seen a horse last night, a horse that looked like Rocky. He'd been standing next to the fire watching her with wide, white-rimmed eyes. He'd acted as if he wanted to come closer, but had been too afraid.

Wait a minute. How silly was that? Rocky was home in the Taggert barn where she wished she, Katie, David and Ty were. She covered her eyes with her palms, massaged her forehead, then dragged her hands down over her face. Freedom's Choice looked just like Rocky and he was . . . he was . . .

No. She'd been dreaming. She dreamed about horses a lot. She'd even dreamed about Rocky before. Sure. That was it. She'd been so tired—still was. Everyone else remained asleep. Smart. They'd all be needing their strength for whatever lay ahead today.

Heather touched David's forehead. Still cool. She studied his leg. No blood showed through the makeshift dressings. David moaned slightly. Knowing how much pain he'd be in when he came to, Heather hoped he'd remain unconscious a while longer.

Easing back down, she closed her eyes, but the vision of her dream replayed itself in her mind. She sat up. Then stood. Ooh. Her feet hurt, as did her legs. Glancing down, she saw why. Her legs and particularly the bottoms of her feet were criss-crossed with scratches and tiny cuts from her barefoot travels on the rocky ground. She looked longingly at the left-over bandages in the first aid kit. No. They'd have to save those for David if help didn't arrive today.

She placed some of the wood they'd gathered the night before on the embers and stopped short. There in the mud, near the fire, hoofprints all but jumped out at her. She hadn't been dreaming. She had seen a horse. She took in a deep breath, then let the air out slowly. Could that horse have been Freedom's Choice?

As she tried to decide whether to wake Ty with her discovery or to see if she could follow the hoofprints herself, she heard a loud, far off humming. It was a minute before she realized the sound was a plane flying overhead.

"Ty!" she cried. Forgetting the soreness of her feet, she darted down to the shoreline, waving her arms and shouting. "Here. We're down here."

Leaping up, Ty joined her, followed by Katie, who waved a towel above her head. "Did they see us?" she cried.

"They're turning. Look." Ty pointed.

As the yellow floatplane passed overhead, its wings dipped back and forth in acknowledgment. It circled once more before disappearing.

"Where'd they go?" Katie's naturally curly hair stood out from her head like a lion's mane.

"I suspect they'll send someone back in a boat." Ty flexed the shoulder Heather had doctored the night before. "Let's get back to David." Picking his way carefully, he started up the hill.

Katie still stood on the shore watching the disappearing plane. Waves, much smaller now, washed against her legs.

"Ty." Heather caught up with him. "I saw a horse last night."

"A horse? You're kidding. Where?"

"By the campfire."

"There are horses on this island, remember?"

"I know, but he looked like . . . he looked just like Rocky, or . . . Freedom's Choice," she whispered.

Ty chuckled. "Are you sure you weren't dreaming?"

"I thought maybe I was until I saw fresh hoofprints this morning." She grabbed his arm. "Come on, I'll show you."

"Show him what?" Breathing hard, Katie caught up with them.

"Well, I'll be darned." Ty stopped short at the mouth of the cave. "Look who's awake."

David had pulled himself into a sitting position, slid over to his camera and now held it up, ready to sight through the view finder. A large lump spread across one side of his forehead over an eye surrounded by purplish green. "Smile," he said and clicked the shutter.

Both Katie and Heather hurried to him.

"Are you okay?" Katie dropped down next to him.

Heather claimed his other side. "That's quite a shiner. How's the leg? Do you want me to hold the camera for you?"

"Tell you what. If I don't think about something else besides my leg, you're gonna see a grown man cry." He handed the camera to Ty who stood above them. "Take a picture of us for posterity, will you?"

"Oh, my hair," Katie cried and tried to smooth it.

"You look better messed up than the rest of us do on a good day." Heather knew her own hair was way beyond worry.

With an arm around each girl, David pulled them close. "You both look amazing."

Ty cleared his throat. "How do you work this thing?" He held the camera at arm's length.

"It's set on automatic so just point and shoot. That little button on the side . . ." Closing his eyes, he tipped his head forward. "Ooh, ouch," he said through clenched his teeth. "It hurts when I breathe."

Ty opened his mouth.

"Don't say it," David returned.

"What?" Ty blinked.

David forced a smile. "I don't remember much, Ty, but I think I owe you my life."

For a moment no one spoke as Ty's expression sobered. Then he cleared his throat. "It was my turn to do the saving," he said, and snapped the picture.

A shiver trailed up Heather's spine as she remembered their experience the summer before when Ty had suffered a madman's beating. She, Katie and Ty could have used David's help then, but, of course, he'd been in Utah.

"I can't take all the credit," Ty said. "These two helped a lot."

"I seem to remember that." David smiled at one girl, then the other. "Do you think it would do any good if I told them I feel a chill coming on?"

Ty handed David the camera. "You could try."

Katie blushed.

Heather nudged David's arm. "Behave."

His smile faded. He grimaced and reached down to touch his leg, still wrapped in the crude bandage. Not much could be seen of the injury, but angry red scratches and purplish green bruising traveled up his leg to where Ty had torn open the pant leg of David's jeans to care for his injury. "I'm assuming that the plane I heard saw us and we're about to be rescued."

"Yep. I think we're saved," Ty said. "Now we won't have to hike to one of those cabins on the other side of the island."

Heather took a deep breath. Thank goodness. She didn't dare think about how another day without medical attention would have affected David.

With a groan, David lay back down. "I hope they bring pain pills—lots and lots of pain pills."

Heather and Katie gathered the towels and life jackets to position his head and leg. Heather stroked his cheek.

"Did you say you saw hoofprints?" Ty asked her.

"I did." Heather leaped up. "Right there." She pointed.

Leaning over to study them, Ty spun around when he heard a motor and saw the big white bulky-looking boat heading their way. "Okay. We got ourselves some rangers." He picked his way toward shore, waving as they approached. Katie did the same.

Heather saw Bea and Wells leaning over the railing of the craft, which looked pretty much like a big fishing boat except it was surrounded by what seemed to be a huge inner tube. Heather stayed behind so Ty and Katie could have some time with their parents before she and David interfered. Bea would have leaped into the water to greet her children had Wells not restrained her.

The tallest of the two rangers edged the boat up next to a wall of rocks, throwing out ropes to secure it. Wells and a second ranger climbed over the bow of the craft and jumped onto the shore. Katie leaped into Wells's arms. Ty joined in a three-way hug. Then he pointed toward the cave. The stocky ranger returned to the boat, where the first ranger handed him a large bag. He slipped its strap over his shoulder.

Katie climbed into the boat with Bea. Ty followed Wells and the ranger.

Wells took Heather into his arms when he saw her. "We've been so worried," he said. Dark circles showed beneath his eyes and his cheeks were hollowed.

"Thank you for coming—all of you." Heather glanced at the ranger, a solidly built man with a bushy mustache and thick graying hair.

"Heather, this is Hank Rollins. Hank, Heather Chambers."

"Glad to meet you," she said. "Really glad." Her heart hurt when she thought about what Wells and Bea must have gone through the night before, having two of their children missing.

"Bea kept telling me that if something had happened to any of you, she would feel it," Wells said. "She was just acting brave, though, so I wouldn't be so worried."

"I'm sorry." Heather touched his arm. "You stress a lot about your kids when I'm around."

"What's that?"

"Last summer," she reminded.

Wells chuckled. "Oh. You mean Charlie Phipps . . ."

"I'm starting to get a complex."

Wells tucked her arm in his as they worked their way up the pathway. "At least we've had happy endings, well, sorta happy endings. Is David hurt badly?"

"Leg's broken." Ty came up behind. "We had to splint it."

"He's hoping you brought pain pills," Heather told Hank, whose biceps stretched the fabric of his short-sleeved blue uniform.

"I'll bet I can find some."

When they reached David, he'd apparently found renewed strength. Once again he sighted through the lens, taking shots in all directions. He lowered the camera as they walked in and nodded a greeting. "Am I ever glad to see you two. You wouldn't happen to have pain pills, would you?"

They secured David on the portable stretcher Ranger Hank had pulled from the bag and carried him to the boat. With hugs and kisses, Bea greeted David and Heather almost as warmly as she had her own children.

"Now we can call Kevin and Laura, and your parents, David," she said. "I couldn't bear to contact them last night. Actually, David, I wouldn't have known where to call your mom and dad."

The rangers came up with pain medication and settled David on a padded bench in the boat's cabin.

While everyone fussed over him, Heather felt a tiny tug in her matted hair at the nape of her neck. Her fingers investigated.

So that was where David's horse charm had hidden. Chuckling at her luck, Heather couldn't help feeling a twinge of joy, not only that she hadn't lost the charm, but that Ty hadn't seen it the night before.

Standing back from the others, she worked the little silver horse free from her hair, pulled the necklace over her head and slipped the chain and both charms into the pocket of her cutoffs.

Moments later, they were headed for home. Katie and Bea opted to stay in the cabin with David, while Ty, Wells, the rangers and Heather rode outside.

As they bid farewell to the island and Old Rusty Bucket for now, Ty said, "Look, Heather. There's the horses."

Four horses stood on a ridge above—a paint, a buckskin, a bay and a black—not one of them looking even remotely like a red stallion.

CHAPTER TWENTY-FOUR

After surgery to repair his broken leg, David stayed in a Kalispell hospital for two days. The doctor would have preferred him to recuperate there longer, but upon David's solemn pledge to remain with the Taggerts babying his leg for another week, the doctor relented.

Since David's parents were in Europe on business and would have been unable to look after him, Bea, and whenever possible, Katie, hovered over David like kids with a new pet. Heather found herself busy in the barn with Ty and the horses. She couldn't determine whether she went voluntarily or if Ty just needed her help more urgently. Besides, David had Bea and Katie.

"I've got to spend some quality time with David," she told Possum one day. She still discussed certain important personal issues with her big gelding. Sometimes a listening ear with no threat of commentary helped mend the moment.

He could have been trying to rid himself of a fly, but Possum nodded. "Yes, you do. After all, isn't David the one you're supposed to love?" his eyes seemed to say.

Possum did have a way of getting to the root of the matter. She had been spending more time with Ty than with David and that probably gave both of them wrong impressions.

"Do you want to ride into town with me to get a couple bags of grain?" Ty rested his arms on the top of the half-door to Possum's stall. "Maybe we could grab a bite after."

"I'd better check on David." She raked the pitchfork through the remaining sawdust.

Ty's lips thinned. "Don't you think Mom and Katie have that covered?"

"No." Heather stopped cleaning Possum's stall and stared Ty straight in the face. "*I* need to check on him."

Tapping his hands on the stall door, Ty leaned back. "Okay, Heather. I get the picture." He turned and headed down the aisle.

Had there been a choice? Had she made it? Then why did she have a twist in her stomach? The time had come for her to get all thoughts of Ty out of her mind. She was, after all, promised to David.

She finished her barn chores in silence—even conversation with Possum ceased. Returning to the house, she entered the downstairs family room where Bea had set up the hide-a-bed so David could rest near the TV during the day.

Their backs propped against pillows, Katie sat next to David and peered into the screen of his laptop computer. They smiled back and forth at each other, pointing and chuckling. Heather noticed how fast her breathing had become. Was this how Ty felt when he saw her with David?

"Hi, Heather." David held out a hand for her. The cast on his leg came to his knee, but he'd been able to get around by himself on crutches even though the doctor had recommended complete bed rest. On the good patient scale of one to ten, David had rated about seven. Had it not been for his computer and being able to download the pictures he'd taken, David would have scored a two or less. "Come join us. I've got some great photos."

He tugged her onto the bed next to him, on the side opposite Katie. "Look at this shot of you and Ty on each other's horses."

"Neat picture." Katie glanced at her watch. "Oh, my gosh. I've got to go." She stood. "See you both later." Jogging off, she took the stairs to the front room above two at a time.

David watched Katie go, then turned to Heather, squeezing her hand.

"I've missed you. I guess you've had a lot to do in the barn lately." His eyes, so blue, matched the color of his shirt almost perfectly.

"It doesn't look as if you've suffered much." She nudged his arm.

"Katie and Bea have been great." David stared at her intently.

"What?" The muscles in the back of her neck tightened.

Releasing her hand, he put his arm around her, pulling her close. "I love you, Heather."

"I love you too." She tilted her head. She really did love David. She always would and if it hadn't been for Ty . . .

"But? . . ." he asked.

"But what?" Her pulse raced.

Since the screen saver had come on, he clicked the mouse on the computer he held on his lap. "Look at this picture."

She straightened to get better light. It was another view of her on Roxie and Ty riding Image—one of the pictures David had taken at the horse show in Kalispell.

"Do you see it?" He shifted the position of his broken leg on the mattress. Katie had autographed his cast, "your friend always" in red ink. Heather had yet to sign it.

"See what?" She squinted.

"Katie even mentioned something about it."

Heather held out her hands, palms up. "About what?"

David nodded his head slowly. "Look at the two of you—you and Ty—you and Ty together—your expressions when you watch the other." Keeping hold of her shoulder, he whispered in her ear. "You and Ty belong together."

She turned to stare at David. "What did you say?" Her heart lodged in her throat.

"You and Ty belong together. You love him, don't you?" His brows raised.

She swallowed.

He cocked his head.

"Yes." Her voice cracked. She cleared her throat. "But I love you, too."

"And I love you. It's a different love, though, isn't it? You love me like a friend. A close friend—a brother. But Ty? It's not the same with him, is it?"

"Ty's a good friend." Heather stuck out her chin.

"Ty's your best friend—your best friend and more. You see, that's the difference between Ty and me. It's the 'more.' I could never be everything to you, but Ty can . . . *Ty is.*"

Tears trickled down Heather's cheeks. "But . . . but . . . how come you know all this?"

He touched her face. "It was pretty plain once I got to noticing."

She chewed her lip. "Really?" Now that she thought about it, sincerely thought about it, all of the emotions she'd experienced since coming to Montana made complete sense.

"Really."

"I'm so sorry." She studied his handsome face, remembering all the good times they'd shared. Right now all she could remember were the good times.

"I guess the better man won."

"Don't say that." She lay her hand across his middle. "You're both the best man."

He pulled her into a hug. "I love you, Heather."

"I love you, too." She snuggled next to him, putting her head on his shoulder. He stroked her hair. Cuddling for a moment seemed the perfect way to end a relationship Heather felt certain had meant as much to David as it had to her.

"Ty, are you down there?" Katie called from the top of the stairs.

Heather pulled away from David so fast she nearly fell off the hide-a-bed. "He's not here."

"What?" Katie bounded down the stairs, changed and ready to go. She wore her hair in a high ponytail. No doubt she'd play "Kim" tonight. "Where is he?"

"We haven't seen him." Heather's mind raced. Katie had thought Ty was here? Did that mean she'd seen him nearby? Oh no. "He was in the barn a while ago."

"I just saw him start down these stairs. Then the phone rang and I ran to answer it." Katie's ponytail swung from side to side as she spoke. "I wonder where he went?"

Pursing her lips, Heather thought about what she and David had been discussing. Had Ty overheard David and her professing their love to each other? "I don't know, Katie," Heather forced herself to say.

"Well, okay. Allie will just have to call back." Katie started up the stairs. "I'll probably stay in Bigfork tonight. See you tomorrow."

Allie! Why was she calling? Heather felt heat rise in her face. Settle down, she told herself. Allie was probably wondering about lessons. She had every right to call.

"Take care." David watched Katie until she disappeared out of sight. When he turned back to Heather, he was still smiling.

A giggle rose inside Heather. She covered her mouth with her hand as her eyes grew wider. "It's the 'more' you don't feel for me too, isn't it?"

He lifted a brow. "What?"

"The 'more.'" She lay her head against his shoulder. "You know."

He put his hand over hers. "You're really something."

"I know." She wrinkled her nose. "Let's have another look at that shot of Ty and me."

He clicked on a new picture, but instead of Ty and Heather, it was one of Allie and Ty at the horse show.

"You could have gone all day without showing me that. Change it, hurry, change it." Heather scratched her head. "Do you think Allie's cute?"

"She is quite attractive."

Heather rolled her eyes. "Wrong answer. You're supposed to say no, she's rather plain. She's not nearly as cute as you."

"She isn't as cute as you."

"Good one. You get an 'A+' on that prompted answer."

Smiling, David selected another picture.

"Oh! Look at my hair . . . and the rest of me—hideous." Heather pointed to a photo of Katie, David and herself in the cave, when David had been trying to get his mind off his pain. "Do you even remember when we took that shot? You were pretty out of it."

"You could never look hideous." He touched her jaw with the tips of his fingers, turning her head to face him. "And sure I remember. I'm the one who asked Ty to take the picture."

"That's right. I guess I was pretty out of it too."

"You? How so?"

"That night we spent on the island, I thought I heard horses. I could have sworn I saw Ty's red stallion standing by the fire." She leaned against the back of the couch which, being part of a hide-a-bed, now acted as a headboard. "The next day, just as we were leaving in the boat, I saw four horses, but none of them looked even remotely like Rocky."

David studied her. "You dreamed of a red stallion standing by the fire—a red stallion that resembled Rocky? He pawed the ground a couple of times, snorted, then acted like he wanted to come closer."

Her mouth fell open. "Yeah. How did you know?"

"I must have had the same dream."

A current of excitement shot through Heather, bringing her head up straight. "You saw the red stallion?"

"I did. I'd forgotten about it until you mentioned it. I had so many weird dreams on the island I figured the horse was just one of them."

"Are you thinking what I'm thinking?" She chewed her bottom lip.

"I probably am." He held up his index finger. "We have a missing horse that looks like Rocky." He held up his middle finger. "Now we have a mystery horse . . . who looks just like Rocky." His eyes narrowed. "If that horse is real, he just might be . . ." He nodded. "Freedom's Choice," they said together.

"I can't believe it." She stood. "I've got to tell Ty."

"About the horse?"

"Yes . . . about the horse." She sighed. "You don't suppose Ty heard us earlier, do you?"

"Heard us saying . . . He might think we care about each other."

"We do care about each other." She patted his cheek. "I thought we went over that."

"Just checking. I still have to get used to the idea that we're not together anymore." He pulled a sad face.

She slipped off the ring David had given her, lay it in his palm and closed his hand around it. "Poor baby. I don't think I've ever known you to be between girls before."

He dropped the ring in his shirt pocket and favored her with a broad grin.

At the bottom of the stairway, she turned. "But I have an inkling you won't be that way for long. In fact, I wouldn't be surprised if someone like . . . well, someone exactly like Katie turned up with that ring on her finger."

His mouth fell open.

"Don't act surprised with me."

"I'm not acting." His bewildered expression appeared for real.

"Oh my gosh, maybe you aren't."

"Hey. Katie's a doll and a riot to be round, but until recently I thought you and I were a thing."

"You're serious, aren't you?"

He closed his computer and snapped it shut. "As a judge."

"What?"

"I'm as serious as a judge and I've known a lot of them." He stared at the wall for a moment. "Katie, hmm?" He smiled.

"Of course, you'll have to wait a while for her to grow up." This was working out far better than Heather would have ever figured.

"I'm not opposed to the idea, mind you . . ." He rubbed his chin. "Actually, come to think of it, Katie is pretty grown up."

"She's not quite seventeen."

He moistened his lips. "You're only eighteen and . . .

"Almost nineteen," Heather said.

David nodded. "Almost nineteen, and . . . patience is my middle name."

Heather chuckled. "Of course it is."

"Katie. Interesting—very interesting." David said. "She's young. I'm young. We'll just have to see what happens."

"Better fasten your seat belt." Smiling, Heather stood to leave.

"I hear you."

When Heather climbed to the top of the stairs, she heard Ty's voice. As she drew near she could tell he was talking on the phone.

"I think I can go, Allie. Thank your dad for me. I've been watching for that horse clinic for a long time."

She drew back into the dining room out of Ty's sight range.

"What was that?" he said. "Yeah, it looks like I'll be able to get away for all three days. Leave Friday? Okay. We'll have fun." He chuckled. "I know what you mean. I'll call and make sure we can get the ring."

Ring! What ring? Had Ty bought Allie a ring? Heather wanted to scream. All at once, telling him about the mystery horse seemed totally unimportant.

CHAPTER TWENTY-FIVE

Heather headed to the barn. This was definitely a two-horse depression visit. In times past, she'd sought out Possum, or Image when Possum wasn't available, to share her tales of woe. This afternoon she'd visit them both. Heck! Maybe she'd stop at every stall in the barn. David had a ring for Katie, and now Ty had one for Allie. Two minus two equals zero. That's how many guys she had left. Served her right.

Automatically her hand went to her neck where her fingers touched the chain carrying only one charm—Ty's key. Even before she and David had their talk, she'd removed the horse charm and placed it in her suitcase. Had she known even then that Ty was the guy for her? She wrinkled her nose. Actually, Ty seemed to be the guy for Allie.

She unlatched the gate to Possum's stall and stepped in. He whinnied. Stretching her arms around his neck, she snuggled close, then stood there for several minutes gathering strength.

"Will you be sleeping out here again tonight?" Ty asked, his voice cool—well, of course it was. He had Allie now.

"It's early yet, but what if I do?" The words slipped out before she could catch them.

"Suit yourself." He started for the door.

Darn, he looked good—white western shirt tucked into great fitting jeans. A little grouchy this morning, but she'd driven him to that. Normally he was sweet and kind. "Ty. Wait."

He whirled around, eyes large, head cocked. "What?"

"That red stallion I told you about on the island . . ."

"The one you dreamed about?" His lips thinned.

"David saw him."

"What are you talking about?"

"Until I said something about seeing a red stallion, David thought he'd been dreaming."

Ty turned, came back and leaned a shoulder against the stall wall. "You say you and David both saw him that night we all slept in the cave?"

"Yep. But as it turns out, we weren't sleeping." Without thinking she touched his arm. "Do you think it could be Freedom's Choice?"

He straightened. "I don't know, Heather. I've just been on the phone with Special Agent Campbell."

Her mouth twisted. That wasn't the only person he'd just been on the phone with. "What did he have to say?" And what had Allie been saying?

Possum put his head over Heather's shoulder and she stroked his nose.

"Their tests determined that Anthony Grange died before he entered the water."

"So it wasn't an accident?" Heather asked. "Someone killed him and made it look like he'd driven off the road into the lake?"

"That's what they figured."

"Who do you think did it?" Heather wasn't about to make any judgments where Ty's family and friends were concerned. She'd been there, done that already, last summer.

Ty closed his eyes for a moment, then opened them slowly. "I'm afraid it could have been McCade. I hate thinking he could do such a thing, but having the watch show up on his property makes me wonder if there was a fight or something and the watch got knocked off. I mean Rolex watches just don't come undone. And then there was that pile of hay and that spot where the horse had been tied. With a barn so close, the only reason someone would tie a horse in the forest would be to hide it, don't you think?" He reached across the stall door, ran his finger under the chain that hung around her neck and pulled, bringing the charm to the outside of her shirt.

Was that a smile that flashed across his face, or a smirk? He probably wanted to give the necklace to Allie. "I'll bet that hidden horse was Freedom's Choice and now, somehow, he's on Wild Horse Island," Heather said quickly, ignoring any reference to the necklace.

"Freedom's Choice on Wild Horse Island? Now, that's a stretch," Ty said.

"It's worth looking into, isn't it? I tell you, the horse looked like Rocky, only thinner and unkept, but there was an eagerness about him . . . he didn't act wild."

"I guess it could be Freedom's Choice. Never say never . . . on anything," Ty said.

What did he mean by that? "So who do we tell?" Heather brushed Possum's long forelock out of his eyes. "Montana Fish and Game, the Quarter Horse Association, the FBI, that Randall guy—Matthew Randall—the horse's owner? We could check it out ourselves. I wouldn't care if we don't tell too many people, though, in case it turns out not to be true."

"We could tell Agent Campbell," Ty said.

"Or Officer Tuttle."

They both laughed.

"Funny thing, Agent Campbell mentioned Officer Tuttle quite a bit during our conversation. I think he's taken our skinny cop under his wing."

"Good for him—good for Officer Tuttle." She dug the toe of her boot into the sawdust-covered floor of Possum's stall. "So it was Agent Campbell on the phone." She could have bitten her tongue for asking, but she couldn't keep the words from bursting out. She held her breath, waiting for Ty's reaction.

"On the phone?"

"Yes. Katie said you were wanted on the phone. She came downstairs looking for you."

"Oh. That time it was Allie."

"How's she doing?" Heather asked.

"Fine."

"Good." Short pause while Heather chewed her lip. "How's her horse coming along?"

"Really well."

"Nice horse."

"Yep."

He was as closedmouthed as before. Heather wanted to strangle him. "So . . ."

"So . . ."

Darn him. "Where are you going with her?"

"Who wants to know?"

"What do you mean, who? Aren't you and I the only ones standing here?"

"There's Possum."

Heather took a deep breath. "Okay. Possum wants to know."

He smiled. "Allie's father invited me to go to a Pat Parelli clinic, Possum. Do you think your master would like to come along?"

"Oh sure. You, me and Allie. Cozy."

"I was talking to Possum." He turned to the gelding, took hold of his ear and bent it down like he was talking into it. "Tell your master it's no different than her, me and David."

"There's a huge difference." Her hands went to her hips.

Ty tipped his head. "And what would that be?"

"Well, you and David are friends," Heather blurted. "I hardly know Allie, and if I did I probably . . ." Enough said. Heather's insides did a flip-flop. Ty was enjoying this far too much. "Let's get back to the horse on the island. When are you going to call Agent Campbell?" she asked. "How do you think Freedom's Choice—if it is Freedom's Choice—got on the island?"

"Good question, just one of the many unanswered mysteries."

"I'll say. Do you have theories?"

"I think Freedom's Choice was here." He shrugged. "Well, we know he was here or how else would there be a Jasmine, who we now know is Freedom's Choice's baby? I think Freedom's Choice was the horse tied to the tree in the forest—the horse someone was trying to hide. I think Anthony Grange was in the forest too because of his watch. Now all we need to figure out is how a live Anthony Grange in the forest ended up a dead Anthony Grange in the lake."

"Do you think McCade and Grange had a fight?"

Ty shrugged. "It's a possibility."

"Maybe it was an accident. Maybe McCade and Grange were fighting and Grange fell and hit his head. Do you think it was about Freedom's Choice?" Heather asked.

"I guess we'll never know."

"Do you think that's why he took off?"

"I think before he went anywhere, McCade should have warned me about the colt, left me a note or something in case the cancer was fatal. Instead my old friend just kept me hanging. I can't believe he'd do that."

"Hmm. That is strange. Nowadays he could have just sent an e-mail, no fuss, no bother. All he'd have had to do was switch on the computer."

"Yeah, but he'd have been afraid I wouldn't get the e-mail. You know how he was always asking if I'd ever learned to use the computer."

She grabbed Ty's arm. "Maybe he did leave you a message—on the computer. Why else would he have kept mentioning it?"

Ty's eyes grew wide. "Oh no. I crashed it. Remember?"

She raised a finger. "Not before I copied everything onto a disk. Do you know where that disk is?"

"I think I stuck it in the drawer in the computer table."

"Let's go see. I'll bet David can bring all the documents up on his laptop."

CHAPTER TWENTY-SIX

Heather followed Ty down the stairs leading into the basement family room. At the bottom, he stopped short. Heather rammed into his solid back. Her pulse quickened.

"Oops. I forgot something." He turned to face her, blocking the view into the room.

"What did you forget?" Heather ducked under his arm, looking at what Ty had tried to hide.

Katie sat next to David on the hide-a-bed. He leaned across her, reaching for something near the mattress edge. Her hand rested on his back.

"I thought you had a play tonight," Ty said, frowning.

Glancing at her wristwatch, Katie jumped out from under David's arm. "Shoot. I am late. I've got to dash." She rushed past them, avoiding Ty's narrow-eyed glare.

Not saying a word, he watched as she ran to the top, taking two stairs at a time, and disappeared from view. Then his gaze riveted on David.

Heat shot to Heather's face as a rush of emotion—she wasn't sure what—consumed her. Jealousy? She'd come to Montana promised to David and even though they'd earlier discussed their feelings, here he was with another girl. Sure, he'd freed her—freed her for Ty, but Ty wasn't available. Did she now want David back? Yes? No? No! David deserved someone to love him as much as she loved Ty. She glanced at the rigid set of Ty's jaw. Unaware of her earlier conversation with David, he had probably felt embarrassed having his sister sitting so close to someone else's boyfriend.

Heather cleared her throat. "Can your Mac read disks from a PC?" she asked David.

He flashed her a quick grin. Pushing with his hands, he slid back on the hide-a-bed. "I think so." He glanced at Ty who said nothing, only kept his steady stare leveled on David.

"Where did you say that disk was, Ty? Ty! Shall I run upstairs and try to find it?"

"No. I'll go." Ty started for the stairs. "I'm sure you two need some time together." He made it to the top in what seemed like two leaps.

Heather took a deep breath. "I guess we better tell him about us?"

"I think so. He seems ticked." David tapped a few keys on his computer. "He's just jealous."

"I wish." She hadn't had time to tell David about Allie. "Maybe he just doesn't want you around Katie." With a wide grin, she perched on the edge of his bed. "Just kidding."

After a few minutes, Ty slowly descended the stairs, one step at a time, as if afraid he might interrupt something. "Is this it, Heather?"

"Looks like." Reaching for the disk, she looked it over before passing it to David. "Moment of truth," Ty said.

"Moment of truth?" Still thinking about telling him that she and David were no longer together, her voice shook.

"The disk, Heather," David said.

"Oh, yeah. What am I thinking?"

"What are you thinking?" Ty asked.

Heather recovered quickly. "A few days before you came, David, I put together a billing program for Ty and made up forms for collection letters. There was some other stuff on the drive too, so rather than select, I just backed up the whole thing on this floppy disk." She glanced at Ty. "Turned out to be a good thing since the computer crashed not long after."

There was a hint of a smile, but Ty said nothing.

"Ty and I got to talking earlier," she gave him a sidelong glance, "and now we're thinking that maybe McCade left some message on the computer."

"That's possible, I guess." David clicked the mouse a couple times. "But why would you think that?"

"It didn't dawn on Ty earlier, but in McCade's last letters and when Ty talked with the attorney after his friend's death, they'd ask Ty if he'd learned to use the old computer McCade left. Ty thought it was a strange question. Now we're wondering if he was hinting at something, huh Ty? Ty?" She stared at Ty. Ty eyed David.

David's fingers rested on the computer keys. "You got a problem with me today, Ty?"

Heather coughed.

"Well, since you asked. Why is it every time I turn around you're flirting with Katie? I thought you and Heather were this great and wonderful couple."

Moving the laptop to his side, David straightened. "I guess you thought wrong then, didn't you?" He winked at Heather.

Ty sniffed. "Is Heather or is Heather not wearing your ring?"

David rubbed his chin. "Heather is not."

She held up her hand for display.

"What's going on?"

"I don't know," David said. "What's going on, Heather?"

"Let's look at the disk first." She slid closer to David.

"No! To heck with the disk." Ty put his hand on her shoulder. "You need to tell me."

Heather leaned away. "What difference does it make. You're running off with Allie."

"How did Allie get into this conversation?"

"I overheard you talking to her on the phone. I'm sorry. I couldn't help it. You said something about going away with her."

"I know. I'm going with her and her father to a horse clinic—strictly business. I asked you to come, remember?"

"But what about the ring?" Heather asked.

"What ring?"

"The ring you were making sure to get."

Arms wide, palms up, he shrugged. "We need to work our horses."

"Oh!" Blood drained from her head as realization hit. "A show ring—a ring to ride in," she whispered.

"What did you think I meant?" Ty's eyes sparkled.

"Nothing!"

David chuckled, hid a smile behind his hand, then cleared his throat. "The three of us need to talk."

Ty stared at one, then the other. "We are talking."

David nodded at Heather. "Your witness."

She opened her mouth, but no words came out.

"Oh, for crying in a bucket," David said. "I told Heather she belonged with you and she agreed. That's all there is to it. Now you two quit fighting. I'm an injured man. I need some peace and quiet to recuperate."

For a moment Heather felt like a bone being dropped by one dog, waiting to be picked up by another. David surely seemed to have gotten over her fast. Amazing how rapidly a pretty redhead could mend a broken heart.

"So what do you think, Ty? Don't you agree the two of you belong together?"

"Stop it, David!" She swallowed hard and studied her shoes, afraid to look at Ty. "You're embarrassing me . . . and Ty."

The only thing keeping her from being totally humiliated for making such a scene about Allie was her relief that Ty didn't have a ring for the girl. Courage up, she stole a quick look at him. The lines around Ty's mouth had relaxed. Her heart lifted.

"Okay for you." David drew the computer back onto his lap and clicked the mouse several times. "Hmm. What do we have here? Okay. Looks like there's seven documents—your billing program, a letter . . . no two letters. Now, here's something. Let's see. Hold on." He peered up at Ty, and with a grin, turned the computer so both Ty and Heather could see the screen. "Take a look at that."

Heather drew a quick breath. "Ty. It's a letter to you dated last October. It's got to be from . . . Scroll to the bottom, will you, David? It's from . . ."

"McCade Saxton!" they all said together.

Ty nudged Heather closer to David, making a place for himself. The three of them—Ty and David on either side of Heather, huddled together on the hide-a-bed staring at the screen. Ty read aloud.

> *Dear Ty,*
> *By the time you read this letter, I'll probably be dead. No doubt it's fair punishment for what I did. My brain since the cancer is not what it used to be, but I want to*

*explain what happened while I still can. I owe you that.
I put my trust in the powers above that someday you will
read this letter and understand my actions. I counted on
your computer aversion to give me a chance to leave the
country, since I cannot bring myself to spend my last days
in jail and didn't want to put you in the position of
having to decide whether or not to turn me in. You have
been like a son to me. Try not to judge me too harshly.
When things got out of control, I had little choice. No
horse deserves such a death.*

David turned the computer so Ty could see it better. Ty read
on, his voice tight.

*Here's the story. I'm not proud of my part in it. Maybe
if I'd had a family—a son like you . . . Oh well, that's no
excuse. There is no excuse for what I did.*

*I killed Anthony Grange. I didn't mean to, but under
similar circumstances, I'd do it again. Someone had to
stop him. I couldn't allow what he and Matthew
Randall had planned.*

Heather held up a finger. "That's just what we thought, huh,
Ty?"

He nodded, then continued.

*I've known Anthony Grange since childhood. He was
the kid in school whose name teachers hated to see on
their rolls. A big bully, he'd pick on anyone he felt he
could best in a fight. Last year while visiting home, he
happened to attend a race in which I'd entered Red
Rock. Tony came up and introduced himself, mentioning
that my horse was a dead ringer for a stallion he'd been
handling in Kentucky. I recognized the name "Freedom's
Choice," but I'd never paid much attention to what he
looked like until after that conversation.*

Some time later, I started following Freedom's Choice's career and discovered that Tony was not exaggerating. The two horses looked so much alike they could have been twins. I researched both pedigrees and discovered the stallions actually had a great grandsire in common and they both looked like pictures I found of Rock of Freedom on the Internet. I wondered if Freedom's Choice had Red Rock's cranky disposition but discovered from my reading that he didn't.

As you probably know, Freedom's Choice was scheduled to race against Black Baron and Double Jeopardy in California last August. The whole Quarter Horse world waited. Insured for ten million dollars, the stallion was supposed to have a fatal "accident" while traveling back from California. For Tony's services in bringing about that accident, Matthew Randall promised to pay him a portion of the insurance money. I couldn't understand why they would sacrifice such a horse, who in his lifetime could probably earn plenty of cash, but apparently Randall needed money fast. His business was in trouble because of gambling debts.

Heather's face burned. An innocent animal! How could someone even dream of hurting any animal, let alone a horse so gallant and beautiful as Freedom's Choice.

Shaking his head, Ty went on reading.

Another problem was that Freedom's Choice had suffered two attacks of colic during the previous year. Randall thought the theft and mortality insurance he'd instructed Tony to obtain covered colic, but apparently Tony had opted not to purchase the colic protection and pocketed the difference in premium. Randall almost fired Tony over that but instead drew him into the plot against Freedom's Choice.

On the way to California for the match race, Tony made a detour and tracked me down. That night while in my barn, Freedom's Choice experienced another attack of colic. Fortunately I had the wherewithal to help and we didn't need to call a vet, but the horse was in no shape to race. At this point, Tony's Plan B came into effect.

"He had a Plan B?" David said. "What a guy! Here, Heather, you hold the laptop. It will be easier for all of us to see."

She slid the computer onto her lap and scrolled down. "Makes my skin crawl."

"Mine too," Ty said, and read on.

Unbeknownst to Randall, Tony had decided that instead of Freedom's Choice dying in a burning horse trailer "accident," it would be my horse, Red Rock. Randall would collect his ten million and Tony would get his blood money, which he'd share with me. Freedom's Choice would assume Red Rock's identity. We'd breed my mares to the champion stallion, producing a stable full of great racehorses. No one but us would realize their potential and we'd win a bundle betting on them. Everyone would be happy . . . well, everyone but Red Rock, but I tried to put that out of my mind. If Freedom's Choice died of colic later, so be it. We'd still have his colts and chances were they wouldn't have inherited his weakness for colic.

The plan might have worked. I'm ashamed to admit I actually thought about going through with it. I didn't know then I had a brain tumor. Perhaps I was in the process of losing the ability to choose right from wrong. I can't understand how else I could have considered it. Oh, Rocky had been a bit of a disappointment, never having the speed I'd hoped. He'd cost me a bundle in training and I found myself short of cash, but that was no excuse.

Maybe I was blinded for a moment, thinking about the colts. Though we probably couldn't have raced them in big races where DNA testing existed, imagine the thrill of owning Freedom's Choice's offspring. And having that stallion in my barn, for however long, would have been unbelievable. As luck would have it, though, last fall I only had one mare open—the sorrel I call Cinnamon. We bred her to Freedom's Choice, so if she has a foal by her side when you read this letter, Freedom's Choice is the sire.

Heather drew in a quick breath. "Jasmine."

"Yep. Jasmine," Ty said, exchanging a grin with her. He nodded at the computer and Heather scrolled down.

We kept Rocky tied in the forest in case we had unexpected company. We didn't want anyone to discover we had two red stallions. When it came time to load him into the trailer for his last ride, I couldn't do it. Rocky can be pretty ornery when he wants, but he didn't deserve what had been planned for him, no creature does. When I told Tony I couldn't go through with it, he was furious. "You'll ruin everything," he said and slugged me, knocking me to the ground. We fought for a while, toppling over one another. I thought he had me once and almost gave up, but then my hand closed around something hard—a rock. I smacked him in the head. He went limp.

I was so mad I struck him a couple more times, then pushed him off. I don't think he'd have died if I hadn't hit him those extra times. I wished I could have felt some remorse, but I couldn't come up with any. I just sat there on the dirt with a dead man and two red stallions, one of them "hot." I couldn't take a chance of Freedom's Choice going back to an owner who'd tried to have him destroyed and I'd just killed a man, so I couldn't turn the horse or myself over to the authorities.

I loaded Tony into his truck and attached a broken halter to the inside of the trailer to make it look like a horse had pulled away. I was lucky. The weather cooperated that night. Rain came down in torrents and waves crashed against the shoreline. Passers-by stayed in their homes, out of my way.

Aside from the fact that I spent a pretty miserable night walking home, it was easy. I drove to that spot by Yellow Bay where there's no guardrail and the lake is deepest. I placed Tony behind the wheel, propped a stick on the gas pedal and let her rip. What a sight! The truck and trailer actually sailed through the air before hitting the water and sinking beneath the waves.

Hiding Freedom's Choice was more difficult. Where could I put him that he'd have a chance to be safe and wouldn't be discovered for a while?

"Wild Horse Island!" Heather said.

"Yep," Ty said, and continued.

I'd read enough about Freedom's Choice that I knew he liked water. Tony had mentioned it too. Early one morning, I loaded the stallion in my trailer and hauled him to the west side of the lake where the distance between land and Wild Horse Island was the shortest. I just climbed on his back and swam him across, pulling a canoe behind so I could get back.

"Like you and I swam on Roxie," Heather said to Ty. He nodded without taking his eyes from the computer screen.

He's a fabulous horse. I think he actually enjoyed the swim. I stayed with Freedom's Choice for a day, taking him up into the cliffs. He seemed pretty happy when the other four horses on the island found us. He galloped off after them without so much as a backward glance. I rowed across the channel to where my truck and trailer waited in a secluded grove of trees.

The following week I had to laugh. I read in the newspaper that someone had sighted the Flathead monster in the water near Wild Horse Island. It occurred on the same early morning that Freedom's Choice and I took our swim.

Strange, isn't it? Had those people known what they were actually seeing, it might have been even more newsworthy—the great Freedom's Choice on Wild Horse Island.

"So there's really not a Flathead monster?" Heather said.

"Some people swear there is," Ty said and scratched his head. "I guess we'll never know for sure unless we actually see it ourselves."

David grimaced. "Now there's a happy thought."

"I'll say—especially if we're in the water with it." Heather shivered.

"I'll pass," David said.

"Me too." This from Ty.

David massaged the skin at the bridge of his nose. "What's colic?"

"It's the mother of all bellyaches. Horses can die from it." Heather paused for a moment, thinking, then went on. "But Ty, when we saw Freedom's Choice on the island, he looked pretty good. Do you think he still gets it?"

"Hmm. Good question," Ty said. "It's hard to tell what makes a horse get colic, but I'd guess since he's been running wild, eating sparsely—no hot grain, no hot hay, no stress from racing, no traveling in a cramped trailer from place to place, I doubt that he does."

"I hope not." Heather nodded toward the computer screen. "Looks like there's only a little left."

Ty cleared his throat.

> *It's been a month now and no clue has surfaced regarding Freedom's Choice's disappearance. I'm pretty good at being bad, I guess. I'd like to stick around and watch, but I better get out of here while I'm still functioning. I wonder if I'd known about the cancer before, if things would have been different. Would Tony still be alive? Probably not. But I'll get mine. My doctor tells me I don't have much longer. I have pretty bad headaches now. I've been able to cope so far, but I know my time is limited.*

In a rough, strained voice, Ty went on.

> *I talked to you on the phone tonight, Ty. What a fine young man you are. I'm sorry to involve you in all this, but I'm confident when everything comes to light you'll know what to do. I'm leaving Red Rock, Cinnamon, and her foal, if there is one, in your charge. Take care of them for me. I'd sure like to see that colt, but I guess it's not meant to be.*
>
> *Have a happy, full life. Stay healthy. When it's time, find some sweet young thing and settle down. Try to remember the good things about me, if any come to mind. I value the time we spent together more than you'll ever know. I wish things could have been different.*
> *McCade.*

Heather sat on the top step of the cement stairway leading down to the lake, its water as quiet as that in Possum's trough. The rising sun cast a golden glow across the water and a lazy breeze toyed with wisps of hair around her face. So much had happened since yesterday, she figured she'd better take a minute to sort things through. Pouring out her feelings to the lake, although beautiful beyond imagination, just hadn't cut it. Normally she'd have shared her thoughts with Possum or Image, but she'd been afraid of encountering Ty in the barn.

Day before yesterday, David had said to Ty, "I told Heather she belonged with you and she agreed. . . ."

Ty hadn't even answered. Darn him, anyway. On second thought, maybe she should be glad he hadn't. Perhaps he'd have said, "Yeah, well, too late. I'm with Allie now. Heather had her chance." And he'd have been right. She'd blown it. She really should go home—call Kevin and see if he could come get her since David couldn't drive. She didn't feel confident driving herself and pulling a horse trailer.

Even if David could, he acted as if he didn't want to leave, but why should he? He seemed like a cow with a new salt lick. After all, he had Katie. Ty had Allie. She herself had Possum and

Image. She could live with that. Possum was a pretty good date—heck to get into movies, but great to spend time with just the same. She shook her head. Yeah, sure. Her heart ached. She kinda missed David. She really missed Ty.

For a moment she brightened as she thought about Freedom's Choice. Just before Ty had disappeared yesterday, he'd called Agent Campbell to report what they'd seen. Her ear close to Ty's, she'd listened to the FBI agent's response.

"We'll look into it," Agent Campbell had said, giving away nothing in his tone.

"Do you want some help?" Ty had offered.

"No. We'll take care of it," had been the short reply.

Would they find Freedom's Choice? Would he be all right? Who would the stallion belong to? There'd been enough questions to keep her mind occupied all day yesterday. Then, after Ty had gone somewhere, probably to be with Allie, there had been more.

Heather's eyes narrowed. Even while putting in long hours on both Image and Possum, she'd been unable to keep her mind off Ty. Normally he told her where he was going, usually invited her along, but yesterday he'd been secretive. He even avoided giving Katie an answer when she asked where he was going. Heather shook her head. She'd better reprogram her thoughts to not include Ty.

"They're going to bring him here," a voice behind her said.

Heather jumped, stiffled a little squeal, and stared up at Ty, her cheeks burning. "What? Who?"

"Freedom's Choice."

"They found him?"

"They found a red stallion who might be him." Ty stepped down one concrete stair.

"The stallion I saw?"

"Yep. I guess Agent Campbell pulled some strings and the stallion will stay here while he's DNA tested and until the authorities decide who he belongs to."

"Who do you think he belongs to?" Heather asked.

"Don't know. It'll probably take some court to determine—David will be in heaven—but I'll bet the insurance company will have some claim, paying all that money to his no-good owner."

Heather took in a big gulp of air. "What about Jasmine?"

"Nobody's taking Jasmine." Ty folded his arms across his chest. "We'll have a little court case of our own if anyone tries."

"Good." Releasing her breath, Heather cast Ty a sidelong glance. "I'll bet Allie likes Jasmine, huh?"

"Allie? I don't know. I suppose. Jasmine's a nice filly." Ty picked up a pebble and skipped it across the water. "David had an interesting thought."

"Uh oh." Heather brought her knees up under her chin and hugged her legs. David had probably decided Katie would make a wonderful child bride.

"He said there could be a reward for information leading to the red stallion's return." Ty sat on the step beside her. "David suggested that maybe whoever offered it would give up any claim on Jasmine instead of having to pay. That's saying a reward's been offered, that we'd get it and that the arrangement was okay with you."

"Why me?" Heather asked.

A boat sped by. Waves from its wake rolled in, splashing droplets of water onto the stairs beneath them. Heather laughed as Ty jerked his boots away.

"If the stallion turns out to be Freedom's Choice," he pointed at her, "you're the one who actually found him."

Heather's heart leaped. Didn't it know it wasn't supposed to do that anymore? "We were all on the island that night. Any one of us could have seen him. Of course it's okay with me, silly. Jasmine's yours. No one should ever question who she belongs to."

Ty stood and extended his hand. "Possum and Image were whinnying for you in the barn. I'd have fed them, but I know how particular you are about their menus."

She let him pull her to her feet, but not keep her hand. "Beautiful morning, isn't it?"

He licked his lips. "Couldn't be better."

He probably wished she was Allie. "You're cheerful today." She turned away from him. "Excited about the stallion coming?"

"Kinda. We should know if he's Freedom's Choice real soon. The Wildlife people took a sample of his mane after they caught and loaded him into the trailer on the barge yesterday. I'll bet Agent Campbell's people are running the test right now."

"It's enough to fry the mind, isn't it?" She glanced at him over her shoulder. "Speaking of yesterday, I couldn't find you."

"You were looking?"

"Yeah. Kinda."

"How come?"

How dense was he, anyway? "Habit, I guess. You're usually in the barn." Yesterday she'd looked for Ty. Today after he'd avoided her, probably in favor of Allie, she'd not wanted to see him. Now, here he was. They never could get it right. "So where were you?" She turned to face him.

"I had an important errand." He leaned against the railing separating the lawn and walkway from the lake.

"Really? Care to share?" She couldn't believe how bold she was being—snoopy, more like it. She just had to find out if he'd been with Allie.

"You really want to know where I was?"

She narrowed her eyes at him.

"Do you really, really, really want to know?" He grinned.

"I wouldn't be asking if I didn't." She tried to keep her voice steady.

"How patient are you?"

"Patient?"

"Yeah. How patient?"

"NOT VERY." She accentuated each word.

"Too bad." He pushed his hat back off his forehead. "What happened? Did Possum and Image kick you out?"

She stared at him a minute, then shook her head. "What are you talking about?"

"You're not in the barn. You're usually in the barn. I was looking for you."

"Like I was looking for you yesterday." The breeze blew some hair across her face. Quickly she brushed the lock aside.

"Yep."

"I guess you're not going to tell me, are you?"

"You do know that curiosity killed the cat," he said.

"So help me, Ty! If you don't . . ." Her voice trailed off as she stared at the rear of the house where Katie, assisted by Wells and Bea, pushed David in his wheelchair up the gently rolling, grassy hillside toward the barn. "Where are they going with David?"

Ty shrugged.

"You know, don't you?" Heather asked.

He studied the sky.

"Let's go." She started forward.

"Go where?"

"To the barn. Isn't that where you want me to go?"

Ty smiled.

"The stallion's in the barn, isn't he?" She clapped her hands.

"I don't think so, not yet anyway."

"Yeah, he's there. You can't fool me."

"Can't I?" His brow raised.

"Come on." She grabbed Ty's arm and yanked him along.

Arriving at the top of the hill, Heather searched for David, Katie, Bea and Wells. She couldn't see them, but little spots of color dotted the pathway leading to the barn.

A beautiful long-stemmed red rose lay on the graveled roadway. Heather stooped to pick it up, then held it to her nose. It had a wonderful scent. Just ahead lay a pink rose and farther on, a white one. Heather gathered a bouquet as she and Ty walked.

"Who'd be dropping roses?" She held them out to Ty. "Oooh. Smell."

"Someone sure has good taste in flowers," he said.

Heather sighed. "Probably David. I think he's got a thing for Katie now."

"Really? Look." Ty placed his hands on Heather's shoulders and pointed her toward the entrance of the barn. "There's another rose in front of Possum's stall."

Scurrying to the spot, Heather bent to retrieve a huge pink blossom. Straightening, she glanced into the stall. "Where's Possum?"

"He's in the arena," Ty said. "I asked if I could borrow his stall."

"So you're the one with the flowers. You're giving Possum roses?" She held up the bouquet she'd gathered.

He shook his head. "No. Possum's owner."

"Me?"

"Aren't you Possum's owner?"

"Why are you giving me roses?" She sniffed them, her mind switching into high gear. Sure. That must be it. Her birthday was July 16th. How sweet of him. Even though he liked Allie now, he still remembered her birthday and didn't want to miss it. On July 16th, she'd no doubt be back in Utah.

Ty raised his hat and rubbed his forehead with the back of his wrist. "You're not making this very easy." He replaced the hat.

"Making what easy? Ouch." She sucked the end of her finger. "Thorns."

"Just follow the flowers. Here, I'll hold those for you." He took the roses from her.

She leaned back for a better view and grinned.

"What?" he asked.

"You look cute with flowers."

"Just follow the darn trail of roses."

"Okey dokey." She saluted. "Here's another red one. Oh, here's hot pink. Awesome."

One corner of the stall supported a feeder box. A white rose peeked over its wooden side.

As Heather stepped closer, her heart began to race. Her brain struggled to catch up. What was going on here? There were a lot of roses, dozens, she was sure. Far more than anyone would give for just a birthday and way more than for just a friend. Ty really wasn't the flower type and she wasn't Allie.

Almost afraid to see, she glanced into the manger. On top of Possum's alfalfa dinner rested more roses, and nestled in the bouquet was a beautiful wooden box which looked . . . *which looked exactly like* a jewelry box.

She stared at Ty.

He smiled. "Well, aren't you going to open it?"

"Open it?" Her voice croaked and she cleared her throat.

"Yeah." He stooped to lay the roses he held on the floor of the stall.

Her hand shook as she reached forward to lift the top. It held tight. She drew back faster than if the lid had been on fire. "It's locked."

"Use your key."

"What key?"

Ty ran his fingers under the chain she wore around her neck, pulling the key out from beneath her shirt as he had the night before last. "This one."

Her mouth fell open. "I never figured it would open anything. I thought it was symbolic, sorta like the key to your . . ."

"Heart?" Ty said.

"Well, yeah." The roses gave her courage. "Was it?"

"The key to my heart?" He cupped her chin in his hand. "Yep, and my barometer."

"Your what?"

"I figured since you were still wearing it, you might care for me a little." His hand moved to her shoulder. "It made me feel like maybe I could . . ."

Heather tipped her head. "You could what?" Didn't Ty know how she felt?

"Just try the key," he said.

She pulled the chain over her head and, with fumbling fingers, guided the key into the lock. It turned slightly. Hearing a tiny click, she lifted the lid. Another much smaller box rested within the velvet confines of the first.

When Heather just stood there, Ty lifted the smaller box out, opened it and displayed the contents.

A solitary diamond atop a thick gold band winked at her.

She swallowed. "Is this what I think it is?"

Ty took the ring from the box.

"You're supposed to kneel," came a voice from the other stall.

"Katie! I know." He frowned and shook his head. "You said you'd keep quiet."

"Sorry." Her red curls appeared above the side of the stall momentarily, then sank down again. "Go on."

He rolled his eyes, bent to one knee, placed his hat on the ground and said, "I'll understand, Heather, if you need more time to think this over, or . . ." he frowned, "more privacy. It's a big step, and we're pretty young, but will you . . . will you? . . ."

"Ty, for crying out loud!" came the voice again.

"Katie! Hush up!"

Heather dropped down in the sawdust beside Ty. "Will I what?"

He took a deep breath. "Will you . . . will you do me the honor of becoming my wife?"

Blinking several times, Heather stared at him, then burst into tears. Could anything be more perfect? Kneeling in her favorite horse's stall, amidst wood shavings and roses, the most wonderful man in the world was asking her to marry him. Even after all she'd put him through with David, Ty still loved her, and oh, how she loved him. Warmth and acceptance settled over her and she couldn't speak.

He pulled her into his arms. "Does this mean yes or no?"

She sobbed against his shoulder. "What?"

"I still don't have an answer."

Drawing back, she wiped her eyes. "Nothing . . ." She sniffed. "Nothing would make me happier. Of course I'll be your wife."

He raised one hand, thumb pointing up. "I did it."

Bea and Katie rushed into the stall, followed by Wells, who pushed David in his wheelchair.

Blinking away tears, Heather chuckled. "Anyone else in there?"

"I believe that's everybody." Ty stood, pulling Heather to her feet. "Well, do you want the ring?"

She nodded and held out her hand.

Ty slipped the diamond onto her trembling finger. Then he held her hand to his lips and kissed it.

Smiling up at him, Heather said, "You're pretty sneaky. You give me a key a year ago that really opens something—something so special. How did you know everything would work out?"

"I didn't. I just hoped." He drew her to his side.

Heather held out her newly-ringed finger. "It's perfect—just like I've always wanted. How did you . . ."

"Katie can be a wealth of information."

The redhead shrugged.

Heather grinned. "It's so beautiful, and big. Can we afford it?"

"We can." He picked up a red rose from the manger and, nodding slightly, handed the flower to Heather. "I sure like the sound of you saying 'we.'"

"It's a pretty big ring." David peered up from his wheelchair and pretended to be blinded.

Ty grinned. "I said it before and I'll say it again, Heather's ring from me is bigger than her ring from you."

"It was a promise ring," Katie and David said together.

Heather took hold of Katie's hand. "And look who's wearing it."

Katie blushed.

"I hope you don't mind, Heather." David said. "Like I said before, Katie and I are both pretty young. Shoot. You and Ty are young. I'm the oldest of all of you."

"Uh—I'm older." Wells raised his hand.

David laughed. "You're already married—and to a wonderful woman, I might add. Katie and I decided we'll still date others, but that there may be possibilities here."

"Heather's taken," Ty announced.

With a smile, David nodded. "She sure is."

Heather snuggled against Ty.

"So, Heather, you're sure you don't mind about the ring?" David said.

"Heck no. It fits her better than it did me." She slipped her arm around Katie's waist and they hugged. Then while Katie hugged David, Wells and Bea hugged Heather.

"Wait a darn minute here." Ty retrieved his hat and positioned it on his head. "What about me? Don't I get a hug?"

"I'll give you one," Katie said.

He laughed and took her into his arms. "That was nice but not exactly what I had in mind."

Giggling, Heather threw her arms around them both. "I'll be looking for you later," she whispered into Ty's ear.

"Promises, promises." He lifted her chin with his finger and kissed her tenderly.

"Wow," Katie said. "On a scale of one to ten, that was an eleven."

"It was a twenty," Heather said and kissed Ty again.

"Ty," a voice called. "Agent Campbell. I've brought a visitor."

CHAPTER
TWENTY-EIGHT

Oh, my gosh. Do you think it's Freedom's Choice?" Heather grabbed Ty's arm.

He smiled and placed his hand over hers. "Maybe. At least I'll bet it's the red stallion from the island."

A horse whinnied from one of the stalls at the rear of the barn. Was it Jasmine? Could she sense she was about to meet her father? Horses didn't care about things like that, did they?

"Let's go see." Katie stepped behind David's wheelchair.

"Ty?" the voice called again.

"Here," he replied and with Heather, Katie pushing David, Bea and Wells following along, he headed toward the barn's entrance.

"Oh, there you are." Agent Campbell met them as they filtered out the door. He wore a business suit, as usual. Had he gone horse hunting in a suit, Heather wondered. He was one up on Kevin, who always looked like he'd stepped out of a fashion catalog.

The FBI agent glanced at them, then stooped and picked up one of the roses that Heather had missed on the pathway. "Looks like a party. Have we come at a bad time?"

"No. Not at all," Ty said.

"It is a party." Katie smiled and touched David's shoulder. "An engagement party."

"Yours?" He glanced at David, then back at Katie.

"No," she chuckled. "I'm too young. It's Heather's and Ty's. They're too young too, but what the heck. When you meet the right person, you don't quibble about the small stuff."

"Congratulations." He shook Ty's hand and gave Heather a formal hug.

"Thanks." Ty shifted from one foot to the other.

"How's the leg, David?" Agent Campbell asked. "Wells told me you had an encounter with a tree."

"It's getting better," David said. "You should have seen the tree."

Everyone laughed.

"They gave us quite a scare the night of the storm," Bea said.

Ty cleared his throat. "So, did you find the horse?"

"Sure did. He's outside in the trailer." Agent Campbell pointed. "Dale's watching him. Turns out our young officer is quite the horseman."

"Really?" Wells said.

"I remember now," Katie said. "He used to haul his sister's horse to barrel races."

"You should have seen him on the island yesterday. He rode right along with our Fish and Game buddies. They said I was too old to go. What do they know?" The agent shook his head. "As far as anyone but us is concerned, we're just relocating a wild horse." He shrugged. "Maybe we are. I'm still waiting for a call from my people at the bureau with the DNA results."

"Can we have a look at this bronc?" Wells took a step forward.

"Certainly. Of course, you realize we don't want to disclose his whereabouts until we have the matter fully investigated. We'd appreciate it if we could keep everything about this horse low profile."

"From what I remember about how he looked on the island," Heather said as she followed along, "I'll bet most people around here will think he's Red Rock."

"I'll just have to make sure the two stallions are never together." Gravel crunched under Ty's boots as he walked. "Probably would be a good idea anyway, if we want to keep things peaceful."

They gathered around the stock trailer. Heather felt like she was going to pop out of her skin she was so excited. She clung to Ty's strong hand. Katie's face glowed and David sat upright in his chair. Wells dropped his arm around Bea's shoulder.

"Okay, Dale," Agent Campbell said. "You're probably the only one who can handle him." He winked at Ty.

Inside the trailer the stallion whinnied and pawed the floorboards.

The deputy climbed out of the truck and, with a nod, all but strutted to the rear of the trailer, opened its back door, and climbed inside. Working a case alongside Agent Campbell had spit-polished Dale's self-esteem. Heather had liked the FBI agent from the beginning, but her regard now doubled.

The red stallion leaped out, jerking Dale along after him.

Ty moved forward, but stopped as the deputy set his feet and brought the horse up tight.

Head up, ears pricked, the stallion sniffed the air and snorted. His coat was a canvas of mud, scrapes and scratches. Twigs and burrs had tangled in his mane, now grown long, and his unshod hooves were short and chipped.

"That's him," Heather whispered.

"Rocky looks more like Freedom's Choice than this horse," Katie said.

"No. Really look at him," Heather continued. "Look at his head carriage, the glow in his eyes."

"There's nobility about him," Bea said.

"He knows he's great," Ty added.

"He's got a nice shoulder and great hindquarters," Wells noted.

Katie glanced at David who said, "He just looks like a horse to me."

"It's him," Heather repeated. "I know it is."

"Let's put him in the corral out back of the barn for a while until he gets used to all this." Ty walked to Dale and the stallion, who snorted at his approach. "Easy fellow, no one's going to hurt you." Ty took the lead shank from the deputy and the whole group headed to the corral.

"So what happens now?" Wells asked.

"First we need proof that he's Freedom's Choice." Agent Campbell said. "We'll investigate his owner. If the guy really did try to have this animal destroyed, arrests will be made. The insurance company will be involved. Ownership will have to be determined by the courts. That's why I wanted him here. He'll need a good temporary home."

"And if he's not Freedom's Choice?" Bea asked.

"We'll try to find out who he belongs to."

"He's no wild horse," Wells said. "He leads. He loads. He's scared but he's been handled before."

"I'm no horse expert, but that's what I thought," the FBI agent said.

The cell phone hanging from Agent Campbell's belt rang. "Campbell here. Uh-huh." Pause. "What were your findings?"

Pause. "It's conclusive?" Pause. "Thank you, Jeff. I know I can count on your strictest confidence." Pause. "Tell your family hello from me. Thanks again." He clicked the phone off and turned to face them. "Heather's right. That's Freedom's Choice."

She grinned. "I told you."

The FBI agent nodded at Wells. "We could save the bureau a lot of money if we always documented first with Women's Intuition."

"Works for me," Bea said.

"You'd be amazed how many times," Wells added.

Ty turned the stallion into the training corral. Head and tail high, the horse pranced around on stiff legs, his hooves flipping up puffs of dust in the sand and soil mixture.

Agent Campbell sneezed. "Oh, sorry." He cleared his throat. "We appreciate you letting us leave him here while we sort everything out. It could be a long time. You know how slow the courts are. I'll see if we can get someone to pay you."

"Better still." Ty checked the latch on the corral gate. "What do you think about this? I'll breed him to one of my mares each year as full payment for his care, and, of course, I'd want to make sure my new filly's ownership is never in question."

"That sounds fair. I'll petition the court, and we'll try to keep the press from getting hold of this story. I don't know how successful we'll be, but we'll try. Until then, it looks like you'll have full custody."

"Oh, Ty. Isn't it exciting?" Heather could hardly keep from jumping up and down. "Freedom's Choice in your barn."

"Soon to be 'our' barn."

She snuggled close to him.

David cleared his throat. "So when is this wedding? Am I invited?"

"You'll be coming as my date." Katie held a hand out in front of her studying her new ring.

"That's right," Heather said, straightening up so suddenly she nearly unbalanced Ty. "We do need to set a date."

"The sooner the better as far as I'm concerned," he said. "I can't have you changing your mind on me."

"Yeah," David said. "Isn't that the pits?"

Katie favored him with a narrow-eyed stare.

David grabbed her hand and held it to his cheek. "It took us a while, but we've got the couples right now."

"Yeah," Heather blew out her breath. "Whew! Choices can be challenging."

Katie jerked her head toward the red stallion. "Freedom's Choice met his challenge."

"That's right." Heather gave a two-handed thumbs-up. "He escaped death and conquered the island."

"The Challenge of Freedom's Choice," Bea said.

Katie raised her chin. "Challenge of choice," she said slowly. "The challenge of choices. I guess we all face them, don't we?"

"Sounds like the title of a book," Heather said, "and what great timing. Day after tomorrow is the Fourth of July. Freedom's Choice met his challenge to survive and was rescued . . . uh, freed, just before Independence Day."

Wells leaned his shoulder against a fence rail. "I vote we take care of the horses and head into town for dinner and a movie. Would you fellows care to join us?"

"We can't." Agent Campbell took a notebook from his jacket pocket and thumbed through the pages. "We've got investigations to head up. Right Dale?"

"Right." The younger law enforcement officer nodded his farewell and started to his truck and trailer. "I've been thinking . . ." he started to say to Agent Campbell, but the rest was out of earshot.

Heather scratched her head. "If Freedom's Choice sires a foal next year, we should name it Challenge of Choice."

"Great idea." This from Katie.

Ty smiled at David.

"You're going to have your hands full, old buddy." David rubbed his injured leg.

"I'll love every minute of it." Ty chuckled. "You're not out of the woods either, my friend. Whatever happens between you and Katie, you'll never be the same."

"I'm beginning to sense that," David said.

Bea smiled at Wells. "If we could just find a nice girl for Colton."

"Oh, my gosh." Heather put her hand over her mouth, then let it drop to her side. "I have a friend back home who would just fit him. Her name's Sheila."

"Hmm. That's a pretty name." Wells took Bea's hand.

Heather gazed into Ty's soft brown eyes. "And you and David think you've got women problems . . ."

"Nothing we can't handle," David said.

Katie's brow raised.

Ty touched Heather's arm, then glanced at David. "I wouldn't be too sure if I were you."

Snapping her fingers, Heather said, "I've got to call Mom and Kevin."

"That's right, you do." Ty nodded.

"Here, use my cell." David unhooked a phone from his belt.

"Mr. Prepared. Thanks." She grinned at him, then at Ty.

As she dialed, she watched Katie navigate David's wheelchair a short distance away. The redhead flopped down on the grass in the shade of a tall pine and sat cross-legged, staring up at him. Bea and Wells moved to the other side of the corral, probably to give her some privacy. When Ty tried to join his folks, she grabbed his arm, slipping hers through his.

After six rings, Kevin answered. "Heather, is that you? What's the matter? Are you all right?"

She wrinkled her nose. "Now, Kevin, I don't always call with bad news. Is Mom there?"

"She and Robby are at the mall. Are you sure nothing's wrong?" His voice sounded tense.

"Very sure." Heather scratched her head. "I just called to ask you something, but when will Mom be home?"

"I don't know. She's shopping. It's anyone's guess. What did you want to ask?"

"Kevin, are you grinding your teeth?"

"Never mind. What did you want to ask?"

She took a deep breath and let it out slowly. "I really wanted Mom there."

"Okay. Well, she shouldn't be too much longer." It sounded like more teeth grinding.

"Oh, shoot." She shrugged and grinned at Ty. "I can't wait any longer."

The teeth grinding stopped. "So, you have a question?

She swallowed once, cleared her throat, then swallowed again. "What are you doing on November 30th?"

"November 30th?" Ty mouthed the words and gave the thumbs-up sign.

"Another horse show?" The tone of Kevin's voice suggested doubt.

"No." Heather paused for effect. "I just wanted to know if you will give me away on that day."

Kevin coughed. "Really, Heather. I think we should get some compensation for you."

Her hand slid down Ty's arm and she grabbed his hand. "At my wedding, Kevin."

No answer.

"Kevin, are you there?"

"I'm here." He sounded breathless.

"Well, will you?"

Kevin cleared his throat. "Sure, Heather. I'd be honored. Congratulations, and congratulations to David."

"I'm not marrying David." She squeezed Ty's hand.

"What? Who . . ."

"Ty, silly. Isn't that what you planned?" She moved the phone away from her ear and motioned for Ty to listen with her.

All was quiet the other end.

"Kevin?"

Still no sound.

"Kevin, are you gloating, doing handstands, patting yourself on the back?"

"Not me," came his slightly muffled voice sounding as if it passed through smiling lips. "Why should I gloat? You know me . . . I never interfere."

Ty smiled and straightened away from the phone.

Heather shook her head slowly. "Well, I'll say this for you. Most of the time you only interfere when absolutely necessary."

Kevin smacked his lips. "Hmm. How's David taking the breakup?"

Walking a few steps, Heather sat down on the grass, patting the ground beside her. Ty lay down alongside, pulling his hat down over his face.

"You know David," Heather said, selecting an especially long blade of grass that had escaped the mower. "There's a beautiful redhead offering him comfort."

"Katie?" Kevin asked.

"Yep." Heather tickled Ty's ear with the grass.

"Isn't she a little young?" Kevin was using his parent voice now.

Ty brushed at his ear.

"She is, isn't she? But not to worry." She poked Ty with the grass again. "Katie and David are going to date others for a few years before they decide on anything serious."

"Unlike you and Ty."

Heather tickled Ty one more time.

Sliding his hat back on his head, he sat up, grabbed the guilty, still outstretched hand and pulled her to him. Wrapping his arms tightly around her from the back, he pinned the offending arm to her side.

"We're serious." She giggled. "How about you getting serious now. Will you give me away?"

"Do you think it would give me leverage on Ty selling me that new filly you told me about?"

"You are bad."

"What's he saying?" Ty asked, putting his chin on Heather's shoulder.

"He wants to know if you'll sell him Jasmine." She pressed the phone against her leg. "He's just kidding, I think."

"I know. Here, let me talk to him." He loosened his arms and let Heather free.

She handed him the phone.

"Hi, this is your son-in-law-to-be speaking," Ty said. "Thank you." He laughed. "I'll just say this. We'll wait to discuss sale of colts until after the wedding." He laughed again. "Here, I'll let you ask her." He handed the phone back to Heather. "He wants to know what the date was again."

"November 30th," she told Kevin.

"That's a long time to wait," Ty whispered.

"I'll check my social calendar," Kevin said.

"Kevin . . ."

"I'm checking. I'm checking. Let's see . . . lunch with Tom Hanks and Steven Spielberg . . . and then there's that meeting with the President . . . guess I could squeeze you in."

"I'm so relieved." She wove her fingers through Ty's. "Shall I invite Tom, Steven and the President?"

Kevin grunted. "Okaaay. Enough of this. Shall I tell your mom, or do you want to call her."

"I'll call her. Thanks, Kevin uh, . . . Dad. Thanks for everything."

Ty pulled her to her feet.

Leaving the shade of the tall pine tree, Katie stood and walked next to David's wheelchair.

"So you're happy?" There was a quiver in Kevin's voice on the phone.

"If I was any happier, I'd have a runaway." She glanced at Wells who along with Bea walked toward them.

"What?" Kevin asked.

"You know. Happy horses love to run. Sometimes they're so happy their riders can't hold them back, get it?"

"Sounds like something Wells would say."

"Yeah. He said it, all right. I guess I'm going to have to get used to these cowboys." She lay her head against Ty's shoulder. "Tough job, but it's a task this city girl chooses to accept."

"Here, here," Bea said.

An eagle circled overhead. A breeze blew through the trees, spreading a pungent pine fragrance. Freedom's Choice whinnied. From the barn a horse answered, probably Possum, if the low whinny was any indication, then another higher pitched neigh joined in, and another.

Ty and Heather grinned at each other, as did David and Katie. Bea and Wells followed suit. Yes, Heather thought, choices were always a challenge, but with Ty by her side, her challenges would be . . . she just had to say it . . . choice.